I Should'a Been a Cowboy

Book Two

D.L. Bjorngjeld

Published by Dennis L. Bjorngjeld
Forest Lake, Minnesota

ISBN 978-0-9981110-1-8.

Layout & Design by Todd Anderson

Cover Painting by Derk Hansen
Saddle Tramp Studio, Woodbury, MN.

Sketches by D. L. Bjorngjeld

Printed in United States of America

Preface

I've lived nearly all of my 70 years in Anoka County, Minnesota. In younger years, my heroes were the great cowboys like Roy Rogers, Gene Autry, Hopalong Cassidy, and others. Through the 50s and early 60s, we'd watch them on TV, and spend many Saturday afternoons watching them at our small town theatre. For over 20 years I enjoyed my own horses. On Saturdays, my family, and several neighboring families, would load up our horses. Then, with coolers of food and beverage, we'd head for one of the Western Gaming shows at local arenas. There we would enjoy picnicking, while everyone rode in the various events, even picking up a blue ribbon or two.

As I continued my writing efforts – making a number of attempts at producing a good novel – I finally decided to follow an old adage and write about something I really love... Cowboys and the old west.

Again, thank you to my sister, Karen Bjorngjeld - Savelkoul. She's a voracious reader, and her professional background as a proofreader was a great help from start to finish. Thank you Sis!

Chapter One

I saw a door closing, ran and reached out for it just as it clicked shut. I hesitated, wondering what waited on the other side, but the knob was in my hand and the door was slowly opening. The coolness of the evening shoved its way in, as the door slowly pulled its way open.

My mind was screaming, *Careful!* But my feet were stepping through the door into an alley full of darkness. I heard the click of the door's latch again, this time behind me. The door pressed hard against my back, as I waited for my eyes to adjust so I could see something...anything.

I listened, straining to hear the slightest movement in the darkness. The alley's air was cool and dank, thick with the smell of rotting garbage and damp concrete. From my right, I heard a chilling sound cut through the silence. It was a familiar sound. One I'd heard more than a few times in my years as a police officer. It was the unmistakable sound of the hammer being pulled back on a revolver.

I dove to my left, banged my elbow hard on a dumpster, then felt the thud of my body hitting the pavement. A shot rang out, and the deafening explosion echoed down the long, tunnel-like alley. My body hugged the pavement, as I reached back for my 9mm Colt Defender.

Another shot rang out, and the explosion slapped my ears again. Through the loud ringing, I could hear footsteps running and pushed myself up to look toward the sound. Down the alley a door swung open, and bright light sprang from inside the building. A silhouette darted through the wedge of light, and the door slammed shut.

I scrambled to my feet and hurried to find the door; the one where the silhouette had disappeared. The first one I grabbed was locked. The second swung open and I rushed into the kitchen of a pizza shop. Two employees, in white shirts and white aprons, had been adding ingredients to pizza crusts. Now they were statues, wearing looks of confusion.

"Did someone just..." I started to ask.

Before I could finish, one pointed toward the main entrance, while the other looked at me and yelled, "He ran out the front."

"Thanks!" I shouted, as I bolted toward their front door. I jerked it open, quickly scanning the area for someone running. Down the street a half block, a honking horn got my attention, and I saw a man dodging through the heavy traffic. I took off after him, grabbing for my cell phone as I ran. I managed to dial 911 and, almost instantly, heard a voice say, "Police and Fire."

"I'm chasing a gunman who shot my friend!" I shouted. "He's...."

"Let me connect you to the police dispatcher," the voice interrupted. "Please hold."

"Hurr..." I started to say, but immediately heard another voice saying, "Police Dispatcher."

"I'm a retired officer," I told him, shouting at the phone. "I'm chasing a gunman who shot my friend. He's running toward Fifth Street and Third Avenue North... just turning east onto Fifth." I was panting heavily, and hoped he'd been able to understand me.

2

"We've got two patrol cars near you," the voice said. "Can you stay on the line with me?"

"Yes! Get 'em to Fifth and Second North. Fast!"

"They're on the way," he assured. "Don't get too close, or try to engage the suspect."

"He's still headed east on Fifth," I said, slowing my pace, and trying to take some deep breaths. "He's nearing the corner."

"Do you know if he's still armed?" the dispatcher asked in a calm voice.

"Yes, I think he's still carrying a revolver. He shot my friend with it, and he's fired twice at me."

I could hear him telling the approaching officers that the suspect was armed and dangerous. "One car should be coming around the corner onto Fifth within seconds," he told me, reassuringly.

The gunman was nearing Second Avenue and must have spotted the approaching squad car. He stopped, wheeled around, and ran back toward me. As he did, the squad car sped around the corner, its tires squealing. I planted my feet, raised my pistol, and yelled, "Freeze!" I was hoping he would feel cornered and give up. I really should've known better.

He didn't slow, or even break stride. Instead, he darted between two parked cars and headed across the street. The squad car screeched to a stop in front of him, but he dodged around that, too. In an instant, the officer was out of his car, shouting, "Stop! Police!"

Just as quickly, the gunman whirled and fired at the officer. The bullet rang off the doorpost of the squad car, and hit the officer in the upper arm. He ducked, grabbing at his arm. When it looked like the gunman was going to fire at him again, I yelled, "Freeze!" and took dead aim at his leg, hoping to knock it out from under him.

His gun swung toward me, so I fired, hitting him solidly in the thigh. It spun him, sending him sprawling, screaming and grabbing his leg, while his gun flew from his hand and clacked on the sidewalk. The wounded officer was quickly on him, kicking the gun away. Just then a second squad car screeched around the corner, and braked to a stop.

I rushed to the first officer. "You okay?" I asked as he was cuffing the gunman.

"I'll be all right," he said, glancing at his bloody shirt sleeve. "Ambulances are on the way."

The gunman began barking about being in pain, and needing help. "You just heard me say an ambulance was on its way," the officer growled. "Shut up and stay put, or you'll have a lot more pain to be crying about."

"This guy shot my friend as we were sitting outside at Gilstead's Pub," I told the officer. "Can your partner bring me there to see if he's been taken care of? I'll come down to the station right after that to give you a full statement."

He hesitated briefly, then said, "Could I see some identification first?"

"Of course," I told him, as I pulled out my wallet. I handed him my driver's license and conceal-carry permit. "My name is Troy MacAlan," I said.

"Thank you Mr. MacAlan. I'm Officer Tom Hartley." He studied my license and gun permit, gave me a long, measuring look, then called to the other officer. "Brad, could you help Mr. MacAlan check on his friend." He hesitated a moment, looked back to me, and asked, "What's your friend's name?"

"Russ Skills," I answered.

He looked back toward Brad. "See if they have record of a gunshot victim named Russ Skills being picked up in the last half hour."

He handed back my license and permit. "Dispatch said you're a retired officer. You look too young for that," he said, sounding surprised.

"Forced retirement... gunshot wound I took in a fight with some drug dealers," I said. "Injured my hip, and left me with a limp. I didn't want a desk job, so I decided to take disability and retirement. As life sorted things out, it all turned out for the best with my family."

He nodded, then winced as he tried to move his bloodied arm. Glancing around, he walked to a nearby brick flower planter and let out a sigh of relief as he sat on the edge of the planter.

"Let me have a look," I said, pointing to his arm. I gingerly tore open the blood-soaked sleeve, trying to get a look at the wound. "Looks like it ripped through some muscle. Probably burns somethin' fierce, but shouldn't give you any trouble with your arm when it heals."

"You're right about it burning," he said, wincing again as he moved to get a look at it himself. "Like being stabbed with a red hot poker."

5

"Yup, no fun at all," I said. "That's exactly what I tell people who ask what it's like being shot – think about getting stabbed with a red hot poker and you'll get an idea of it."

Officer Brad Henson, the second officer on the scene, walked over to tell me that Russ had been taken to the emergency room at St. Adolphus Regional. "He's reported to be in good condition."

"Thanks Brad," I told him. "I really appreciate it. I'm going to head over there as soon as Tom can let me go from this situation."

I heard sirens coming fast, and soon two ambulances turned onto Fifth. One carried two police officers, along with the emergency staff, to escort the gunman to the hospital and stand guard over him. The other ambulance was there to take care of Officer Hartley. Before they closed the doors, I reached to shake his good hand. "Thanks, Tom. Good luck with your arm."

He thanked me, and added, "Good luck with your friend Russ. Hope he's okay."

The other officer dropped me at my car, and I headed over to St. Adolphus Regional Hospital. When I asked at the nurse's desk about Russ, the nurse told me he was being prepped for surgery. "They need to remove the bullet, and stitch him back together, but the doctor said he'll be okay."

Later, as promised, I met with Officer Hartley to give my statement of the incident for his report. He said he'd be finishing his report, cleaning up a few other odds and ends, then going on a six week leave of absence while he healed. Finished with my statement, I wished him well and headed for home.

The next morning, I found Russ in room 327, where he was reading the sports section of the morning paper. As I stuck my head in the door, I said, "You look pretty good for a guy who was shot yesterday."

"Actually, I feel pretty good for a guy that was shot yesterday," he replied, showing a big grin, and waving me into the room.

We sat visiting, and I told him the entire story of what happened after the gunshot knocked him from his chair at Gilstead's. "The gunman was running from a rival gang, and thought you were moving to stop him. That's why he shot you."

Later, with the story-telling done, I said, "I'll be back to see you tomorrow evening, anything you'd like me to bring?"

"Yeah," he said, with the same big grin he'd showed earlier. "A bag of peanuts and a couple cold beers."

I laughed, shaking my head. "I can do the peanuts. But the beer? I'm not so sure."

Headed for home, I was cruising north on Lake Blvd. The speed limit there is fifty-five and I was being a good citizen, keeping it under sixty. I had my windows down, enjoying the fresh air, and singing along with "As We Waltz 'Round the Floor," one of my favorite tunes by a local singer/songwriter.

Relaxed, enjoying the music, I didn't give the Chevy pickup coming toward me much thought... until... suddenly... everything seemed wrong. In an instant of panic, I thought, *No! He can't be!*

The pickup cut in front of me, trying to make a quick left turn. I stomped hard on my brake pedal, my back pressed against the seat. Before I felt the brakes lock, or tires claw at the pavement, I felt the collision and heard the chilling explosion of metal and glass. As I crashed into the side of the pickup, a split-second vision flashed through my mind. A vision of torn flesh, broken bones, blood everywhere, and this being the end for me.

Death — some say it brings life to an abrupt end and there's nothing more. Others believe it transforms us to an eternity of everything that's beautiful. Many, because of its recondite nature, deeply fear it. Those of strong religious faith sometimes embrace it. I choose to not question it, and to be content with the mystery.

In the next moment, time stood still, and my body began trembling violently. Somehow, this trembling seemed familiar. Then I had the sensation of being pulled from my body, also strangely familiar. My car, which was collapsed like an accordion and stuck in the side of the pickup, began to shrink in the distance below.

In a sudden burst of speed, and an explosion of light, I was catapulted through space and time. The dimensions were distorted, as I beamed through space – a small mass of energy. Then it seemed as though I slipped through a tear in the fabric of time.

Suddenly, everything shifted into slow-motion, and I found myself in an old west town. It was early summer, 1868. A large crowd of people were listening to a hard, raspy voice that was shouting. The voice was attached to a big, rough, mean looking character, and was shouting at a cowboy. The cowboy was a black man.

Chapter Two

"I don't give a rip what yer Abe Lincoln said. You still owe me, and yer gonna work it off," the big one growled.

"No suh," the cowboy said, giving his Stetson a tug. "You doan owns me no mo', an' ah owes you nuttin'. Not one t'ing. Ah gonna be workin' for Mista Clusky on his cattle drive startin' tamarra."

"We'll jus' be seein' 'bout all that," the burly one bellowed, as he lowered the hand holding the whip.

It looked to me like he was about to uncoil the whip, and maybe use it against the cowboy, so I shouted to get his attention. "Hey! You! Hold it!" Then I quickly pushed through the crowd and headed toward him.

His head jerked around, and he glared at me. Shaking his whip, he barked, "Mind yer own affairs stranger, or you'll git a taste of this, too."

"No, I don't think so. You're not usin' that whip on anyone," I said, slowly shaking my head, while I continued strait toward him.

Without hesitating, he raised his fist, still full of the coiled whip, and swung toward me. I slapped at his arm to deflect the blow, stepped into him, and struck him hard in the chest with the heel of my right hand. He staggered back a few steps, gasping for air, and clutching at his chest. For a brief moment he looked dazed, then he went for his gun. My .44 Army Revolver was cocked and aimed at the middle of his chest before he'd cleared leather with his Colt. He froze, staring at me with a questioning look.

9

He cautiously lifted his hand from his pistol and continued staring. He seemed confused, and asked, "Who in blazes are you, anyway?"

With a measuring look, to be sure he wasn't about to try anything else, I said, "Just a friend of this fella." I nodded my head in the direction of the cowboy, never taking my eyes from the burly menace. "And I suggest you just let him be."

His glare moved from me to the cowboy, and back to me. "We'll jis see," he snarled. Then, as he slowly back-stepped away, he repeated, "We'll jis see."

I stood firm, holding his stare, until he turned and walked away. *Probably haven't seen the last of him*, I thought. Then I turned to meet my new friend.

As I passed one of the bystanders, I heard, "Wha'cha doin' stickin' yer nose in things... Neegra lover!"

I ignored him, and his comment, and reached a hand toward the dark-skinned cowboy. "Howdy," I said.

He hesitantly shook my hand. "Thank ya, suh."

"Glad t' help," I told him. Then, glancing over my shoulder, I asked, "Who is that ornery cus?"

"Mista Cody Powell. Use'ta own me, an' still figgers he does... or dat uhm still in debt 't him."

"Well, hopefully he'll give up on that notion, and on threatening you anymore."

"Doan know if dat'll happen, suh," the cowboy said, slowly shaking his head.

I gave him a smile, saying, "You don't have to call me sir. My name's Troy MacAlan. Folks call me Mack."

"T'anks agin... Mack. Muh name's Eustace. Eustace Mitchell." He paused in thought, then added, "Not many white folk eva call me a fren', likes ya tol' him."

"Glad to call you friend, Eustace." I moved to sit on the edge of the boardwalk under a sign that read, "Jerry's Dry Goods Emporium." Sitting down, I slapped the plank, saying, "Sit down, Eustace. Take a load off."

Nervously, he glanced around, then finally walked over and sat next to me. Down the street there were a few of the folks that had been in the crowd, and now were gathered again, whispering to each other.

Ignoring them, I asked, "What's the deal with this Powell fella?"

He stared at the ground, scratched at it with the toe of his boot, then said, "Likes ah say'd, me 'n some othas usta belong t' him. Afta da war, 'n we was free, some of us stayed on t' work fer 'im. We had no place t' go, an' least we got us a roof 'n meals wit him. Been mor'n two yeahs now, 'n cordin' t' his figurin', we still owes him mor'n we's got comin'."

"That's some figurin'," I said.

"Yup. Claims we owe mo' fer meals and rent den we earned workin' fer 'im."

"Sounds like you'd never catch up by his figurin'."

"Das jus it. He jus worried 'bout losin' all his free hep, an' havin' t' hire men fer real wages."

A stagecoach thundered into town, covering us in a cloud of dust as it rolled past. The teamster, both fists full of reins and his foot braced against the front of the box, shouted, "Whoa thar... Whoa now!" I watched it stop, wondering, *Where had it come from? Where was it bound? Where am I?* Staring at the coach a while longer, I finally asked, "Eustace, what town is this?"

He gave me a puzzled look, then said, "Glen Springs, Texas. Why you askin'?"

"I'm not sure," I told him slowly. "Only been here a short while, and guess I already forgot what town it is."

Along with not knowing *where* I was, I wondered how and when I'd got here. I took off my hat, scratched my head, then decided to keep those thoughts to myself.

The Stetson I held was a tan colored beaver skin, with a dark sweat stain around the band, and two wooden matchsticks tucked in the band. I stared at it, then put it back on my head, liking how comfortable it felt.

My puzzled, bewildered wondering was interrupted, when Eustace said in a whisper that was almost the size of a shout, "Oh, Lord-a-Mercy!"

"What is it?" I asked, looking toward him.

He nodded, looking past me down the street. "Mista Powell 'n two hired hands a-comin'."

Turning and studying them for a moment, I whispered, "Let me handle this, Eustace."

"Suit'cha se'f," he said. "But dem two's real mean."

12

We got to our feet, and I said, "Hello Mr. Powell."

Ignoring me, and staring at Eustace, he said, "Time you got back to the ranch, Eustace."

Eustace was just staring back at Powell, as I said, "Eustace tells me he doesn't work for you anymore."

"Ain't none of your affair," Powell snarled, turning his angry glare to me. "You jis stay clear of it."

Holding his stare, I tugged down on my Stetson a bit. "Seems to me Eustace could use a little help... you havin' him outnumbered three-to-one like you do."

As I'm saying this, one of his hired men stepped to the side trying to flank us. I told him, "You just stay close by your boss over there."

Acting unconcerned, he continued to move, so I drew and fired at the ground, just inches from his foot. He froze, looking seriously concerned now. Waving the barrel of my revolver, I said, "Back by your boss."

I saw Powell staring past me, so I took a quick glance over my shoulder. Eustace was on the boardwalk, moving quietly along the building. With my attention quickly back on the three standing in front of me, I heard a loud yelp from behind me at the boardwalk. Next, it sounded like some serious wrestling was going on.

I moved a few steps to the side, flanking Powell and his thugs, so I could keep an eye on them, and see what was happening behind me. Eustace had a man pinned down on the boardwalk. He pulled a pistol from the man's hand, and threw it into the dusty street.

"Dis one figgered t' git ya from bahine," Eustace said, as he leaned harder with his knee in the middle of the man's back. "Ah saw 'im comin', 'n when he reached 'round the corner wit his gun, ah grabbed his arm 'n yanked him out onto da boardwalk."

I quickly turned my attention back to the three, and stepped back in front them. The second hired hand had stood expressionless, but now moved as though going for his gun. In a blink, I cocked my revolver and had it aimed at his chest, telling him, "I don't think so." His hand slowly moved away from his gun.

I looked back at Powell. "Like I said before, Eustace is a free man. Let him be."

Now Powell's glare was like fire shooting from his eyes. "This ain't the last of it," he growled. He spun around and stomped away, his thugs slowly following at a distance, not wanting to get too close to his fury.

As they moved farther away, I holstered my revolver, then stood staring down at it for a long moment. I was more than a little surprised by the ease and speed I had with handling this gun. It was a .44 caliber Remington Army Revolver, similar to the one currently carried by James Butler Hickok – better known as "Wild Bill Hickok." *Interesting*, I thought.

Chapter Three

Sitting back down on the boardwalk, I said, "Eustace, you mentioned a cattle drive... for a Mr. Cluskey I think it was. Know if he's takin' on any more hands?"

"Ahm thinkin' so," he answered.

"Where can I find him?"

"He got a spread 'bout t'ree miles east-a town."

"After I see if I can buy me a good horse," I said, "I think I'll look him up. When's he startin' the drive?"

"T'ree days. Ahm startin' for 'im tamarra, but da cattle drive startin' in t'ree days."

After thanking me again, Eustace saddled up and headed for the Cluskey ranch. He'd be moving his gear into the bunkhouse this evening, and starting work in the morning. I told him I was gonna ride out to the ranch this evening, and asked him if he'd let Cluskey know for me.

I started to stroll the boardwalk, checking out the town of Glen Springs. Mostly I wanted to find the livery stable, and see if they had a good horse for sale. At the far end of town, a ways beyond where the boardwalk ended, I saw a sign for "Capella Brothers Livery, Blacksmith, and Feed Mill." *That'd be the place*, I thought.

I met Andy, the youngest of three Capella brothers. "I run the livery," he said, as he shook my hand. "My older brother, Mike, is the blacksmith. And my oldest brother, Chris, runs the feed mill."

"Sounds like a nice family business," I told him.

"Yup, it is. So... what can I do for ya, Mack?"

"I'm in need of a good horse. Hopin' to catch on with Cluskey's cattle drive, and I'm looking for a good workin' horse. Whatcha got?"

He gave a wry grin, then said, "May sound a bit like a salesman's pitch, but I've got just the right horse for ya." He waved for me to follow, as he headed toward the far end of the livery. He stopped at the last stall, and pointed. After a pause, he said, "This Palomino is a real beauty. And, more important for you, she's as good a cattle horse as you'll find anywhere.

"She was John Cobb's until last month. Ol' John's crowdin' fifty now, and he's worked cattle all his life. Fell from a loft last month, 'n broke up his hip real bad. He needed money for doctorin', and knew he'd not likely be sittin' a saddle for some time, so he sold her to me."

"How much you want for her?" I asked.

"W-e-l-l." he said, drawing it out. "Gave ol' John sixty-eight dollars for her, plus thirty dollars for his saddle and bridle... they're Heiser Denver made, and you can't get finer tack. S-o-o-o, I've got ninety-eight dollars tied up, plus feedin' her fer a month."

He paused, rubbing his chin in thought. Finally, almost apologetically, he said, "I gotta have a hundred 'n twenty-five dollars for the works, just to have some profit in the deal. And you get the dog for free."

"Dog?" I asked.

"Yup. Two things I had to promise ol' John. First, that I'd sell her to someone who'd keep workin' her around cattle. Second, that I wouldn't let the dog be separated from her. They're both seven years old, and have always been together. Ol' John treated 'em like they was royalty."

I hesitated a bit, then said, "Guess I wouldn't mind a good dog."

"I don't know fer sure just how good the dog is," Andy said. "Fact is, seems he'd just-a-soon bite yer hand as lick it. Mighty protective of that horse, too."

I'd always been good with animals, so this seemed like a bit of a challenge. "Got any jerked beef handy?" I asked.

"I do," he said, and went to his tack room to fetch some from his saddlebag. I tucked it in my shirt pocket, stepped into the stall, and saw the dog lying in the corner. He rose to his feet in one fluid motion, and started a low growl. I ignored him, talking to the horse and stroking her neck. Then, rubbing her leg, I slowly knelt to be down at the dog's level, while still ignoring him. I continued speaking to the horse, and rubbing her leg. Soon the dog began inching closer. I could tell he'd caught scent of the beef, as he came closer, sniffing around my pocket. Finally, I began talking to him.

"Hey big guy, what's that you smell?" I spoke softly, still rubbing the horse's leg, and still not looking at him. "It smells pretty good, huh?"

I slowly reached in my pocket, tore off a chunk of the beef, and closed it in my hand. I rested my arm on my knee, my fist held toward him. He sniffed and nudged with his nose. Then he nudged again, trying to get at the meat.

"Easy now," I said, softly. "Don't be takin' a finger with that meat."

When he got more gentle in nudging my hand, I slowly opened it for him. "Good boy!" I whispered, scratching his head.

"Well, don't that beat all," Andy said, as he leaned against the stall. "Looks to me, that you'll treat 'em like royalty, too."

Royalty, I thought. "Yup, royalty they are," I said. "This here's the Duke, and she's the Duchess. Think that's what I'll call 'em... Duke and Duchess!"

I decided to go grab a little supper before heading out to the Cluskey Ranch. I paid Andy a little extra to feed Duke and Duchess, so they'd be set for the night.

Walking into the Linwood Hotel, I paused to take in the impressive place. The lobby was built of finely finished wood. The wide registration desk had curved stairways on each side that met in the middle behind the desk. To the left was the hotel's Diner, and on the right was their Saloon. I went to the door on the left.

In the diner, a very pleasant gal named Theresa said, "Hello. How are you this evening?"

"Doin' just fine. How 'bout you?"

"It's been a good day," she said, smiling.

She was a petite woman, barely five feet tall, with a pretty face, and a pleasant smile. She handed me a paper with food selections written on it.

18

"If I may," she said, bending toward me and pointing at the paper, "I would highly recommend the beef brisket. Our chef, Jack, is one of the very best, and the brisket he's cooked is wonderful. He's seasoned it to perfection."

I looked up, saying, "Brisket it is, then."

Later, finished with supper and feeling full, I wasn't sure if the brisket was that exceptional, or maybe I was just exceptionally hungry. Maybe both. In any case, it was just about as good as anything I'd ever eaten.

I paid for the meal, left her a little extra, and headed to the saloon for a beer. From there, I'd round up Duke and Duchess and ride out to find the Cluskey ranch.

Chapter Four

I rode east, and came to a large gate wearing a sign that read, "Cluskey Ranch." The ranch was very impressive. Their buildings were well-maintained, the wood fences were straight and solid, and the house was neatly trimmed.

I saw Eustace sitting with two other cowhands over near the bunkhouse, so I nudged Duchess and rode to where they sat. Swinging down from the saddle, I said, "Hey, Eustace, how ya doin'?"

"Fine. Jus' fine, Mack." He stood to shake my hand and, after introducing me to the others, told them, "Dis heah da fella dat hep me wit' Powell."

Eustace and I visited for a while, and finally I asked, "Know where I'd find Mr. Cluskey?"

Pointing, he said, "Up t' da big house."

Eustace had been a slave virtually all of his life. First, it was in Louisiana for the owner of a large sugar cane plantation with his papa, mama, brother, and his sister. Then he was sold to Powell, who moved him to Texas, where he learned to handle horses and cattle. When slaves referred to the plantation owner's house, they called it the "big house."

I smiled at him, saying, "Ranch house... you mean up at the ranch house."

He grinned at me, and shook his head. "Ol' ways, Mack. Hard t' change dem ol' ways."

I tied Duchess to a hitching rail, had Duke lay down near her, then walked to the house to meet Cluskey. I knocked on a huge, wooden door, and in a few moments it swung open. A handsome looking buckskin shirt filled the doorway. The man wearing the shirt stood about six-three, with broad shoulders. He said, "Yes sir? Can I help you?"

"Mr. Cluskey?" I asked.

"Yup. Call me Jim," he said.

I reached out to shake his hand. "My name's Troy MacAlan. Most call me Mack." He had large, powerful hands, and a firm handshake.

As he shook my hand, it looked like something occurred to him. "You the fella Eustace mentioned?"

"That's me," I said. "I was hopin' you could use another hand for your cattle drive."

"Come on in. Grab a chair," he said, waving me in as he stepped aside. "Care for a cup of coffee?"

On the table I saw a cup at one place, so I took the spot across from it. "Sure I would," I replied.

"So, you'd like to hire on?" he asked, setting the coffee in front of me.

"I would."

He sat, sipped his coffee, then said, "Be two months before we reach Abilene, Kansas."

"Yup, kinda figured that."

22

He leaned back in his chair, staring into his coffee cup. "So... you like the notion of spendin' time ridin' your trusty horse, watchin' cattle mosey and graze all day. Then lyin' out under starry nights, listenin' to cowboys sing, and tell stories around the campfire."

I could see where this was headed. He was settin' me up, seeing if I knew anything about a cattle drive. I interrupted him, saying, "Well, I don't really know about any of that. I figure herdin' cantankerous cattle through the day, and keepin' 'em calm all night is what the job is. It's hard work, eatin' dust all day, and maybe gettin' rained on all night. That, and puttin' up with horses, and cowpunchers, that might be just as cantankerous."

I paused to sip my coffee, then added, "As far as those other frills, I don't know much about 'em. Just figured they was mostly made-up tales to make it sound fun."

He grinned as he set his cup down. Then he leaned forward, and stood from his chair with his hand extended. "There's room in the bunkhouse for you." I shook his hand, and he added, "You can move in tonight, and start work in the morning. I'm payin' ninety bucks for the drive, which will take two months... maybe a bit longer."

"Thanks, Mr. Cluskey," I said. "That's mighty good wages."

"It's Jim, call me Jim. And you can thank me when you collect your pay in Abilene." He paused, then asked, "Say, you're not a cook are ya?"

I shook my head. "I guess I can fry my own breakfast alright, but cookin' for a full crew of hungry cowhands? I don't think so."

"Just thought I'd ask. We lost our cook, Stewey, a few days ago. He got throwed bad, 'n broke his ankle and wrist. So he won't be travelin' with us." Rubbing his chin, with a far-off stare in his eyes, he added, "Gotta round one up pretty quick. Hopin' to start the herd north in two or three days."

At the bunkhouse, Eustace pointed out an empty bunk next to his. I threw my saddle bags and bedroll on it, then went out to unsaddle Duchess, and put her in a corral. Duke would stay with me in the bunkhouse. Eustace had a gentle way about him, and Duke warmed up to him right quick. It didn't hurt that Eustace had some jerky to bribe him.

Later, we were relaxing on hand-hewn, split-log chairs outside the bunkhouse. The evening air was fresh and cool. The sun was glowing golden-orange, slowly easing down on the western horizon. Duke lay next to me, his head resting on his outstretched paws.

"Mack..." Eustace said.

"Yeah?"

"Ya knows how ya say'd ranch house, when ah say'd da big house?"

I paused, feeling a little flush in my face. "I hope I didn't offend you."

"Oh no-o-o, not one bit," he said. "You seem to be a smart man, an' you talk good. I'd 'preciate it if you'd hep me learns t' talk good."

I smiled, a little surprised, and said, "Learn... learn to speak well."

24

"Learn - to - speak - well," he repeated, slowly.

"Yup. As long as you're not offended by it, I'll help you... and correct you sometimes."

"Ah'd likes dat," he said.

"Like that," I corrected. "I'd like that."

Slowly, again, he repeated, "I'd - like - that."

Another one of the cowhands joined us, and Eustace said, "Mack, dis here's Rocky Daggert."

I shook his hand, saying, "Pleased t' meet ya, Rocky."

"You jis hire on?" he asked.

"Yeah. Just this evening."

"Cook?"

"Nope, just another cowhand." Then, wondering, I asked, "How 'bout you, Eustace? Cowpuncher too?"

"No suh, I's da wrangler."

I hesitated, then said, "I'm... I'm the wrangler."

"I'm – the - wrangler," he said, with effort.

I looked at Rocky, sheepishly, and said, "Eustace asked me to correct him, help him speak better."

"Well, I'll be," he said, nodding to Eustace. "That's a mighty good thing."

Eustace smiled and shrugged. "Anaway, Mack, I's good wit' horses, an' Mista Cluskey needed him a wrangler."

Cattle drives, depending on how many head of cattle, and how many cowhands, will have a herd of extra saddle horses called a *remuda*. Cluskey's would have thirty head or so. It's the wrangler's job to herd these horses, and to graze, water, and care for them. He also takes care of the mules that pull the chuck wagon.

Just then we heard Jim Cluskey's voice, asking, "What's goin' on boys?" We all turned, and saw him coming around the corner of the bunkhouse, a handsome woman walking at his side.

"Jis takin' it easy," Rocky said.

"I figured we'd walk over, so I could introduce you to Mrs. Cluskey." With a proud wave of his hand, he said, "This is my lovely Rebecca." She gave a soft smile, and a slight nod of her head.

Then Jim told her, "And Becca, this is Eustace, Rocky and Mack." She gave us each a firm handshake, saying, "Very pleased to meet you."

She slowly scanned the horizon, and said, "I see why you boys are sitting out here. You've got a great view of that beautiful sunset." They grabbed chairs and sat with us, visiting about the setting sun, the copper painted sky, and the coming cattle drive.

Chapter Five

"Mmm mmmmm," Eustace hummed, as he chewed a bite of breakfast the next morning.

"Now, this is the way to start a day off right," I told Eustace, as I held a chunk of ham up on my fork, ready to devour it.

Mrs. Cluskey overheard us, and said, "Thank you, gentlemen. Glad you like it."

She was an attractive, curvy kind of woman. And though she stood five-foot-six, she looked petite next to Jim. Her light brown, wavy hair was tied back with a ribbon and, with her sleeves rolled up and apron tied snug around her waist, she was all business in her large kitchen.

"It's the best," I said, saluting her with my fork.

The Cluskeys had a large dining room, with a long table that could seat twelve hungry hands. Most mornings there weren't more than five or six, but today there were eleven hands, plus Jim, while Mrs. Cluskey and a helper cooked our breakfast.

Rocky piped up, saying, "Oh, he's just tryin' to get on yer good side, Mrs. Cluskey."

She smiled. "Well, he's doin' a fine job so far."

After breakfast, six of us relieved the hands that had been riding nighthawk, keeping the herd bunched up about a half-mile north of the ranch house. They came in for breakfast, and then would catch a few hours in the bunk.

Later that day, I was helping Eustace work on the chuck wagon, making sure it was ready for the long trail. As Eustace worked on repairing the harnesses, I checked the wheels. Beside the fact that there was no spare wheel, I found one that had a cracked hub.

"Best we get this one fixed, and get a new one so we've got an extra," I said.

"I'll go ask Mista Cluskey can we use da buckboard an' go in t' see da blacksmith," Eustace said. After getting Jim's okay, we hitched a team of horses, loaded the wheel, and headed for town.

At Capella's Blacksmith Shop, we slid the wheel off the buckboard and rolled it in the open doorway. The smithy looked up, and shouted, "Howdy."

"Hello there," I said. "I'm Mack 'n this is Eustace."

He grabbed a rag and wiped his hands, saying, "I'm Mike Capella. How can I help you?"

"We need a new wheel, and wondered if you can fix this one for us, too."

"What's up with this one?" he asked, bending to give it a closer look.

I pointed, and said, "The hub's cracked here."

He knelt to study it. "Well, I can wrap a steel band around it good 'n snug. Be best if you use it as a spare."

"Yup, we kinda figured that. That's why we need a new one, too."

"I can have 'em ready for you to pick up before noon tomorrow. Whose name do I put on the order?"

"Jim Cluskey," I told him. "See you tomorrow."

Back on the buckboard, rolling through town, I said, "We're gonna be late for supper at the ranch. Why don't we eat here before we hit the trail? It's on me."

He shrugged, and I could tell he wasn't too sure about it, so I asked, "Don't like the idea?"

"Der's some don't like us comin' in a place."

"There's... There's some folks who don't like it," I said, correcting him.

He grinned a little. "Das right. Dey don't."

I laughed and slapped him on his big shoulder. Through it all, he always kept a good sense of humor.

"Well, we're here together," I said, "so let's give it a go. How 'bout we try the dining room at the Linwood Hotel? They should have a pretty good supper."

We parked the buckboard at the side of the hotel, and climbed down. When we walked in, a fella in the lobby paused, saying, "Don't think you want to bring *him* in here."

"Oh, sure I do," I said. "He's with me, and we'll be sittin' down for supper." This brought sideways glances, and grumbling from others in the lobby. We walked in the dining room, and, just as we got situated at a table, there was a loud commotion in the kitchen.

The swinging door flew open, and a guy, who looked like he was their cook, tore off his apron, kicked the door open again, and tossed the apron back into the kitchen. "I'm done with all yer grief," he barked, as the apron flew.

After he stomped away, I tapped Eustace on the arm. "Come on. Let's go catch up with him."

"Wh... wh..." Eustace stuttered, then hurried after me.

Out on the boardwalk, I saw the guy crossing the street toward a saloon. "Hey! Cookie!" I yelled.

He whirled to see who was shouting, then relaxed a bit. "Yeah, what is it?"

"Are you the hotel's cook?"

"Was!" he said, emphatically. "*Was* their cook."

"Might sound a bit strange, but can I ask how much they paid you?"

"Not nearly enough," he said. "Barely forty bucks a month."

I paused in thought, then asked, "How'd you like to make seventy bucks a month for the next two months? And you run your own kitchen."

That seemed to get his attention. "A hunert 'n forty bucks fer two months cookin'?"

"Yup, 'n no one givin' you orders."

"Who's it cookin' for?" he asked, warily.

30

"Jim Cluskey. He needs a good cook for his cattle drive, startin' in two days."

"Hmmm...." He pulled on his ear, so I could tell he was giving it some serious thought. "Maybe it'd be good to get outta town for a while," he finally said.

"We gotta be back here tomorrow to pick up two wheels at Capella's. Why don't you get your gear together, and we'll pick you up at noon."

He hesitated again, and then said, "Okay. Pick me up down at Rochelle's Boarding House... east end of town."

"We'll be there at noon," I told him. "Oh, by the way, I'm Mack, and this here's Eustace."

"Name's Jack," he said, thumbing his hat. "Folks call me Flap Jack."

As we left Jack, I told Eustace, "Why don't we head for the ranch. I'm sure the Cluskeys'll be excited to hear we found 'em a good cook. Maybe Mrs. Cluskey will rustle up somethin' for us to eat."

"Aw'ight," he said brightly, as we headed for the buckboard. He sounded relieved that we weren't going back in the hotel for our supper.

At the ranch, we sat at the Cluskey's dining table with a fresh cup of coffee. "Well I'll be," Jim said. "I know Flap Jack. Never thought he'd leave the hotel... 'specially for a chuck wagon."

"Must've got fed up with his boss there," I said. "He ripped off that apron and flung it with a fury."

"Good work, Mack. Now we can head north on schedule," Jim said, sounding relieved.

"I hope seventy a month was okay to tell him," I said, with a shrug.

"Sure was," he said. "Probably would've gone more if needed – to get a good cook – and Jack's a good one."

Meanwhile, like I figured, Mrs. Cluskey asked if we'd had any supper. "Nope," I said. "We got interrupted chasing after Flap Jack." She went to work fryin' up venison steaks and potatoes for us.

Next morning in town, Eustace and I picked up some last-minute supplies for Jim. Then, after getting the wheels at Capella's, we rounded up Flap Jack at the boarding house.

"Always wondered about workin' a chuck wagon," Jack said. "Now... guess I'll find out first hand."

Chapter Six

The next day, Eustace and I had finished breakfast, and were getting ready for the trail. It was still an hour before the sun up, as I walked over to saddle Duchess. Duke sat close by and watched. I asked him, "Ready for the long trail, boy?"

He rose to his feet, and came closer. His tail wagged, making his whole body swayed. I bent and scratched him around the ears, then pulled a hunk of jerky from my shirt pocket. We played our usual game of me holding it wrapped in my hand, and he gently nudging with his nose until I say, "Okay," and give it to him.

I had put some sweet oats in the cuff of my new work pants. When Duchess saw me shake them into my hand, she perked up, and snatched 'em from my palm with her lips. "A special treat for Her Highness," I told Duke. He sat up and gave a muffled bark.

"Poor boy. Just don't get enough attention do ya," I said, and scratched behind his ears, laughing at his antics.

Pulling the saddle's cinch tight, I patted Duchess on the rump, bent to pick up my bedroll, and hiked over to see Flap Jack at the chuck wagon.

Along with food, cooking gear, medical supplies, and tools, the cook hauls our bedrolls in the chuck wagon. It's one less thing to be in the way when we're herdin' cattle. And it's a little less weight on your horse. The job can wear a horse down, and it's why you have a remuda of extra saddle horses. A cowboy might switch mounts once or even two times in a hard day on the trail.

In my bedroll I have two ground sheets, a wool blanket, my rain slicker, my few extra socks and underwear, and my rifle — a .52 caliber, Model 1852 Sharps. It may be the most accurate rifle at long range that the west has seen. It'll stay in my bedroll on the drive. Again, it's one less thing to be in the way when you're herdin' cattle.

Eustace was helping Flap Jack harness the mules to the chuck wagon. When they finished, Jack climbed in the box and drove the wagon over to the well to fill the water barrels. Instead of one large barrel, Cluskey had two smaller barrels, one strapped to each side of the wagon.

Over the last two days, with Mrs. Cluskey's help, Jack had stocked and organized the chuck wagon with everything we'd need for the trail. On one side there were two drawers. They would hold pots 'n pans, tin plates and cups, utensils, and miscellaneous cook gear.

Covering the drawers was a large, hinged board that dropped down, and was supported by two wooden legs. This served as a counter for fixing and serving meals. Under the wagon there is a boot for more miscellaneous storage. The food supplies included cured ham and bacon, jerked beef, beans, rice, coffee, flour, and some sugar. Out on the trail there was plenty of game to be taken, giving the crew fresh meat every now 'n then. Hunting had to be done well away from the herd though, so we wouldn't risk gunshots spooking the cattle and causing a stampede.

Jim Cluskey walked up. "How ya doin' Flap Jack?"

"Ready to roll, boss."

"All right. You'll be out front with me, so head for the north end of the herd. I'll catch up to you there."

As trail boss, Jim will spend much of his day scouting for the best route, and the best places to ford streams and rivers. The drive will cover twelve to fifteen miles in a day, and by mid-afternoon he'd be looking for a good place to bed the herd down for the night.

"How's your remuda?" Jim asked Eustace.

"Good shape, boss. One come up lame las' night, so we got twen'y-nine head of good hosses wit' us."

"That should do just fine," Jim told him. He turned to walk toward the house, then called back to me. "Mack, would you tell the hands to gather-up by the bunkhouse in ten minutes."

"Will do," I replied.

Ten minutes later we were getting our marching orders. "Mack, you and Rocky'll ride point," Jim said.

Cattle follow the dominant steers in their ranks. If you herd those, the rest will follow along. A herd of twenty-eight hundred head, like the Cluskey's have, can stretch out nearly a mile on the trail. Cattle like to follow in line, and will seldom be more than five or six abreast.

Jim paired up the rest of the crew as swing and flank riders, to spread out the length of the drive. Their job was keeping the cattle in line, and moving forward. The first couple days took extra work trying to keep the cattle headed in the right direction, and not let them turn back. Eventually, they'll get used to the trail, and become more cooperative.

"Whitey, you and Tuck are the youngest, and haven't been on the trail before. So, you're ridin' drag."

"Kinda figured," Whitey said, with a shrug.

There's not an experienced cowhand around that wants to ride drag... bringin' up the rear, and eatin' dust all day. Depending on the wind, any puncher might eat dust for a while. But ridin' drag you're eatin' dust most every day, all day long.

"I'll meet you boys up on the north end in a half hour," Jim said, and headed to the house for some final goodbyes. He wouldn't be home for two and a half months.

At the north end, Jim, Rocky, and I began pushing the steers that Jim knew were the dominant leaders. Jack was already rolling out ahead in the chuck wagon. With the swing and flank riders whoopin' 'n hollerin', the large herd of cattle soon began to follow. Eustace and his helper, Jebodia, herded the remuda of horses alongside the cattle.

About a mile north of the ranch, we were moving up a gradual grade, and I turned to look back. I could see the line of cattle that was five or six wide all the way back to the ranch. Soon, the last of the cattle would be moving, and Whitey and Tuck would bring up the rear.

"That's a pretty sight," Jim said, lookin' back.

"It is for a fact," I agreed.

"I'm gonna ride on ahead," he told me. "Check out that first creek crossing. Be back to you in a while."

"I'll be watchin'," I said, then reined Duchess around to shag two strays back in line. A while later, I glanced in the distance, and Jim was nothing more than a dust cloud against the horizon.

Chapter Seven

Under the hot, white, mid-afternoon sun, I shaded my eyes and could see a dust cloud against the horizon again. It appeared to be moving toward us. *Has to be Jim*, I thought. A while later he rode up, swung his horse around, and took up beside me.

"Things look good up ahead," he said.

"How's that stream lookin'?"

"Good. It's been pretty wet the past couple months, so it's runnin' a little deeper than usual. Shouldn't be any trouble crossing it though." He pointed ahead, and a little to the right. "You wanna veer to the right a bit. See that rock-faced ridge out there?"

"Yup."

"It's probably a little more than six miles out. That's where we'll bed down for the night. Cross the stream in the mornin'."

"You got it boss," I said, with a quick nod.

"Mack, it's Jim... call me Jim."

"Okay... Jim," I said, smiling.

"You need to change mounts?" he asked.

"I don't think so. Duchess here," I said, patting her neck, "is a real stayer. She's got a lotta bottom to her."

"That's good," he said, reaching to scruff the mane of his horse. "Ol' Dunny here is that way, too. He'll go all day, and into the evening. I need to put him out to graze, just to get him to rest at night." Dunny, a line-back dun, is big and strong, and looked to be from hearty stock.

"Veer 'em a little to the right, and I'll see you in a while," he said, then reined Dunny around to check things back down the line.

I turned Duchess, and we started to nudge the lead cattle to the right. Rocky was coming up the right side, so I held my arm out, pointing toward the rock-faced ridge, then waved to signal our direction. He nodded.

The day had been a good one, much better than we expected. There'd been no troubles, no strays that were lost, no stampedes, or even near stampedes, and we were makin' good time. Jim figured it to be fourteen miles to the first creek crossing, and we'll be layin' up just short of it. A good first day.

The late evening sun had turned to molten orange, and had slipped down to where the broad Texas range held it on its fingertips. Soon, the last of the herd came in, with Whitey and Tuck pushing them. Not stopping, they rode on to the north end, where Flap Jack had set up camp, and was cookin' our supper.

He had a kettle of beans hangin' over one edge of the fire, a pot of coffee hangin' over the other, and his Dutch oven set off the backside keeping some biscuits warm – the biscuits he'd baked in it earlier. As cowhands rode up, he fried 'em a slice of good ham to go along with the beans 'n biscuits. And, of course, it was all served with a good portion of grumbling from Jack.

Meals on the drive weren't fancy. Most of the time we had beans and fried salt-pork for breakfast, generally served before sun-up. Jerked beef from your saddlebag, and water from your canteen, was it for many lunches on the trail. Then we'd hope for some good meat or fresh game with supper. The fresh game would usually last for two meals, then Flap Jack would chop up the rest for stew meat.

When he'd made stew, and the drive was going okay, Jack parked the chuck wagon at mid-day, and built a fire to heat it up. The cowhands would stop for a quick plate full, then get right back in the saddle.

Night watch was in shifts of six riders that would change-up every three hours. Getting by on five or six hours of sleep, after a long day in the saddle, was something few cowhands ever really get used to. You just do your job, and tried not to think about it.

When you're on watch, you're duty is keeping the cattle calm and quiet. Many cowboys found that it helped to sing a soft melody, as they slowly circled the herd. Some, obviously, were better at this than others, but, no matter. It always seemed to help, even with the poorest voice.

Next morning we crossed Cedar Creek, and started the herd toward Austin, where we'd cross the Colorado River. The next three days went by without a hitch, including crossing the Colorado.

Early on our fifth day we reached Brushy Creek, near Round Rock, Texas. Jack urged his mules into the creek and, as they struggled up the far bank, the wagon got mired in muck. Rocky and I skirted around, and up onto the bank. We tied ropes to the front corners of the wagon, then spread out to each side to help the mules pull it out.

With ropes cinched around our saddle horns, and pulled tight against the wagon, Jack slapped the reins, yelling, "Heeya... Git up thar... Heeya!" The mules chugged with short, choppy steps, while our horses did the same against the ropes. The wagon creaked, barely moved, then finally broke loose, and climbed the bank.

Meanwhile, Jim saw that we had things well in hand, so he checked upstream searching for a more solid bank. We only had to shift a short way to the right, and the herd crossed easily.

That afternoon, as we headed toward Waco, I could see storm clouds building in the western sky. Jim rode up beside me, and said, "Looks like it could be a gully-washer headed our way."

"Think yer right," I said. "Been watchin' it build. Gettin' pretty black out there."

He tugged on his hat. "Let's start circlin' 'em up before it hits. Got your slicker handy?"

I reached back, and pulled the edge of it out of my saddlebag for him to see. "Got it real handy."

"I'm gonna check back down the line, make sure they're all on their toes, 'n let 'em know what we're doin'." He reined Dunny around, and waved as he spurred him into a gallop.

Keeping a close eye on the threatening storm, we began pushing the cattle to the right, starting to circle and bunch them up. The storm was building fast, and closing in on us. At the leading edge of the heavy black clouds, was a rolling line of white clouds. Beautiful... and eerie.

Pulling on my slicker, I noticed Rocky doing the same. I felt the wind gusting, and tugged down on my Stetson. I knew the rain wasn't far behind. Hopefully, we'd have the herd bunched up before the sky opened up.

Then, suddenly, the very thing that we didn't want to happen, happened.

A huge, fiery bolt of lightning struck a tree, not more than a quarter-mile from us. It was instantly followed by a bone-rattling clap of thunder. I knew what would come next. The cattle began to bellow, and break away in fright. We had the makings for a serious stampede on our hands.

I spurred Duchess, and yelled, "C'mon Duke! Get out in front!" In a few strides, we were at full gallop and overtaking the lead steers.

A stampeding herd, if it reaches full force, is like living thunder. The deep, roaring sound is like nothing you've ever experienced. It can freeze some men to their core with fear, and shoot panic through their hearts.

"Keep 'em movin' to the right, Duke!" I shouted, as I began to ease Duchess over, crowding the steers, and forcing them to be circling to the right again. In a stampede situation, cowhands all know to turn the cattle to the right, so we're all working together. And you keep pushin' to the right, until you have 'em going in a circle that begins to spiral in on itself. This will eventually slow the herd, and bring it under control.

Rocky, knowing what would happen, cut his horse to the left through the line of cattle, getting out on their left side before it was a full-fledged stampede. From there, he could help crowd the herd, pushing them to the right.

As I worked Duchess out in front, continuing to push to the right, one steer broke loose and tried to head straight out, which could start real trouble. "Get on him, Duke," I shouted, but he was way ahead of me. He was already running at the steer's shoulder, stride for stride, barking and trying to nip at its front shoulder. Finally, frightened enough by Duke's harassment, the steer cut to the right, and joined the herd that was continuing to circle.

With Rocky's help, and that of the next riders, we soon had the front of the herd bending around, and circling tighter and tighter. We seemed to be gaining some control.

Farther back in the herd, one of the flankers was trying to cut through the stampede. Galloping and weaving through the cattle, his horse stepped in a hole left by a burrowing animal. The horse flipped, tossing the rider and, though the cattle would instinctively try to jump over or around him, the cowboy figured he was done for. Trying to cover himself, he hid behind a small boulder, but was kicked and stomped repeatedly.

His flanking partner saw what happened, and reined his horse into the herd. He knew this might mean getting thrown and trampled himself, but didn't hesitate. He rode toward his fallen partner, then tried to block and divert the cattle around him.

Amazingly, it worked. Dillard and his horse held their ground, and the cattle jumped, cut, and dodged around them, until a gap had opened up in the stampeding herd. The move had saved Lefty, his fallen buddy.

Soon, we had the front of the herd circling in on itself, and things were beginning to come under control. The whole herd was slowing, as they continued to circle.

I noticed Dillard dismounting way back in the herd, and wondered what he was doing. *Gonna get himself trampled*, I thought, feeling a little panic. Later, I learned he could see Lefty's horse struggling, screeching in pain. When he slid from the saddle and looked closer, he saw the horse had a badly broken a leg, and was in terrible pain. Knowing it had to be put down, he reached for his gun. He stopped, realizing he could start the herd stampeding again. He took his hand from his gun, and knew what he had to do.

When he drew his knife, his heart sank. It seemed like such a cruel act, but it would be much more cruel to allow the horse to go on in agony. He stepped around, reached under its chin, and slit its throat. In moments, it stopped its writhing, and Dillard was left with a deep sense of sadness.

Watching it all, Lefty knew it had to be done. When Dillard moved to help him up, he told Lefty, "Sorry pard'."

"No need," Lefty replied. "You had to do it."

Lefty was a mess of torn, bloodied clothes, and Dillard noticed how gingerly he was holding his right forearm. "Bust it?" he asked, with a grimace.

"Reckon so. My wrist I think."

"At least it's on your right arm," Dillard told him, trying to make light of it.

Lefty is Gregory Lewis Mayweather III, but he always thought the name was too pompous. So, since he wore his gun on his left hip, and worked his lasso with his left hand — he'd never learned to read or write, so didn't know which hand he'd use for writing — he was branded "Lefty" at a young age and preferred that to his real name.

"Let's get you to the chuck wagon," Dillard said. "See if Flap Jack can do somethin' with yer broken wrist." He climbed back in the saddle, grabbed Lefty by his good arm, and swung him onto the back of his horse. He heard Lefty's groan, and asked, "You okay?"

"Yeah, let's go," Lefty moaned, trying to hide his pain.

Before the storm hit, Jim had told Jack to make camp. "We're gonna bunch 'em up quick as we can." So Jack had parked the chuck wagon and built a fire. Then, knowing the storm was gonna hit soon, he put up the extra canvas he carried under the wagon. This would give the hands a place to gather, and be out of the rain. When the stampede started, all Jack could do was watch.

As Dillard and Lefty rode up, Jack saw the trouble, and helped ease Lefty from the horse. When they told Jack the story, he slowly shook his head. He stared silently for a moment, then finally whispered, "Lordie me, Lefty. Surprised yer still breathin'."

Chapter Eight

"I reckon a trail cook is usually 'spose to know somethin' 'bout doctorin' stuff," Flap Jack said. "But... 'fraid I don't know the first thing 'bout a broken arm. And probably not much about any other doctorin' kind of stuff either. We hafta round up someone who knows a thing or two about broken bones."

Dillard saw me near the herd, and waved his hat to get my attention. When he knew that he'd caught my eye, he frantically motioned me over. He looked like it was really urgent, so I reined Duchess around, and galloped over to them. I called out, "What's up?" as Duchess eased to a stop near the canvas.

"Know anything 'bout a broken arm?" Dillard shouted, to be heard over the noise of the cattle.

I swung down, saying, "Might be able to help a little." As I dropped the reins to ground hitch Duchess, I saw Duke head toward Jack. He was hoping, I'm sure, to get his usual chunk of leftover meat, and lots of attention.

"I saw you struggling back there in the herd," I told Dillard. "What happened?"

He explained about Lefty's fall, and how he tried to shield him from the stampeding cattle. "We got real lucky, and the herd began to separate. Must'a been someone's guardian angel lookin' after us."

Seeing how torn up Lefty was, I said, "Looks to me like the whole stampede ran you over."

45

He forced a grin. "Feels like it, too."

Jack started cleaning the cuts and bruises around Lefty's head and neck. He said, "Best git yer shirt off so's I kin clean more wounds, whilst they work on that arm." Lefty unbuttoned the shirt, then held out his good arm for Jack to pull it off. The sleeve on the broken arm was nearly ripped apart, and Jack carefully slid it off.

As Jack continued cleaning the wounds, I asked Lefty to raise his arm a little. Wincing, and with a fair amount of effort, he slowly lifted it. I carefully put my hand under his elbow to help hold it, and could see right off that it was a bad break just above his wrist.

"See this bone running from the heel of your hand up to your elbow," I said, pointing just above his wrist.

He nodded, as he responded, "Mmm hmm."

"See how it's bulged out here?"

"Mmm hmm," he hummed again.

"That says it's not only broke, but it's pushed out of place." To show him, I held up my index fingers, touching them together tip to tip. "There's breaks..." I said, and angled my fingers to show a break.

"And then there are bad breaks." This time, I moved my fingers so they were angled, and out of line with one another.

As he watched this, his eyes squinted and he cringed, as though it hurt just to see it. He glanced down at his arm, and said, "That's what I got... ain't it."

"'Fraid so," I told him. "And, we gotta get it back in line or it won't heal right, and you'll have trouble with it the rest of your life."

He shuttered. "Think I know what that means. And don't think I like it."

"'Fraid so," I said, again. "We'll have to give it a tug to get it back in line, and it'll likely hurt more than when you broke it."

With the cattle mostly under control, and the crew slowly circling to keep 'em calm, Jim rode over to check on us. He slid from the saddle, and shook the rain from his hat as he stepped under the canvas awning. "I hear you took a bad fall, Lefty. How you doin'?"

"Been better," he told him.

"We gotta set his arm, Jim," I said.

As Jim looked closer, I added, "I know drinkin' on the trail is against the rules, and can get us fired. But, you also told me that you carry a bottle of whiskey wrapped-up in yer saddlebag... for emergencies."

He nodded, waiting for me to continue.

"We got a serious emergency here, and some of that whiskey sure could help."

He glanced back at Lefty's arm, then squinted saying, "Busted bad, ain't it."

"Yup, and a few shots of that whiskey would sure help him when we try to set it."

Without hesitating, he fetched the bottle, pulled the cork and slid it in his shirt pocket, then handed the jug to Lefty. "Take a couple good pulls on that," he told him, with a quick nod of his head.

Lefty held it up, saluting Jim, and then took two long swallows. He shook his head, smacked his lips, and, in a croaking whisper, said, "Smooooth!"

After a short while, and two more tugs on the bottle, he said, "Amazing how it starts to ease the pain." Then he looked up and forced a grin.

"Think we should use his belt for him to bite down on?" Jack asked.

"Nah," I replied, shaking my head. "Tastes like old leather. Got a thick chunk of jerked beef in the wagon?"

His eyes brightened. "That does sound a mite better."

Eustace rode up to see what had happened. "Anything I kin do t' hep?" he asked, as he slid from the saddle.

I thought a moment, then said, "Yeah, there is. We're gonna need a splint for Lefty's arm when we get the bone reset. Think you can round somethin' up from that clump of trees yonder?"

"Ah sure kin," he said. He swung back in the saddle, and headed toward the trees.

"Time to try and set it," I said. "Jim, you're the tallest. You wanna hold him from behind?"

"Sure thing," he answered.

48

Helping Lefty to his feet, I told Jim, "From behind, you can wrap your left arm over his shoulder and across his chest. Then hook your right hand under his arm pit, so you can hold back 'n keep him steady when I pull."

He nodded, saying, "Got it."

Jack handed Lefty a thick chunk of jerky. "Here you go pard'. Clamp your jaws down on this." As Lefty slid the jerky in his mouth and bit down, Jim took hold of him.

"Ready Lefty?" I asked.

He hesitated. Then, with a lot of fear showing in his eyes, he nodded.

Looking at Jim, I said, "We'll do this on three. One, two, and pull on three."

Jim nodded, and Lefty did too. Tiny sweat beads were forming on Lefty's forehead, and I figured more waiting wasn't going to help him. "Here we go... one... two... three." As I grunted three, I was pulling on his hand.

Lefty let out a muffled scream that I tried to ignore. I felt his wrist move and the bone shift, so I eased off on the pressure. He showed relief, and sagged into Jim's arms.

"Think we got it," I said, seeing that the bulge in his arm was gone.

Jim relaxed his hold, and then softly patted Lefty on the chest. "I think it was worth it, pard'. Is it feeling any better yet?"

"Not yet," Lefty groaned.

Eustace was near the clump of trees working on getting a splint. Soon, he was in the saddle and headed back to us. He reined his horse to a stop, and leaned to hand me what he'd found. "Will dis work?"

I took the chunk of wood and studied it, as he slid from the saddle. It was a curved piece from a dead tree trunk that was about a foot 'n a half long. Eustace had cleaned up the jagged edge on one end, and, on the thicker end, he'd carved a smooth, round edge.

"Kin ah shows ya?" he asked.

"Sure," I said, and handed it back to him.

"See here... he kin lay his arm in 'da curve of 'da wood, 'n wrap 'is hand over 'da roun' end... like 'dis."

I was a little surprised and glanced up, as Jim said, "Now, that's what I call a splint."

Eustace added, "If ya lays a folded cloth on 'da wood fer a pad, 'den wrap it up snug, it'll hold da arm good."

"Thanks Eustace," Lefty said, staring at the splint. "That's really somethin'."

Eustace nodded, and then looked down at the ground, not used to compliments from white folks.

Flap Jack tore bandages from a piece of cloth, while I folded a piece to lay in the splint as a cushion. When I moved to lay Lefty's arm in it, Eustace quietly interrupted, asking, "Kin ah check his arm?"

A little surprised, again, I stepped back making room for him. "Sure you can, Eustace."

Eustace carefully took Lefty's arm in his hands. He looked closely, nodded his head, then slowly put his hands around the break. Closing his eyes, he gently squeezed.

Lefty's eyes grew wide. "It feels real warm," he told us. "And it's easing the pain some, too."

Not sure what to think, I glanced at Jim, who seemed to have the same puzzled feeling that I did.

As Eustace slowly removed his hands and stepped back, I asked, "What did you do there, Eustace?"

"Jus' put muh han's on it," he said slowly, and shrugged. "Seems t' hep folks when ah does it."

JIM CLUSKEY

BRANDING IRON

Chapter Nine

Later, eating some supper, I asked, "Eustace, did you say folks feel better after holding your hands on them?"

"Yeah, dey say it heps."

"That it helps," I said.

"That - it - helps," he repeated, slowly.

I nodded at him. "When did you learn you could do this for people?"

Scratching his head — and his memory — he slowly said, "Mehbee when I's 'bout twelve yeahs ol'."

"How did you figure it out... that you could do this?"

"My li'l sis break her ankle," he started to say.

"Broke..." I said, interrupting. "Broke her ankle."

"Yeah, she *broke* her ankle, an' while we waits fer *help*, ah try t' calm her, so ah gently put muh han's 'round her ankle, hopin' it might help. Muh Gran-ma-mah – she live ova' neah Baton Rouge – she a healer, 'n ah see her do dis t' folks who's hurt. So, ah try'd it."

"What happened?" I asked... more interested in his story now, then his speaking correctly.

"Sophie, das my li'l sis, she calm down 'n say it feel better. She say it feel warm, 'n not so much pain."

"That's what Lefty said, too, when you held his arm. Do you know what you do? How you make it work?"

Shaking his head, he said, "No... ah jus' puts muh hands on. When I tol' Gran-ma-mah 'bout what happen wit' Sophie, she say dat ah was like she is. She a healer 'n knows lots of good medicine, 'n some folks say she has magic, too."

"What kind of medicines?" I asked.

"She grow'd up in Florida, 'n her daddy was frens wit' a Seminole medicine man. After da Shaman see dat Gran-ma-mah has her magic, he began t' teach her all 'bout da medicines. When Gran-ma-mah see dat I's blessed too, she start showin' me da medicines. Der's lots of t'ings in nature dat help wit' healing."

"There's lots of things," I said slowly. "What kind of things?"

"*There's things*," he struggled to say. "Things that grow. Like da prickly pear, it heals wounds. Or dandaline, it helps a bad stomach. White willow bark can ease pain, 'n ahm gonna cook summa dat fer Lefty."

"You have some of that stuff with you?" I asked, surprised.

"Yeah, ah carries a medicine pouch dat has lotta stuff fer medicines."

I knew a lot about Eustace already – that he's a friendly, generous sort; that he's good with animal's; that he's a big, strong man, standing six-two and a solid two hundred 'n thirty pounds; and, that he's a very hard worker. But, it seems, I'd given him way too little credit for being knowledgeable.

"I never noticed you had a pouch," I said.

"Yup. Ah carrys it in muh saddlebag. Ah learned from Gran-ma-mah what t' look fer, n' what t' keep in muh pouch. Most folks doan know what t' search for – what dey look like, or where t' find 'em. Ahs always on da lookout fer plants, 'n roots, 'n such."

I can tell he likes that I'm interested. "I'd like to see your pouch sometime. Maybe you can show me tonight when you make that willow bark remedy for Lefty." A quick nod of his head, said he'd show me.

It rained all that night, and into the next day. Flap Jack had been sharp enough to park the wagon on a small knoll. We could spread our bedrolls under the awning and wagon, and the rain drained away in all directions.

Taking our shifts ridin' herd that night, kept every man soaked from his hat to his boots. It was warm enough to stay comfortable, though, in spite of being soaked. The camp fire, just outside the canvas awning, gave off plenty of heat, if anyone needed warming.

Being wet is as much a part of the cowpuncher's life as being coated in dust. Next day, the hot Texas sun would bake everything dry. Soon enough, we'd be caked with trail dust again, until the next rain or river crossing washed it away.

I spread my bedroll beneath the wagon. The ground was still dry and, though I was mostly soaked, I was comfortable under my wool blanket. Duke followed me under the wagon, and curled up next to me. After a little scratching behind his ears, I told him, "Time to get some shut-eye, boy." He tucked his nose into his fur, then drifted into dreamland, and the dreams that dogs dream.

55

Asleep in no time, I enjoyed the peaceful bliss we somehow sense as we slip away. After a few hours of deep sleep, I felt a nudge, and heard, "Hey... Mack. It's near midnight. Time for your watch."

"Mmm hmm," I groaned, forcing myself up on an elbow, and rubbing my eyes. "Okay, Josh," I said, and began to crawl from beneath the wagon.

I nudged Eustace and Rocky, saying, "Time to ride." They were on watch with me, along with three others, for the next couple hours. Then we could sleep again. I walked toward Duchess, Duke by my side, and saw her slumbering. Her rump was pointed into the northwest breeze, her head was hung low, and her eyes were closed. "Time to go to work, Duchess," I said softly, as I neared her. She raised her head, shaking off the rain... and the sleep.

I put her bridle on, and tightened the saddle's cinch. Then, with a hop and a tug on the horn, I stuck my boot in the stirrup and swung into the saddle. Seeing Eustace and Rocky ready to do the same, I said, "I'll ride out and tell Johnny, Muley, and the others, that they can head back to camp. See you guys out there.

Muley's real name is Walter Schmidt. He's known among the crew as a stubborn German, and Flap Jack had branded him with the name "Muley." He figured the man was just as stubborn as the mules pulling the chuck wagon. Surprisingly, Walt accepted the nickname with a grin. He even had a sense of pride about it.

Chapter Ten

At daybreak, I was yanked from my sleep by Flap Jack banging on the bottom of a tin pot with a big ladle. "Rise 'n shine you yayhoos. Coffee's hot."

Jim was up before daybreak, and had decided to move the herd. In the soft, steady rain, the cattle were calm, and grazing on good Texas range grass. It's not like the lush, green stuff they have in other parts of our country, but most western ranchers claim there's as much nutrition, maybe even more, in the range grasses.

"When we're through with breakfast, and camp is packed," Jim said, "we're gonna move 'em out. They've had a good long night restin' 'n grazin', so I figure we can get ten, maybe eleven miles behind us... even in this rain."

Sure 'nuf, by three o'clock that afternoon, we'd moved the herd nearly nine miles. It was beginning to clear, showing a slice of beautiful blue sky at the horizon. By the time the last raindrops had moved off to the east, the afternoon sun was shining bright.

I glanced over to check where Rocky was, and saw the brightest, most beautiful double rainbow I'd ever seen. Leaning back in my saddle, I rested my hands on the horn, and whispered, "Wow!"

I scanned the area, looking for Rocky, and didn't see him anywhere up and down the line. I was puzzled, and a bit concerned. As we continued north, I kept checking for him. Just about the time I was gonna have Muley ride out to try 'n track him down, I spotted the silhouette of a rider.

I pulled Duchess to a stop, and turned to get a better look. As I reached in the saddlebag to get my spyglass, Duke sat near, and was staring up at me with his head tilted as though puzzled.

"Gotta find Rocky," I said, as I raised the spyglass. He lay down, and rested his head on his outstretched paws, satisfied with my explanation.

I focused the glass, and sure 'nuff, it was Rocky. His rope was wrapped on his saddle horn, and pulled tight behind. With its head lifted slightly by the rope, I could see it was a deer he was dragging.

"Let's go get Flap Jack," I told Duke, as I tucked my glass back in the saddlebag. We rode up beside the wagon, and I shouted to Jack, "Rocky's comin' up the east side draggin' a deer. Maybe you should swing around 'n meet him and get his deer."

"Will do," he said, with a big nod. He slowed his mules, then swung them to the east, circling wide of the cattle. He drove the wagon partway back, then stopped to wait for Rocky. A bit later I glanced back to see Jack standing behind the chuck wagon, getting out his gear.

Soon, I saw the two of them on their knees, dressing out the deer, skinning the hide, and putting the carcass in the back of the wagon. It was ready for carving at suppertime. Jack took a dipper-full of water and slowly poured it over Rocky's arms and hands to wash away the blood. Then Rocky did the same for Jack.

With his mules at a smooth, steady trot, Jack rolled out front of the herd again. I galloped Duchess up beside the wagon, and asked, "What is it?"

"He got a nice, fat doe. Be good eatin' tonight."

"Alright!" I shouted back. "I'm hungry already."

"I'm gonna roll ahead and find Jim," he said. "See where he plans to hunker down for the night. I'll set up camp, and start carving that venison. I'll have it ready to cook when you boys get 'em circled up."

With a nod, and the tip of the hat, I reined Duchess around. "C'mon Duke," I shouted. He had been trailin' the wagon, tryin' to figure out the rich scent coming from inside. He turned toward me, glanced back at the wagon, then came on a run.

Later on that night, as we feasted on fresh steaks and chops from Rocky's nice deer, I asked him, "I didn't see you up near Jack... when did you round up your rifle from the wagon?"

He waved his fork, while he finished chewing and swallowing, then said, "You'd swung back to pick up three strays just about the time I'd caught sight of a small herd of deer going over a rise to the east. After getting my rifle, I rode out to the ridge where I'd last seen 'em."

He reached for his coffee cup, took a couple sips, and then continued. "I got to the ridge, swung down from the saddle, and took off my hat to sneak to the top. When I peeked over the ridge, I saw seven deer drinking at a small pond. They were maybe sixty yards down the slope."

He drank some coffee again, and I could see it was as much to let the drama build, as to quench his thirst. After glancing around at his audience, he went on.

"On the far side of the pool there was a big buck... a real dandy. But he was already on alert, and I figured he would be tough meat. So, before he alarmed the rest, I took aim at this doe, and dropped her right there."

"Did the right thing," I said. "Sure is tender."

"No thanks to the good cookin', I s'pose," Jack snarled, "that it's nice 'n tender like it is."

"Oh yeah," Rocky, and several others, hurried to say. "It's mostly thanks to you!"

"Cooked to perfection," I added, saluting him.

He stopped poking at the campfire and, with the cockiness of a cactus sparrow, gave us a big grin.

We rolled along, day upon day without a hitch, much to Jim's satisfaction. We hadn't lost more than a few cattle to straying, or the stampede, or any other natural cause.

Late morning of the tenth day, we were nearing Kimball's Bend where we'd cross the Brazos River. As we came to the river, both Jim and I noticed three canvas-covered wagons. They had come across the river from the other direction, and were headed southwest.

Though the wagons were a little ways off, something struck me as not quite right about the look of things. Each wagon was driven by a woman, with another sitting at her side. And there were one or two women in the back of each wagon, who sat quietly, staring out the back.

I saw only four men, two riding out front, and two trailing behind. They didn't have the look of family men, and the women all wore a somber stare. I nudged Duchess and rode over next to Jim.

"Anything strike you funny about that bunch?" I asked, as I nodded toward the wagons.

"Yeah," he said, still staring out at them. "Not quite sure what, but it must've struck you as a little strange, too."

"Well, they're a ways off, but looks to me like the women are all young, and attractive, and all wearing a sour look. Not a single one has glanced our way, either."

"Now that you mention it, that's right," he said. "Normally, you'd expect at least a polite wave."

"Strange," I said, almost whispering.

It took us nearly two hours to get the herd across the Brazos, while Flap Jack was setting up camp a half-mile to the north. We bunched the cattle up for the night, and I rode over to talk with Jim.

I took my hat off, and pulled out my bandana to wipe my forehead. "You know those wagons back there..." I paused, staring back across the river. "That whole situation seems strange, and it's kind of gnawing at me."

"I've been thinkin' about that thing a bit myself," he admitted. "What'cha thinkin'?"

"If you don't mind, I'd like to take Eustace, and ride back there. Check things out a little closer before dusk. May not find anything, but it's worth a look."

61

Rubbing his chin, as he stared in the direction the wagons had gone, he finally said, "Guess that'd be okay. But... if somethin's not right, you come back and get us before tryin' to do anything."

I told Eustace what I was planning to do, and asked if he would ride with me. "Sure will," he said, and tightened the cinch on his saddle once again.

"Gonna be late for supper," I told him.

"Makes me no neva-mind," he said, as he swung into the saddle. "I ain't been starvin' none."

I swung up on Duchess, and we took off at a gallop. As always, Duke was beside us, running stride for stride. We crossed the river, and had the wagons in sight in a half hour. As we got closer, I motioned for Eustace to slow his horse to a walk. A couple of the men with the wagons had taken notice of us, and before we got close I wanted to tell him what I was thinking.

"When we get to these folks, Eustace, I'm gonna say we're in need of medical help for one of our hands. So, just go along with the tale."

"I'll be watchin' close," he said.

Chapter Eleven

By the time we drew near, the four men riding with the wagons were on full alert. The women stared straight ahead, as though afraid to even glance around. We slowed our horses as we came to the trailing pair of riders. I nodded, and thumbed my hat. "Howdy," I said politely.

The riders barely nodded to acknowledge the greeting, so we rode toward the front. Studying each wagon as we passed, I noticed that all the women continued to stare strait forward. When we passed the front wagon, and neared the lead riders, one of them turned his horse toward us and stopped. He held up a hand, shouting, "Hold up!"

The wagons came to an immediate halt, and the rider, evidently the man in charge of this troop, gave a menacing stare at Eustace, and then turned to me, asking, "How can I help you?" He looked bothered by our being there, and his tone was less than friendly.

With a quick glance back at the wagons, still puzzled, I said, "We were hopin' someone in your party might know a little doctorin'. We got a cowhand that's come down with a terrible fever. He's in real bad shape."

He gave me a long, measuring look, then said, "Sorry, but we got no one can help you. And I just-a-soon you move aside so you don't spread such a fever to us."

He raised a hand, shouting, "Let's roll 'em." Then, without another word, he reined his horse around, and rode away. Eustace and I backed our horses out of the way, as the wagons began moving.

I studied the woman who was driving the first wagon, and the woman sitting next to her. The one riding shotgun nervously glanced from me to the lead riders, and back to me. Then she gave a quick flick of her thumb, pointing back over her shoulder. I stared, not sure what she meant. I wanted to try and get more from her, but saw her sit up straight, rigidly staring forward. Then I noticed one of the lead riders was looking back at her. I tried to act as though unconcerned, and took a drink from my canteen.

When the second wagon neared, I noticed the driver give a quick glance front and back. Then, holding the reins in one hand, she showed me something white held in the other. I nodded to let her know I saw, but I was not sure what it meant. Next, she lowered her hand beside the wagon seat, and let the something white flutter away.

"See that, Eustace?" I said, barely above a whisper.

"Mmm hmm," he hummed. Now it was his turn to try to look unconcerned with the whole thing, as he took a long drink from his canteen.

When the trailing riders passed by, I thumbed my hat toward them again. I guess it was to agitate them more than anything. "Let's give 'em time to move away before we pick that up," I said, studying the wagons.

"Mmm hmm," he hummed, again.

A short while later, a breeze fluttered the something white, blowing it closer to us. "Glad it didn't blow when those riders were passing by," I said, glancing in their direction to be sure they hadn't seen.

Once again, he hummed, "Mmm hmm."

Staring in the distance, I told him, "Wish you wouldn't go on-and-on the way you do, Eustace."

He leaned on his saddle horn, giving me a serious look. "Ah'll try 'n keep it down," he said, then grinned.

Studying the wagons, as they moved away in a dust cloud, I said, "I think they're far enough out. If you nudge your horse ahead just a bit, it'll block their view, while I get down 'n pick that up."

As he moved, I swung down from Duchess, grabbed the piece of material, and got back in the saddle. It looked like cloth torn from a petticoat, or some other garment. On it were letters that looked like they were scrawled with the burnt end of a stick. It read... *HELP - KIDNAP.*

For a long while, I stared down at it, then out at the wagons shrinking in the distance. *Must be... gotta be,* I thought.

"What's it read?" Eustace finally asked.

"I think those women are being kidnapped," I said, showing him the note.

He gave it a quick glance, then looked out toward the wagons. I remembered he once said that his reading wasn't too good. "What we's gonna do?" he asked, looking from the wagons back to me.

I paused, staring down at the note again, then pushed my hat back on my head. "Guess we'd better ride back to see Jim before we do anything," I said.

He tugged his hat down. "Let's hightail it back dere."

We swung our horses, and spurred 'em into a gallop. I grabbed at my hat, almost losing it to the wind. We crossed the Brazos River, and in a short while caught up with the herd. Seeing us coming on the run, Jim reined Dunny around and rode to meet us.

As we pulled to a stop beside each other, Jim shouted, "What'd ya find out?"

As Duchess settled, I reached out to hand him the piece of white material. "Trouble," I told him.

He took it, studied it a moment, then looked back at Eustace and me. "Kidnapped?"

"Yeah..." I said, slowly. "And the way the women are acting, I can believe it."

He took off his hat, wiped his forehead, and then blew out a long, slow breath. "What ya thinkin'?" he finally asked.

I scratched the back of my neck. "I was hopin' you'd be okay movin' the herd for the next two days without Eustace, 'n Rocky, 'n me. We can track down where they make camp for the night, then figure out what to do."

"Ya know, if it's kidnappin', you're likely dealin' with some nasty hombres that can handle themselves... and their guns," he said.

"You're right," I said, "but Rocky 'n I are pretty fair with guns, and Eustace is darn good with his knife and shotgun." Eustace carries a cut-off ten gauge Parker that no man would want to face, and a big Green River knife."

"Any ideas what you'll do?" he asked.

66

"Nope. Have to play it as it's dealt."

"Guess we can't ignore it," he said. Then he gave me a serious look. "But... you be mighty careful. I don't want to be diggin' no graves."

"We will," I told him. "You can be sure of it."

"You kin be dern sure of it," Eustace added.

We rode over to talk with Rocky. I explained what we figured to do, and that we'd like his help. "There'll be plenty of risk..." I started to say.

He interrupted me, saying, "Count me in."

Rifles in our scabbards, and ammunition in our saddle bags, we were ready to ride. I told Jim, "We'll catch up to you in the next three days."

"I'll be countin' on that," he said, with a quick nod of his head.

Chapter Twelve

We rode back to where Eustace and I had left the wagons, and picked up their trail heading southwest. It led us into rolling country, with more trees and rocky buttes. We slowed our pace, keeping a lookout for where they had made camp. The last remnants of a long day lingered on the western horizon. A bright, full moon was rising in the east with a golden glow.

Figuring we had to be getting close, we dismounted and led our horses on foot, watching and listening for any sign of life ahead. Slowly cresting a rise, I saw the flicker of a campfire through the trees. "Hold it," I whispered, pointing down the slope. "Down there."

Three or four hundred yards ahead, we could see the glow of a campfire. In the quiet darkness, we could hear an occasional voice echo up the slope, though we couldn't make out what they were saying. "Let's tie the horses back down the rise a bit, out of range," I said. "We can move in on foot, quiet and slow."

Rifles in hand, we circled left to move through an area thick with trees, hoping not to be seen or heard. We came to a small rocky ridge and guessed they were camped not more than ninety yards beyond. We peered over the rocks, and had a good view of them – not more than sixty yards beyond.

The wagons, dimly lit by the moon and the small fire still burning, were all parked in a row. To the right was mostly open range, and to the left were trees and rocks. I counted eleven women, each lying on a blanket, with their hands and feet tied. The ropes were looped through the wagon wheels to thwart any escaping.

Two men were spreading bedrolls to the left of the fire, and a third was already stretched out on his. Where was the fourth man?

I ducked behind the rock ridge and, when Eustace and Rocky followed, I whispered, "See the three hombres by the campfire?"

"Ya... but where's da fourt' one?" Eustace asked.

I nodded. "That was my next question. We've gotta stay put 'till we spot him." We slowly stood to scan the area again. After what seemed like a long while of staring hard into the darkness, I wondered what we would do if we don't spot that fourth guy, who was very likely standing guard somewhere nearby.

Just then Eustace touched my forearm. "Up der," he whispered. "See dat clump of rock t' da left of da fire, den up? He sittin' in dose rocks. Ah seen da firelight shine offa his rifle."

I studied the shadowy rocks, then finally caught part of his silhouette. "See him, Rocky?" I whispered.

"Not yet," he said.

"Keep watchin'. You'll spot him if he moves."

In moments, he whispered, "There you are. Now I see you number four."

Again, I ducked behind the rocks. When they knelt beside me, I said, "Think we should get comfortable here, and give 'em some time. Make sure everyone in camp is sleeping, before we try move on the one standing guard."

70

"When we's ready t' move," Eustace said, "Ah kin git dat one standin' guard."

"*We're*... when *we're* ready to move," I whispered.

He grinned. "When *we're* ready."

"Alright," I said, checking my watch. "Let's give 'em a half-hour, then we'll make our move."

Sitting there, waiting in the darkness, time passed slowly. Finally, a half hour later, we stood to check things again. The fire had burned down to glowing embers, but in the moonlight we could see everything was calm and quiet in the camp, except for the loud snoring of one of the hombres sleeping by the fire.

"What'cha thinkin', Eustace?" I asked.

"Gimme ten minutes t' circle 'round, 'n sneak inta da rocks bahine 'im. Den you snap a twig, loud, t' git his attention. If he doan move, snap anudder one. When he move... ah gots 'im."

"Okay podner," I said, checking my watch again. "You got ten minutes." He turned, and snuck away.

While we waited, Rocky and I talked about rushing the camp as soon as Eustace had control of the guard. We'd get the drop on the other three, before they were fully awake and knew what was happening.

Soon, I said, "It's been eleven minutes. Hope Eustace is ready." I reached for a dead branch, stood and snapped it, loudly. Staring into the shadows where the guard was hidden, I saw moonlight glinting off metal, telling me he had probably moved, but only a bit.

"He's still in the shadows," Rocky said. "Better snap another one."

Grabbing a second, larger twig, I reached up and snapped it. Then we both spotted the silhouette coming out of the shadows, slowly moving toward us.

Eustace had worked his way to the backside of the rocks where the guard was perched. Like a big cat waiting patiently for its prey to make a move, Eustace waited to hear the snap of a twig, then see the movement of his prey.

He heard the first snap, and was on high alert, adrenaline pumping. He watched, and listened for any sign of the guard moving from his shadowy perch.

Nothing.

Then he heard another crack, and saw the silhouetted figure slowly moving from his blind in the rocks. *A li'l futher*, Eustace thought. *Jus' a li'l futher.*

If the man moved ahead a little more, Eustace had a clear path across a large, flat rock to silently rush him. Second by second, he waited for his prey to move farther.

The guard, attention focused on where the noise had come from, crept ahead slowly, cautiously, rifle at the ready. Eustace decided it was time and, like the big cat, rushed his prey in silence. Before the man knew what was happening, Eustace had an arm around him, and knife blade pressed to his throat. He quickly whispered in the guard's ear. "Make a move or a sound, 'n dis blade cuts yer t'roat."

From where we stood, we could see the shadowy movement play out. "He must have him," Rocky said.

"Think yer right," I told him. "Otherwise all hell would be bustin' loose. Let's move!"

We rushed the camp and, as we neared the sleeping men, I shouted, "Hands up! Nobody touch a gun!" As they came to life, I shouted again, "Touch a gun 'n ya get shot!"

Two of the men, startled awake, instinctively raised their hands. The third, who hadn't heard or wasn't gonna listen, scrambled for his pistol. Rocky fired at the man, shattering his shoulder. A pain-filled scream ripped through the quiet night air.

"My shoulder! Ya shot my shoulder!" he yelled.

"I'll do worse," Rocky growled, "you try anything stupid like that again."

Just then, we heard Eustace say, "An' here's da udder one." I saw him coming through the trees, nudging the fourth man toward us with his shotgun.

Suddenly, the man whirled on Eustace, trying to grab his shotgun. In one fluid motion, Eustace hit him hard in the stomach with the butt of his shotgun, and then as the man bent forward, Eustace came up hard with his knee.

I heard the sickening crunch of the man's nose being broken. It slammed him backwards to the ground, where he covered his nose with both hands, and lay there groaning in pain, blood streaming through his fingers.

"Stop da groanin'," Eustace told him, "'n git over der by da udder woman beatin' cowards."

"Rocky," I said, "Eustace and I can keep these boys covered. Why don't you cut the ladies loose."

73

"Yes! Please," one of them shouted, sounding very relieved.

Soon, with all the women cut free, I said, "Alright boys, each one of you go sit by a wagon wheel. Your turn to spend the night tied up to 'em. We'll see how you like the kind of treatment you been dishin' out."

"Just gimme a gun," one of the women shouted, as she rubbed her wrists where the ropes had been cut free. "I'll take care these butchers!"

"No... we're not going to do that," I said, trying my best to calm her.

She walked over to where the one with the shot-up shoulder lay. Looking down at his blood-soaked shirt, and the pain etched on his face, she said, "Good!"

Then, suddenly, she lashed out with a kick to his shattered shoulder. That brought another blood-curdling scream, ripping through the calm night air.

"Beat on us, you mangy cur!" she shouted, then moved to kick him again, as I stepped in to stop her.

"Easy, easy..." I said, holding her back. "They're all gonna get what they deserve."

Chapter Thirteen

With Rocky standing guard, I began tying each of the kidnappers to a wagon wheel. While I did that, Eustace patched the shoulder on the one Rocky had shot. I tied that guy up last, trying not to pull the rope quite as snug on his bad arm. Even so, he flinched and cussed as I strung him to the wheel.

Meanwhile, the women had rebuilt the fire, and were sitting on blankets, consoling one another. When we finally joined them, they poured out their thanks to each of us, over and over.

Lillian, the wagon driver who had dropped the note, said, "I just knew when you saw me drop the note, that you'd be back to help. I just knew it!"

I smiled at her, asking, "What's the story with them kidnapping you?"

"They planned on selling us into prostitution in Mexico," Jackie, the one who'd kicked the man's shoulder, scowled.

"Must be big money in it," Rocky said.

"Eight hundred bucks a piece," Jackie barked. "You boys sell yer cattle fer thirty or forty bucks a head, 'n they git eight hundred fer each one of us. The lousy, no good...."

"Easy, Jackie," Lillian interrupted.

"So, how'd this all happened?" I asked Lillian. She seemed to be the one the others looked up to.

"We're all from the Little Rock area," she said with a soft, sweet drawl. "They kidnapped us, one by one, and kept us in a house on the outskirts of the city. In a few days there were twelve of us."

"The cowards beat on us, too," Jackie, the feisty one, growled, as she glared at the kidnappers.

"Easy Jax, it's all going to be okay," Lillian said calmly. "They're gonna get theirs." Then, staring into the campfire, she went on.

"They would beat on us for any little reason. Put the fear of God in us... I figured. They did it right from the start to cower us, and have us under control."

"And we'd heal up just in time to sell us," one of the other women interjected. "It's frightening just to think...." She stopped, covered her face, and began to weep. Two other women tried to console her.

"Lillian, you mentioned there were twelve of you. I've only seen eleven," I said, glancing around.

"You're right," she said, sadly. "Candace was number twelve. She was a feisty one. Even more than Jax," she added, smiling at Jackie.

"What happened?"

Pausing, thinking back, she showed a sad smile. "Just a little too much fight in her. On the third evening out, we stopped to make camp and have supper. She sassed Johnny over there; he's the head rat that you talked to earlier today. Anyway, he didn't like her sassing him, so he moved to slap her... teach her another lesson.

76

"Well, she'd just poured herself a hot cup of coffee and, when he raised his hand to her, she threw it in his face. It hit the side of his face and neck, and he spun away yelling. Then, instantly, he spun back with his gun drawn and shot her." Lillian stopped and put a hand over her mouth, seeing it again in her mind.

I waited, letting her calm. Then she said, "That put us all in our place. From then on we behaved like slaves, knowing what could happen." She quickly put a hand to her mouth again, saying sheepishly, "Sorry Eustace."

"No need," he said, giving her a soft smile. "Ah surely knows da hell y'all went t'rough."

After a few moments of staring into the fire, I asked, "What did they do with Candace?"

"We asked if they'd let us bury her proper-like, and they reluctantly agreed. There was only one shovel, so we all took turns digging. Then Sadie," she nodded toward a woman who was smiling sadly, "said some words over her. Things she knew from the Bible.

"From that point on, we only talked with each other when we were on the wagons, while the men were riding front and back. I've been carryin' that note in my pocket for more than a week, waiting and hoping to see someone who maybe would help. And, like I figured, you did. God bless all of you! You did!"

The next morning, I awoke at daybreak to the sound of the women cookin' breakfast, and the sweet smell of fresh coffee. Eustace, Rocky and I had traded shifts throughout the night, standin' watch over the four varmints lashed to the wagon wheels.

As we ate breakfast, there was a noticeable change in the women. Their mood was brighter and more cheerful, and they talked of getting back to their lives in Little Rock. Freedom is a precious and wonderful thing.

"Like I mentioned last night," I said to Lillian, "we gotta be getting' back to the cattle drive. We've left 'em short-handed, and I'm sure our boss is lookin' for us."

"Are you certain we can handle these rats?" one of the other women asked, nervously.

"Yes," I told her, "I'm sure of it. When we're done tying 'em up, they won't be able to do anything but walk behind the wagons. And you've got all their guns now. You'll have four rifles, four revolvers, and two shotguns. From now on, you don't do anything near them without a few others standing guard.

"And you don't let 'em get near each other. That's the only way they could get free. We're gonna have 'em trussed up, then tied to the wagons by their neck. One of 'em will be hitched to the lead wagon, one to the rear wagon, and one on each side of the middle wagon. That way they can't get close to one another. And they're gonna walk all the way to the jailhouse in Waco."

Waco was the closest town with a sheriff, and they would be there in a day and a half. Then they could head home to Little Rock with the wagons and horses.

"What if they won't walk?" one woman asked.

"Then they'll get drug by their neck," I said with a grin. "Don't think they'll be tryin' anything like that. I think they'll be steppin' right along to stay upright."

Finished with breakfast, the women broke camp while we tied up the kidnappers for the hike to Waco. With each of them, we tied a piece of rope above the elbow of one arm, then behind their back to the other elbow. We snugged it tight so their elbows were drawn back. Then we tied another piece of rope to one wrist, and across the front to the other. Again, we snugged it up good 'n tight. This had their arms and hands completely immobilized, with no way for them to get at the knots.

Next, we tied pieces of rope into hangman's nooses, and tightened one over the neck of each man. Leaving seven or eight feet of slack, we attached each man to a wagon. This gave 'em plenty of rope to walk along during the day, and to lie down at night.

Showing Lillian, Jackie, and several others, how we'd tied 'em up, I told them, "You'll have 'em under complete control this way. But... no one should get near 'em without several others standing guard. Not even to give 'em a sip of water."

"I think we can do it," Jackie said. Then, plenty loud to be sure that all four of the varmints heard her, she added, "And I can't wait for any one of 'em to try somethin', so I can crack his skull with the butt of this shotgun."

Then, getting louder still, she yelled, "Hear that! Ya lousy, no good...." She cut herself short, and shook her head, as though trying to clear her mind of the whole experience.

I quietly told Lillian and Jackie, so not to be heard by the men, "You don't have to let them know, but if one stumbles and falls, I'd stop to let him back on his feet. No sense dealin' with a dead body. Punish 'em by makin' 'em walk all the way to the jail in Waco."

79

"You're probably right," Jackie said, softly, "even though I'd rather drag 'em by the neck."

Soon, we mounted up and were moving out with the wagons. We'd ride with them for about five miles, then we'd head northeast to catch up with our crew. The women would head southeast for Waco, and from there on to Little Rock.

At the point where we figured to turn north and leave them, we stopped to say goodbye. All eleven women hugged and thanked each of us again. Lillian was the last one to hug me, and tell me thank you. Looking up at me with a smile in her eyes, she said, sweetly, "I can't help but wish it had been another time 'n place that we'd met, Mack."

I took her in my arms again, squeezed her, and said, "I've thought the same." Then, studying her face, I added, "You take good care of yourself, Lill."

She rose to her tip-toes, gently kissed my cheek, and said, "You do the same, Mr. MacAlan."

Chapter Fourteen

We watched the wagons roll away, headed toward Waco. Staring in silence, I took a long drink from my canteen, as Rocky asked, "Think they're gonna be okay?"

"I think they'll be just fine," I said, slapping the cork into my canteen with the heel of my hand. "They've got all the guns now, and enough feistiness to keep those cur-dogs on the leash."

"Yeah... yer probably right," he said, as he put his hat back on his head.

"We bes' be gittin' back t' da herd," Eustace said, reaching for his saddle horn. We swung into our saddles, and nudged our horses into a steady lope. After crossing the Brazos — for the fifth time in two days — we turned north.

A cattle drive travels in a general direction, following the wide path of trails used by others, which lead to the best places to cross rivers and travel through rugged terrain. We knew they'd be working north toward Fort Worth, then they'd head for Trinity Ford. We figured to be catchin' up to them long before Fort Worth. The trail left by twenty-eight hundred head of cattle was no trick to follow.

In a couple of hours we came to a small creek that was winding its way across the range. It had just enough water flowing to let the horses a drink their fill and give them a breather. I slid from Duchess, loosened the cinch a bit, then let her step into the creek. Eustace and Rocky did the same with their horses, and soon the three of us were stretched out on the grassy bank of the creek.

As we lay there, I reached in my vest pocket for my watch, clicked it open, and said, "Just comin' up on one o'clock. Reckon we oughtta be seein' the herd before too long."

"Think yer right," Rocky said. "The cattle flop is lookin' pretty fresh. Can't be too far ahead."

"Bafoe we stop, ah seen a dust cloud 'gainst da horizon," Eustace said quietly. "Bet we catches 'em in an hour."

Eustace was right. Shortly after two o'clock we could see Whitey and Tuck pullin' up the rear of the herd. They gave a big wave when they saw us coming. Then, as we passed, Tuck cupped his hands around his mouth, and shouted, "Can't wait to hear yer story."

I waved, and shouted back, "See you in camp."

Before long, we could see Flap Jack's wagon rolling at the front of the herd. As we rode up beside him, he gave a surprise look, then leaned back on the reins shouting, "Whoa thar... Whoa now!" When the mules had come to a stop, he said, "You boys got back quicker'n I figured. And you don't look none the worse."

"It all went good," I said. "We'll tell ya all about it in camp tonight."

"Can't wait t' hear," he said. "How 'bout a plate of stew? Still got some that's warm in the kettle."

We were more than happy to take him up on that offer. He pulled his wagon to the side, and said, "I jis got done givin' all the crew a plate full of fresh stew for their noonin' as they passed by."

82

He handed each of us a plate of the stew, saying, "You'll have to drink water. I poured out the last dregs of the coffee when I packed up."

As I ate, I asked Jack, "Is Jim out scoutin'?"

"Yup. Haven't see'd him yet this afternoon. Should be back soon, though, t' let us know where we'll hunker down fer the night."

We finished eating, and, as he cleaned his plate with some wet sand, Rocky said, "Mighty fine vittles there, Jack. Pretty good stew."

Jack straightened, looked at Rocky, then snarled, "What? You expected somethin' less?"

"No, jist as good as I expected," Rocky shot back. "An' jist as ornery as expected, too."

Jack let out a hearty laugh. "You boys give as good as you take. That's why I like workin' with ya."

That evening, as we bunched up the herd, Jack made camp and started cooking supper. Everyone was anxious to hear our story of the kidnapper experience, but Eustace, Rocky, and I had decided to let their eagerness build, while we all finished eating. Then the suspense would end, and the story tellin' would begin.

First, we told of how we found their camp, and about Eustace's plan to take out the guard. Though he was a little embarrassed with all the attention, I could tell Eustace felt good about getting approval and praise from all the men.

"How'd you pull that off, Eustace?" Lefty asked.

"A li'l bit like huntin', ah guess. Muh Pappy showed me how t' be a good hunter... how to stalk real quiet like. Pappy was favored by da Masta, 'n he'd let us use guns t' hunt. We hunted deer, 'n bear. We even hunted gators 'n wild hogs a time er two.

"I figured wit' dis coyote's attention locked on Mack 'n Rocky over yonder, I could git up on him in a hurry."

"Think I'd been mighty nervous standin' there in yer boots, Eustace," Jim said. "One mistake, 'n that coyote whirls, and starts shootin'." Eustace nodded, knowing the complement Jim was giving him.

Next, we told about rushing the camp when we knew Eustace had the guard under control and about Rocky shooting the one in the shoulder to stop him from pulling a gun. "The guy was just a plain fool, going for his gun like he did," Rocky said, shaking his head.

When I explained how the feisty gal, Jackie, kicked the man in his shattered shoulder, some of the men around the campfire squeezed their eyes shut, cringing at the thought of it.

For nearly an hour, they asked questions about the kidnappers, the women, and the details of what happened. Finally, Jim said, "Well boys, time we get some shut-eye. And, don't forget that Muley 'n the others need to be relieved in two hours."

In the mornin', as we ate our breakfast, the six who'd been out ridin' herd at supper time wanted to hear the whole story. So, we retold it all, and most of the hands were right there, eagerly listening to the details all over again.

Chapter Fifteen

With the breakfast vittles picked clean, and the story telling wrung out, we broke camp and started the herd north. Soft blue light was seeping from the eastern horizon, and the sun would soon show itself. Through early morning, the sky filled with fluffy white clouds, and it was cooler than it had been for many days. It was a good day to be in the saddle, and it made the occasional diet of dust more bearable.

Early that afternoon, Jim rode up to let us know it'd be a long day. "I found a spot, near a large pond, where we can bed 'em down. But it's a couple miles farther north than I wanted. So we'll be pushin' 'em 'till dark."

"That'll be all right," I said with a shrug. "It's a good day for it."

"Would you have the boys spread the word back down the line. I'm going to take Jack on ahead, 'n show him where we'll make camp for the night." I nodded, as he reined Dunny around, and headed off to get Jack.

Like he figured, it was near dark when we circled the herd for the night. Jack was workin' on supper, and I was workin' on a mighty hunger.

"Man, what smells so good, Jack?" I asked, stopping in my tracks to take another whiff of the mouthwatering smell. Duke had raised his nose sniffing earlier, and now I knew why. It smelled mighty tasty.

Jack looked up with a big grin, and waved a chunk of meat. "Prairie chicken," he said. "Yer lucky day. Jim 'n I shot a bunch of 'em this afternoon."

After taking the saddle and bridle off Duchess, I turned her loose to graze. At the wagon, I took a long drink of water, then dipped some into a bowl for Duke. Now I was ready for some prairie chicken.

Jack put a large scoop of beans on a plate, then laid a big chunk of chicken next to the beans. As he handed me the plate, I asked, "How'd you come by the chickens?"

"Well, when Jim and I was headed up here, we spotted this flock in among the scattered trees – it was back down the trail a half-mile 'r so." He interrupted his story to take another bite of the juicy chicken. Then, swiping his mouth with the back of his hand, he went on.

"I stopped the wagon, grabbed two shotguns, 'n handed 'em to Jim to hold, while he hoisted me up behind him on Dunny, and we rode after 'em. I'll tell ya, it was the biggest bunch of prairie chickens I ever did see. And they didn't seem to be bothered by us as we rode closer.

"We rode slow and kinda zig-zag as we got closer to the chickens, tryin' to stay behind trees as much as we could. Then, behind some trees and boulders, thinkin' the birds were just twenty or thirty yards on the other side, Jim turned and whispered, 'They're pretty close... on the other side of these trees and rocks. I caught a glimpse of one now 'n then through the trees as we got closer. Let's slide off 'n you go right... I'll go left. When you've got a good view of 'em, start shootin'. Take as many as you can on the ground, before they're in the air, then just keep loadin' 'n shootin' 'till you don't have any left in range.'

"I slid down from Dunny and he handed me one of the shotguns. Then he swung down and started moving left, so I headed to the right."

"How many did ya get?" I asked, and took my first bite from the chicken leg I held.

"Got fourteen of 'em," he answered, and grinned when he saw me swoon over the flavor.

"Tastes every bit as good as it smells," I told him, licking my lips and smiling.

"There's a-plenty... so eat 'em up," he said, proudly.

I walked over and sat down to lean against my saddle. Duke followed close, and sat in front of me, his whole body wagging with excitement. His eyes were pleading, as he looked from me to the chicken, then back to me.

"Okay, boy, I won't make you wait," I said, as I tore a piece of chicken, and held it toward him. He gently took it, then chomped it down. It almost looked like he was smiling, while his front paws subtly pranced, and his eyes pleaded for more. Suddenly, his ears pricked, his head turned, and he began a low growl.

"What's wrong, Duke?" I asked, as I stroked his neck.

In a few seconds we heard, "Hello the camp!" It was dark enough that no one had seen a rider approach. And, with the camp chatter, and the cattle noise, no one heard their approach either.

"Come ahead," Jim shouted.

It turned out there were three riders. They rode in close enough to be seen, then slid from their horses.

"Howdy," one of 'em said, removing his hat. "Name's Dub... Dub Horn. Mind if we join ya?"

He was a stout man, probably five-foot-eight, with a thick, strong frame. He looked like a mighty tough hombre, built of rawhide, wire, and spit. His old leather chaps were well-worn, as was the holster that held his revolver in a cross-hand style near the front of his left hip. A style used by some gunslingers.

"Don't mind a bit," Jim said, stepping toward the man with his hand held out. "I'm Jim Cluskey. You boys had any supper yet?"

Dub hesitated, then said, "No sir, we sure ain't."

"Well, yer in luck. We happen to have plenty enough to share this evenin'."

"Smells mighty good, too," Dub said. "We were hopin' you might offer. We ain't et a thing since yesturdee."

"Well, grab a plate full," Jim told them. "Jack's cooked some good prairie chicken we shot this afternoon. There's more'n enough to go 'round."

"We'd surely 'preciate it," Dub said, as he turned and pointed to his sidekicks. "This here's Jess Hill, and that's Clete Brown."

Both men stood near six feet tall, with lean, strong frames. The one named Jess had a thick, red scar running across the hard planes of his face. It started above his right eye, and ended under his right jaw.

The fella named Clete had blond hair, and eyebrows that where almost white. Against his dark, tanned, weather-beaten skin, it was a striking look. They each wore a fancy holster that hung low on his hip, and was tied to his leg. The whole situation made me wonder just a bit.

88

All three dropped their reins to ground hitch their horses, and walked to where Jack was filling plates. It was easy to see they hadn't eaten in a while by the way they tore into the chicken. They gnawed on big chunks of meat, and shoved beans in as fast as they could. Being polite eaters wasn't in their thinkin' at all. They couldn't shovel the food down fast enough.

Soon, the whole crew, including the three strangers, was well fed. There wasn't more than scraps left from the chickens. Jack had saved four to feed the men riding watch. He would heat 'em up later, when they came in from their watch and had their turn at supper.

"That was mighty, mighty fine," Dub told Jack. "Ain't had any vittles that tasty since leavin' my mom's good home cookin'... nearly three weeks ago."

"By-gum I think yer right," Jack answered, with a big nod of his head. "If'n I do say so m'sef."

We sat around the fire, drinking fresh coffee and pumpin' Jack up with some more praise about the delicious prairie chicken. Jim asked, "Where you boys from, 'n where you bound for?"

"Well, we're from Alabama," Dub said, "'n workin' our way west... maybe all the way to Californee."

"Goin' after gold?" I asked.

"Nah. Just lookin' for work of any kind," he said. "There's too many that's gone bust chasin' after gold." He paused, then said, "Don't wanna wear out our welcome, but we was hopin' maybe you had a couple days work. Make us a couple dollars to carry us futher west."

Jim stared into the fire, thinking on it. Finally, he said, "Might just be that we could use the help for a bit. In three days or so, we'll be crossin' the Red River, and that'll be the toughest one we've faced. Can't promise more than three or four days' work though."

"That'd be real fine," Dub told him. "Can't ask for more'n that."

"I'll pay a dollar 'n a half a day and you'll take a shift on night watch, too."

Dub looked toward his friends. They both nodded in agreement. "Agreed then," Dub said.

Chapter Sixteen

The new-comers didn't seem to fit particularly well with our crew. They were pretty rough, and didn't seem much like experienced trail hands. A few times I had to calm Duke from voicing his low growl deep in his throat when they came near.

Our next day on the trail was a little better, though the three showed they weren't particularly good cowhands. That night as we finished supper, Dub sat leaning against his saddle, picking at his teeth. After a bit, he reached out toward Eustace with his cup.

"Hey, boy," he barked. "Fetch me some coffee."

I was talking with Rocky, and stopped mid-sentence when I heard Dub giving orders to Eustace. I quickly sat upright. "Hey, Dub, he ain't yer boy, and we fetch our own coffee around here."

His first reaction was to stiffen, as his head snapped to look at me. At the same time his hand started toward his gun, but then he thought better of it. "Sorry," he said, easing back. "I meant no offense." Then he turned to Eustace, saying, "Sorry there... Eustace."

"S'awright," Eustace told him, with a slight nod of his head, but a stern look. There wasn't much that would scare Eustace, this character included.

I noticed Flap Jack had his arm stretched into the chuck wagon. I'm sure when the ruckus started, he'd reached in for a shotgun, and then, when Eustace said it was okay, Jack let go of the gun.

As Dub stood to get his coffee, Rocky leaned over and quietly said, "Be glad when we're across the Red River, and Jim cuts these three loose."

"Mmm hmm," I hummed.

Later that night the newbies rode graveyard. It seemed to go okay, and the other three that rode with them said they'd done just fine. The next day brought us within four miles of the Red River, where we made camp. We'd be moving the herd across the Red by mid-morning the following day.

Things with the newbies from Alabama seemed to be smoothing out. Maybe some of us had been little quick to judge. Maybe, like Jim had said, it'll be good to have the extra help when we cross the Red.

That night Rocky and I caught a few hours' sleep, then joined four others to ride the midnight watch. At three o'clock, the newbies, Muley, and two others relieved us. They would ride watch 'till daybreak, when we'd push north toward the Red River.

Before daybreak, I was awakened when I heard Flap Jack rousting Jim from his sleep. "Somethin's not right out there," he said, with an urgency that I'd not heard from Jack.

"What is it?" Jim groaned, pushing himself to his feet.

"I haven't seen a rider out there since I woke up twenty minutes ago, 'n things just don't sound like they should with the herd."

Jim noticed me propped up on my elbow listening. "C'mon Mack. Let's check it out."

We saddled our horses, and began circling the herd. In a short while, we spotted Muley's gray Appaloosa, but no Muley. Searching more, we finally spotted him on the ground, tied to a scrub tree.

"What happened, Muley?" I asked, as I removed the bandana that gagged him, and then began to untie the ropes.

He hacked and spit, then snarled, "They got the drop on me, the lousy...."

"Who did?" Jim asked.

"Those Alabamans," he barked, and spit again. "I'm sure they'd already hog-tied Lance and Billy. They cut out about eighty or ninety steers, and started pushin' 'em west. From what I heard 'em sayin', I think there were two or three other riders out there, waitin' to help."

"Ya know..." I said, gazing west. "I saw three riders, yesterday afternoon, riding that ridge out there. They disappeared, and I didn't give 'em any more thought."

We brought Muley to his horse, then Jim said, "You two find Lance and Billy. I'm goin' back to camp to get a few more riders out on the herd. Meet me back at camp, and we'll figure out what were gonna do."

We found the other two tied up and gagged, just like Muley had been. They told the same story about the three from Alabama.

Lance said, "I figgered they was just stopping to chew the fat. Next thing I know'd, they'd got the drop on me. Dub told me I was dead if I made a sound, and he kept his gun on me, while the other two tied me up."

Back at camp, Jim had rounded up the rest of the crew to talk about what had happened, and what the next move would be. When I rode up and slid from Duchess, I asked, "What'cha thinkin', Jim?"

He slowly shook his head. "Thinkin' I got suckered... real good." He paused, staring into the campfire. "I'm not quite sure just what we should do. Head out after 'em, or write it off, and keep the drive movin' north."

"Well," I said, "the thought of lettin' 'em get away with it leaves a mighty sour taste."

"I'm with Mack," Flap Jack said. "I reckon we should go after the no good side-winders."

Jim nodded. "Guess that's what my gut tells me, too."

I knelt to pet Duke. "I know there's more than twenty-seven hundred head still needin' to be herded to Kansas. But, those eighty or ninety steers they took are worth the better part of three thousand dollars. That pays the wages for this whole crew, Jim, plus some of your other expenses."

"Plus... them gettin' what's dern right comin' to 'em," Jack snarled.

"You give the word, Jim, 'n we're ready to go after 'em," Rocky said.

Jim listened, thoughtfully, which was his nature. He seldom made decisions without careful thought. "Guess it wouldn't hurt to hold up here for a couple days. Fact is, it would rest the cattle, even fatten 'em up a little."

"Now yer talkin'," Flap Jack said, tugging on his hat.

"I know you'd like to go with to track 'em down, Jack, but I need you here to feed the crew, and look after things for a couple days."

"Yeah... 'spose yer right," Jack said. "Though I'd sooner be along t' give them varmints a little what-fer."

"Any ideas Mack," Jim asked.

"They've got five or six men out there," I said. "I think four of us would do, and leave the rest back here to watch the herd. They've only got a few hours start on us, so I'm sure we can run 'em down in half a day. The tricky part'll be how to avoid an all-out gun war when we do catch up to 'em."

"Any ideas on that?" Rocky asked.

"Nope," I answered. "It's kinda like it was with those kidnappers back near Waco... we'll have to play it as it's dealt to us."

Chapter Seventeen

We decided that four of us would do, as we should have surprise on our side, so Jim, Eustace, Rocky and I were headed west, hot on the rustlers trail. We rode at a steady lope, knowing we'd likely be on 'em by late-afternoon.

The trail was easy to follow, and our biggest concern was not being spotted by them. After nearly two hours, we slowed our horses to a walk. Partly to give them a breather, but mostly to keep the dust down, so we couldn't be noticed from a distance. They were sure to be on the lookout for a dust cloud trailing them.

In a short while, we spread out and nudged our horses into an easy trot, still trying to keep the dust under control. After a couple more hours, we spotted a large dust cloud on the western horizon, and figured it to be the herd. Again, our real concern was that they hadn't spotted us.

"We'd better ease up, keep a sharp lookout," I said. "They could have a man watching their back-trail."

I'd barely got those words out, when I heard the crack of a rifle, and saw Jim thrown forward against Dunny's neck. He struggled to stay in the saddle, but slid off, hitting the ground hard.

"Help him!" I shouted, and whirled Duchess around, heading toward where the shot had come from. There was a group of boulders and scrub juniper about eighty yards to the side, and I figured that's where the gunman had to be. Veering to circle him, I laid out on Duchess' neck trying to be less of a target. Another rifle shot let me know the shooter was still there.

As I circled, a third shot rang out, and this time it came so close that I heard the hum of the bullet, as it ripped through the air past my head. I caught a glimpse of movement in the junipers, then a horse broke into the open, its rider still clawing his way into the saddle. Finally seated, he drew his pistol, and turned to shoot. I took aim, and squeezed off a shot. The gunman's back stiffened, then he slumped forward, and fell from his horse. The horse ran on, eventually coming to a stop.

As I neared the shooter, he looked to be dead, as he lay there, motionless. Just the same, I moved in slow and stopped twenty feet away. I slid from the saddle and, with my gun aimed, walked slowly toward the still body. As I neared him, I could see that he was indeed dead. My bullet had exploded through his neck.

I took off my hat, and shook my head in disgust. "What a waste," I whispered. I hated shooting anyone — no matter who they are.

Just then Rocky rode up. "Figured I'd give you a hand," he said, "but it looks like you've got things under control."

"What about Jim?" I asked.

"He'll be all right, Eustace is workin' on him with his medicines."

"You wanna ride over and grab that guy's horse. No sense takin' a chance that it runs back to them, 'n gives 'em warning."

"What about this one?" Rocky asked, pointing.

"Got no shovel to bury him," I said. "So, guess we'll let nature take its course."

We rode back to check on Jim, and Eustace gave us a quick nod. "It be a good, through and through kinda wound," he told us. "He's gonna be aw'ight." Eustace made a thick poultice then spread it front and back, squeezing some into the open wound. Then sewed him up.

"It'll fight infection, 'n ease da pain," Eustace told us, after seeing Rocky cringe.

"Can you ride back to the herd?" I asked Jim.

"I'm ridin' on with you," he said.

"You sure?" I asked, looking a little sideways at him.

"Yup... I'm sure," he said. "Be just fine after gettin' fixed-up here by Eustace."

I knew that it was a stretch, but he was in charge and it was his call. Still, I questioned him once more. "Can't convince you to head back?"

He straitened his posture, and said, "Glad you're concerned, but I'm good to go."

Before long we were back on the trail, spread out again so we wouldn't be easy targets. By late afternoon, we were closing in on the herd... and the rustlers. I reined Duchess to a stop, and waited for the others. "When we clear that next rise," I said, "I think we might have 'em in sight. That means we could be spotted by them, too."

"We'd better hold up 'till dark," Jim said.

"Maybe on that treed slope," I said, pointing. "We can rest there a while, maybe even nap for a couple hours. When it's dark, we can move in on them."

Jim turned Dunny, saying, "Let's do it."

We found a good comfortable slope in the trees, and, though trying our best, nobody could sleep.

Chapter Eighteen

When the sun had set, and the last faint glow was slowly disappearing in the western sky, we decided it was time to move in on the rustlers. I mounted the horse that the shooter had ridden, while the others swung up on their horses.

"Remember," I told them, "hang back far enough that you're out of sight."

I'd suggested earlier, that we tie up the rustlers, one by one, just like they'd done to our men. Before we left him, I'd taken the dead shooter's hat and vest. In the dark, wearing his vest 'n hat, and riding his horse, I figured I could get close enough to the rustlers to get the drop on 'em.

"When you hear an owl hoot," I said, "you'll know I've got one, and you can come ahead to help."

I started toward the herd, moving slowly and staring hard into the darkness. I was still leery of them having another rider watching their back-trail. In a short while I stopped to listen carefully, and look deeper into the darkness. As I nudged the horse again, I saw something that made my heart jump. Ahead, on the left, was a flare of light, then a small red glow.

Someone lit a cigarette, I thought.

I nudged the horse ahead, walking him faster so the one standing guard would hear me coming toward him. In a few moments I heard the lever of a rifle jack a cartridge into the chamber. Then a man's voice ordered sternly, "Hold it right there!"

I stopped the horse and raised my hands. Soon I saw a silhouette step from behind some boulders. I was sure I was only a silhouette to him as well, but held my head low so that much of my face was hidden by the hat.

The shadowy figure came closer. "That you Judd?"

"Mmm hmm," I hummed, trying to sound peeved.

"When we didn't hear from you by sundown," he said, as he eased the hammer down on the rifle, "we weren't sure you'd make it back."

I swung down, keeping my face low. When I got close and looked at him, I saw the surprise in his eyes. Before he could react, my gun was cocked and aimed at his chest.

"Make a sound and you die right here," I told him. I could see the disappointment, as he slowly raised his hands. I took his rifle, and threw it to the side. Then I took the pistol from his holster and did the same with it.

"Now, get on your knees, hands behind your head," I told him.

I turned and let out an owl hoot. Then another. *Not bad! Sounds pretty good*, I thought.

I waited, and soon could hear approaching horses. Then I heard Eustace softly say, "Mack?"

"Come ahead, Eustace," I answered.

They helped me gag the rustler and tie him up, so he was hobbled and wouldn't be going anywhere soon. He had his horse tied to a pinyon, but we hobbled it, too, to be sure it wasn't going to get loose.

102

Ready to repeat this, I headed toward the herd while the others hung back. I could see the glow of a small campfire on the southwest side of the herd, so I circled around the northeast side. I stared hard, trying to see any riders in the darkness.

Moving slowly, I finally spotted the silhouette of a horse and rider coming toward me. His arm was out in front of him, as though aiming a gun. It was Jess Hill.

I stopped the horse, and mumbled, "Easy there...."

He came closer, then finally stopped and leaned forward in his saddle. "That you Judd?" he asked, softly.

"Yup," I said, with a long, slow, drawl.

He holstered his gun, and rode up beside me. As before, when I looked up and he saw my face, my gun was drawn, cocked and aimed at the center of his chest.

"Make a sound 'n yer dead," I told him, softly.

We repeated all this one more time. Now we had accounted for four of the rustlers; one was dead, three were tied and gagged. That left two at the campfire — Dub and Clete. We spread out on foot to surround them at the fire.

As we move in, I shouted, "Dub... you boys raise yer hands real slow like," I paused, then said, "We got eight guns on you." *A little exaggeration couldn't hurt.*

His first instinct, as usual, was to grab for his gun, but he evidently decided against it. He slowly eased his hands above his head. Clete did the same. Looking hard into the darkness, Dub mumbled, "How the...."

103

We moved in on them and, as we got into the firelight, his head jerked around looking at the four of us. "Thought you said there were eight," he snarled.

"Can't count so good I guess," I told him.

"Think it really matters?" Rocky growled.

I took Dub's gun from his holster, and checked to see if it was loaded. Most everyone carries their revolver with the hammer on an empty chamber for safety. Not him. He carried six bullets in the wheel.

Chapter Nineteen

With Dub and Clete hog-tied, we stoked up their campfire, brewed a fresh pot of coffee, then proceeded to eat most of the grub they had. The two rustlers sat scowling, as they watched us enjoy their food.

"Whatcha do with our boys?" Dub asked with a snarl.

"Ooohh, their tied up here 'n there," I answered.

"Just gonna leave 'em layin' out there in the night?"

"Yup... figured to," I said. "Just like you were doin' with our men."

Then he said, "What about coyotes or wolves."

I finished chewing and swallowing a bite of jerky, then finally said, "Hadn't really given it much thought."

"Be a real shame," Rocky added. I could hear the sarcasm in his words.

At daybreak, we put Dub and Clete on their horses, and gathered up the two rustlers that we had left tied up at the edge of the herd. Then, with the four of them cinched up, and a rope stringing their horses together, Jim took the lead with them in tow. The rest of us began pushing the cattle back to our herd.

Jim decided to deliver the rustlers to the sheriff in Fort Worth. It would mean more delay in moving the herd north, but he felt it had to be done. He also hoped to hire a few cowhands to help push the herd across the Red River.

Later that morning, we stopped to pick up the rustler we'd left tied up beside the trail. Then we stopped to check on the body of the one I'd shot. When we left him, we'd covered him with some heavy brush, and the scavengers hadn't been able to get to him to do much damage. We strapped the body across the man's horse, and would deliver him to the Fort Worth Sheriff with the others. By early evening we were back with the main herd, and Flap Jack was relieved to see us. Duke came on the run, excited to see Duchess and me.

When Jack saw Jim's arm in a sling, he shouted, "I let you outta my site fer more'n a day, 'n you go gettin' yersef busted up."

"I missed you, too, Jack," Jim said with a smirk.

Jack growled some more, then looked at the string of rustlers lined up behind Jim. "An' lookee here! That's some string of pole-cats you got behind you."

Jim glanced at the wrustlers, grinning, then looked again at Jack again, asking, "Got any supper cookin'?"

"W-e-l-l, what-a-ya think I do 'round here anaway?" Jack snarled, as he tugged his hat down on his head. "Course I got supper cookin'. But none for them varmints strung out behind ya. They kin starve fer all I care."

Jim fought back another grin. "They're gonna do that very thing, Jack, until we get 'em hauled to the sheriff's office in Fort Worth tomorrow."

At daybreak, Jim and I headed out to deliver the rustlers. By late morning we'd located the sheriff, and Jim explained the whole circumstance to him.

"Well," the sheriff said, "we'll put 'em in lockup, but the Judge won't be here for three days. I'd like you two here for testifying."

"Can't do it," Jim told him. "Already lost three days, and can't afford to lose three or four more."

The sheriff rubbed his chin.

"How 'bout we both write out a statement for the Judge," I offered.

He raised his eyebrows, still rubbing his chin.

"Best we can do," Jim said. "If the Judge doesn't figure it's enough evidence, he'll have to cut 'em loose. Texas will be all the worse for it."

On our way into Fort Worth we'd noticed what looked like a small feed mill and stockyard. When we left the sheriff's office, Jim said, "Let's stop there 'n see if we can find a few experienced hands willing to work for a couple of days." We did, and found four that were glad to take the job.

That evening, back at camp, Eustace checked on Jim's shoulder and said it was healing good. "Gonna let it air out some," he told Jim. "Whilst I fix up some more poultice. Then we'll wrap it up good again."

"Is it hurtin'?" Flap Jack asked, cringing a little at the sight of it.

"Not much," Jim replied. "Whatever Eustace is puttin' on it seems to dull the pain, along with healing it."

"Where'd you learn yer magic, Eustace?" Jack asked.

"Long story," Eustace said. "The short of it is, muh Grandmama learned me."

"Taught," I said to Eustace. "Your Grandmama taught you."

"Yup. She *taught* me," he said with a grin. "An' Mack here has taught me lots, too!"

Chapter Twenty

While Eustace was doctoring Jim, I introduced our four new hands to the crew. We spent that evening around the campfire, telling how Jim had been shot, and how we'd rounded up the rustlers. The highlight of the night was when Jim told of the headcount on the cattle we'd recovered.

"I knew right off," he said, "that there were more'n eighty or ninety head in the herd they were pushin', just from the look of it. Turns out there were eighty-seven head of our cattle, and seventy-four head with other brands... a few of this one, a few of that one, 'n so on." He paused, looking around at our crew, thinking on his next words.

He rubbed his chin a bit, then continued. "I figure those seventy-four head of various brands are free-range cattle, and part of our herd now. Anyone claims some are theirs, they just have to prove their brand."

Whitey, one of the young drag riders, was scratching his head and had a puzzled look on his face. Jim took advantage of the moment, and asked, "You look puzzled Whitey, whatcha wonderin'?"

"Well, guess I don't see how it affects us much. Seventy-four more added to our twenty-nine hundred."

"Yer right. It shouldn't add any more work," he said. Then, looking around at the crew, he said, "But the way I figure, it *will* add a little to your pay. Way I calculate it, from the sale of those extra cattle, each man that started out with us will get an eighty-two dollar bonus on top of his ninety dollar wages."

Whitey's eyes grew wide, and he let out a loud whoop. "Now yer talkin' my kinda lingo," he said.

There was a split-second delay as it sank in with the rest, then the whole crew was whoopin'. Flap Jack waved his hat, and did his version of an Irish jig. Soon, the whole crew was roaring with laughter at his antics.

Next morning, before daybreak, Jack was feeding us a hearty breakfast from his new supplies. When we'd taken the rustlers to Fort Worth, Jim brought along a pack horse. We brought back a fresh supply of flour, rice, beans, coffee, and bacon. So, Jack treated us with an extra tasty breakfast.

It felt good to have the herd moving again. We would reach the Red River in the late morning, and Jim had told us that we'd be bunching the herd up about four miles north of the river in the late afternoon.

He asked me to ride ahead with him to check the crossing. Along the way he told me that he'd be taking Grizz and Flap Jack across the river to find a good spot for us to set up camp. Then he and Grizz were going to do a scouting trip up into the Indian Territory.

"Back at home," he said, "I'd heard rumor of a small cattle drive that was jumped by a renegade band of Kiowa a month or so ago. Killed every man on the crew, then took the whole herd and all of their horses."

"Didn't think there'd been any trouble of that kind recently," I said, shaking my head.

"I didn't either, and don't know if it was truth or bad rumor. But it'd be nice to stay a step ahead of any trouble, and Grizz should be a big help with that."

110

Grizz was a big man. He had to be near six-three and two hundred sixty pounds. He wore long hair, and thick, full beard, probably left over from his years living in the mountains. His real name is Gregory Stine, but prefers "Grizz." He'd lived as a mountain man for six or seven years, trapping and hunting in the Big Horn Mountains. He had a keen eye, and became an expert tracker of animals... and of men. And he had learned the ways of the Indians in the northern territories.

No one knew, nor asked, what had brought him from the Big Horns back to Texas, but he lived near Glenwood Springs, and had become a good friend of Jim's.

Jim was a pretty fair tracker himself and, between the two, they'd likely find sign if there were any renegade bands in the area where we'd trail the cattle. Being a step ahead of such possible trouble was definitely a good idea. Hopefully, the word of a hostile band was just bad rumor.

The Indian Territory had become peaceful. The tribes of the Cherokee, Seminole, Creek, Chickasaw, and the Choctaw — known as the Five Civilized Tribes — would likely demand a tariff for crossing the Indian Nation's Territory, usually about five cents per head, but as long as you paid the fee you'd have no trouble.

As we rode on, Jim told me about Salt Creek, where we'd cross the Red. It was situated at a wide, sharp bend in the river that helped to slow the current considerably, and made crossing easier. It had been used for ages as a crossing point by migrating Buffalo, by the Indians, and, for the past century or so, by whites moving through the area.

"This spring and summer has been unusually wet," Jim said, "so I'm hoping the Red hasn't swelled its banks too much."

111

From a long way off, we had seen the long, winding line of trees following the Red River. Jim pointed to a sharp turn in the line of trees, and said it was where we'd find Salt Creek bend.

"If it's up, it'll likely mean that it's twice its usual width of eighty or ninety yards. And likely, a foot or two deeper; And likely, a stronger current; And, likely... well, I think you get the picture."

"Yup... and not such a pretty one," I replied. "Let's hope for the best."

In a while, we stopped to give our horses a short breather. Jim stood in his stirrups and turned to look back up the long, gradual slope that stretched out behind us. In the distance he saw a stream of hides and horns moving under a long cloud of dust, slowly rolling toward us. "That picture back there I like, though," he said.

I finished wiping my forehead and hat brim with my bandanna, and turned to look. "Yup," I replied. "Nice to see that line moving."

As Jim had feared, the river was up considerably, and had swelled to a width of about a hundred and fifty yards at the crossing point. He said, "I'm gonna check to be sure where we have solid ground. We gotta avoid the pockets of quicksand that the Red River is known for. Why don't you ride back and bring 'em on down. I'll have it all laid out by the time you get here."

I reined Duchess around, and said, "C'mon Duke. Let's go find Eustace." His ears perked up, and he fell in stride with Duchess.

As we neared the chuck wagon, Duke took the lead, running up to see Jack. By the time I reached the wagon, Duke was prancing alongside, and Jack was throwing him a piece of leftover meat.

"He knows where he'll find the good stuff," I said.

"Got that right," Jack said, grinning.

114

Chapter Twenty-One

Pushing the cattle across the Red River came off without a hitch, though we were glad to have the extra four hands to help us. Jim got Flap Jack set up about three miles north of the river, and soon we were circling the herd near the chuck wagon. We would make camp here until Jim and Grizz returned. I paid the extra men with money Jim had left with me, and sent them back to Fort Worth.

It was mid-morning the next day when Jim and Grizz came back from scouting the area. As Jack threw together a little breakfast for them, Jim told us, "Didn't see anything that would make us think there was any trouble in the area. Only thing we ran across was a small camp of five Kiowa." Glancing at Eustace, he added, "They had one Negro woman with them."

Eustace stared at Jim for a few moments. "Hmm," was his only reply.

"But it looks like," Jim said, "we've got seven or eight days of good trail ahead of us, then we hit three or four days of rougher terrain."

"How rough?" Rocky asked.

"Oh, a little rougher than we've traveled so far, but we can handle it." He took a long drink of water, then continued. "Somewhere up there we'll likely hear from the tribal leaders about the fee for crossing their territory. This year, I heard they want six cents a head. For us that'll be about a hundred 'n seventy-five dollars. I plan to give them $200, and let them split it among the tribes. Hopefully, that'll give us clear sailing to the Kansas border."

I noticed Grizz staring past me, and I turned to look. In the distance was a rider coming at a steady lope. "Looks like company comin'," Grizz said, nodding in the direction of the rider.

Everyone turned to watch the approaching rider. He continued toward us at a steady lope, wearing a broad smile. When he was about twenty yards from us, he pulled his horse to a stop. Knowing he had the attention of all of us, he removed his sombrero with a flourish, then bowed at the waist and lowered the sombrero with a wide, sweeping motion. "Rafino Raphael de Perez at your service, mis amigos."

"Rafino?" Jim asked, as he stepped toward the man and extended his hand.

"Si Señor. But please, my friend, call me Fini (Feenee)."

"Well, Fini, climb on down."

He did, then took Jim's hand and shook it with great energy.

"Where are you headed Fini?" Jim asked.

"I am heading back to South Texas, or maybe to my home in Meheeco, and my beautiful wife, Estrella," he said. "I have just finished working for a cattle drive a week ago, and am heading back south hoping to find another cattle drive to work. If not, I will head for my home and spend some time with my family and friends."

"Well, Fini, you're welcome to join us for lunch" Jim said. "Jack will be cooking up some grub in a short while, and you're more than welcome to stay and eat with us."

"Muchas gracias, amigo, I will gladly accept your generous invitation. It will be a welcomed improvement over my own cooking for lunch," Fini said. Jim introduced Fini all around, and as he met Eustace, he said, "I have not met many of your dark race before, though there was one woman I saw with a band of Kiowa, a little ways north of here. I am glad to meet you Eustace."

"Glad t' meet you, too," Eustace said. "You mentioned your wife's name... what was it again?"

"Estrella."

"Ess...tray...ya," Eustace repeated slowly.

"Si, amigo. It means 'Star' in Spanish. And my Estrella is more beautiful than all the stars in the heavens."

Fini was a grand storyteller, and had great stories of his adventures as an amansadero. Cowboys who broke raw broncos were usually referred to as "busters" or "peelers." In Mexico they were called "amansaderos." Fini had been breaking horses since he was a young teenager. Soon, he had the whole camp enthralled with his flamboyant storytelling.

He talked about throwing a "Houlihan" with a rope, and that there was no one better than he with it. "Most caballeros don't even know what it is, much less ever used a houlihan. But it can be very effective, especially with a jumpy horse," he said.

A nervous, jumpy horse will usually spoke when they see you whirling a lasso overhead. Someone handy with a houlihan can throw a loop with a single backhand motion and send a vertical lope over the animal's head before they see it and get spooked. Not many can do it well, but, evidently, Fini was an expert.

"I would love to demonstrate for you, mis amigos," Fini said. "If someone has a particularly jumpy horse, I would love to show you how effective it can be."

"We got one in our remuda," Eustace said. "One that's always givin' us fits."

When we'd finished with lunch, and helped Jack clean up a bit, Eustace walked over to bring out the horse he had mentioned. Soon we were all gathered to watch Fini. Then, as Eustace walked away from the horse to join us watching, Fini slowly stepped toward the animal with a lasso draped at his side. With one sweeping backhand motion, he sent a loop that was over the horses head before he'd flinched. It was only after the rope was already being tugged around his neck, that the horse reared a bit, then settled.

"You can see, my friends, how helpful the technique can be with an edgy animal," Feeney said as he gently stroked the neck of the horse. "I would be glad to teach anyone who is interested."

"There are more than a few of us interested," I said. "And it would be the perfect time for it. We'll be here for the rest of the afternoon."

"The only thing I'll offer you for pay to spend the afternoon teaching us," Jim said, "is to invite you to join us for supper and spend the night here with us in camp."

"I accept your offer, and will take great pleasure in working with your men this afternoon. In fact, if you are willing, I would like to spend the next day or two working for you at no charge. Then, if you feel I am helpful enough, you can hire me for the remainder of your drive to Kansas."

"Deal," Jim said, with a nod.

Chapter Twenty-Two

That night, Eustace seemed preoccupied with something. He was staring into the distance as he brushed down his horse. I finally asked him, "Eustace, what's got you off balance? You don't seem your usual self tonight."

"I been doin' some thinkin' 'bout what Jim and Fini said. 'Bout them seein' a colored woman wit' the band of Kiowa Indians," he said slowly, then paused. "When I was wit' Powell back in Texas, I got word that my little sis, Sophie, had been sold to someone in North Texas, and later dat she was taken by Indians. I'm jis wonderin', could it be her dey seen?"

This stopped me cold and I stood there speechless for a while. Finally I said, "There's no way to know for sure unless we can track them down. I think Jim would let us do that as we move the herd north through the Indian Territory. You sure you'd recognize her after all these years?"

"Yeah, I'm sure."

"Of course you are. That was a stupid thing for me to ask. I'm sure Jim wouldn't have a problem with us checking it out. In fact, let's go talk to him about it right now. Settle your mind."

"You think it be awright wit' him?"

"I'm sure of it."

We found Jim sitting with some of the other hands by the fire. "Got a minute?" I asked.

"Sure. What's up?"

"Come on over by the chuck wagon. Eustace and I want to talk to you for a moment."

I reached out and helped him to his feet. "Sounds important," he said. "What is it?"

"No... it's nothing to worry about. Just something we wanted to ask you."

Eustace began explaining about his sister, and the possibility that the Negro woman they had seen with the Kiowa might be her. He asked if it would be okay to track them down as we push the cattle north.

"I've got no problem with that," Jim said. "But, and it's a mighty big '*but.*' What do we do if it is her?"

Eustace and I stared at each other for a long while. Finally I said, "I guess we hadn't got that far yet. I suppose there's a chance that the Kiowa would think they own her, and wouldn't just let her go with us. What do you think Eustace?"

Eustace looked down at his hands and stared for a long while. As he began to look up toward Jim, he said, "Yer right. I hadn't thought 'bout what we'd do. Guess, like some of the other things we run into on this drive so far, we'd have to deal wit' it as we find it."

Now it was Jim's turn to stare into the distance for a while, rubbing his chin, thinking it through. When he looked back at Eustace, he said, "Guess that's all we *can* do. We'll deal with it as we find it."

"Okay," I said. "We just wanted to make sure you knew about it, and were okay with it."

Jim looked at Eustace again, saying, "Yeah, I'm okay with it. It's too important not to check it out. We'll be headin' north with the herd at first light. I'm guessin' we'll be near where Grizz and I saw the Kiowa's camped two days from now. We'll figure it out when we get there."

"Thanks Jim," Eustace said. "Not many white men dat I've known would give two hoots 'bout what concerns me."

Jim put his hand on Eustace's big shoulder saying, "You're welcome." Then he squeezed the shoulder, and said, "You're forgettin', Eustace, that you're talking to men who don't see you as anything less than we are." Eustace could only respond with a soft smile and a nod of his head.

The next morning we were pushing the cattle north as the sun began painting the sky. The few clouds that drifted overhead went through a beautiful array of colors. As a cloud slid over the sun, it looked as though it had been givin' a metallic, golden edge. As the day wore on, the landscape slowly changed. In the distance, we began seeing more rolling hills with thick patches of trees covering the slopes.

As evening was setting in on us, I was getting concerned that we hadn't heard from Jim about where we'd make camp. Soon, Rocky rode over and voiced the same concern. As we talked, we caught sight of Fini coming toward us on his big, gray Andalusian. The Andalusian is a rare breed from Europe, and is a majestic looking horse. Fini called his horse "Domino." I was curious, but hadn't had a chance to ask him about the name.

Waving to us as he neared, Fini rode up, turned Domino, and fell into stride with us, saying, "Señor Jim says to turn the herd to the northeast as we pass this rock face on our left. About a mile up ahead we will find Jack and the place to bed down for the night."

"We were getting a little concerned," Rocky said. "Glad to see you."

"Fini," I said, "how did you come up with the name Domino for your horse?"

"Oh, Señor, it is a simple but fun story. Back in my hometown we love to play dominoes, and we love to gamble. So, one lucky night, I win this beautiful horse in a game of dominoes," he said. Then, with a shrug, he added, "So... the name Domino."

Rocky and I smiled and slowly shook our heads. "As good a reason as any," I said. "He's such a beautiful horse."

"Thank you very much," Fini said. "He is fine example of a very great breed of horse."

As we passed the rock face, we could see a wide trail headed northeast and smoke rising from Flap Jack's fire in the distance.

Chapter Twenty-Three

We circled the herd near Jack's chuck wagon, and I rode over to where Eustace was corralling his remuda. He always built a rope corral that he tied to the back corner of the chuck wagon. From there he would drive two posts to stake out a triangle. The horses could easily break down the rope corral if they wanted, but, unless stirred-up for some reason, they never bothered to even push on the rope. They were glad to rest and graze in their confined area.

I unsaddled Duchess and gave her a quick brush down. After checking her hooves, I gave her a couple handfuls of oats. I scratched Duke all around his ears. I knew he didn't need much to eat, with all the snacking that he got through the day from Jack. He was spoiled, running alongside the chuck wagon, or, occasionally, riding in it, perched next to Jack.

But it was good seeing him, and having him by my side after a long day. I grabbed some jerky and we played our usual game until I thought he'd had enough.

Jack had our supper ready, and all the hands were grabbing a plateful, when Fini shouted, "You better grab a plate Señor Mack, before it is too late."

"I'm on my way," I said. "Thanks Fini."

By the time we all had a plateful, darkness was setting in, and we finished eating by the light of Jack's fire. "Been a long day," Jim said. "But a good one. We covered nearly sixteen miles today. We should have fourteen or fifteen miles of good, open trail tomorrow, too. So, I don't think we'll need to start so early in the morning. We'll head out after we get some light in the sky."

He sipped on his hot coffee, then continued, "I think you remember Grizz and I talking about the band of Kiowa we saw when we were out scouting. And, that there was a colored woman with them. Eustace has reason to think it could be his sister, Sophie, and would like to check it out. So, when we make camp tomorrow night, we'll be near where we spotted those Kiowa. I'm not sure yet what we're going to do, so this is just a heads up for everyone to keep an eye out as we're pushin' the herd tomorrow."

"Señor Jim," Fini said, raising a finger as though to make a point. "I speak a little of the Kiowa tongue, and might be of some help when you encounter them."

"That's good to know, Fini," Jim said. "It'll be very helpful if we find them. It's not likely they would be able to communicate in English, and it may save us a lot of trouble."

The next day was a good one. We were making good time moving the herd north, and Jim sent Grizz and Fini ahead to scout for where the band of Kiowa were camped, and see if there was any sign of them still around.

I could see a small dust cloud moving toward us, and thought it must be them returning. As they got closer and I finally saw the riders, I was more than a little surprised to see it wasn't Grizz and Fini. Instead, I saw two Indians coming at a steady lope. One wore a group of Eagle feathers tied in his headband. I figured he must be the leader, probably a chief.

Jim had been riding with the remuda, talking with Eustace. He noticed me waving to him, and soon was riding at a gallop toward me. As he eased Dunny to a stop, he had already noticed our approaching guests.

"I'm sure they're coming to collect money," Jim said.

"Can you tell what tribe they are?" I asked.

"They look to be Cherokee, I'd say, but, to tell you the truth, I don't know for sure."

We sat watching them approach, and Jim asked, "Know anything about the Cherokee?"

"Not much," I said.

"During the war, they were divided just like the rest of the country. The Cherokee out east generally supported the Union. Those in the west, including much of the Indian Territory, supported the South. By the end of the war, those supporting the north began confiscating much of the land from those who had supported the Confederacy. Those Cherokee who had held slaves, were forced to release them or adopt them into their tribe."

As the riders drew closer, Jim waved. The one we figured was the leader, or chief, nodded his head. They rode up and stopped so close that our horses were nearly nose to nose with theirs.

"Is one of you owner of this heard?" their leader asked.

"That would be me," Jim said. "You speak English very well."

"For a time, one of our great leaders was a man named John Ross. He was a man who was mostly of Scottish blood. His Cherokee name was Koowisguwi, which means 'Mysterious Little White Bird.'

"Though he was only one-eighth Cherokee," the leader continued, "John Ross grew up with the Cherokee Nation and was as much Cherokee as I am. He taught me much of the English language."

"I've heard of this man, and understand he was a great Chief of the Cherokee nation for many years," Jim said.

"You understand correctly. He has not been well recently, and soon will travel to the other side."

To save them asking for the toll, Jim said, "I suppose you are here to collect a toll for our crossing the Indian Territory with our herd."

"Again, you understand correctly," the Indian said. "How large is your herd?"

"We have about twenty-nine hundred head. What is your toll this year?"

"Six cents per head."

"That would be about one hundred seventy-five dollars total."

Pausing to think for a moment, the Chief responded, "That is about the right amount."

Jim reached in his pocket and brought out some folded money. "This is two hundred dollars. I trust you will share it evenly with all the tribes."

His eyes widened, and a slight smile showed in them. "Thank you, sir," the Chief said, with a nod of his head. "You will have safe travels through the territory."

"And I hope you have safe travels as well," Jim said. "We have two men out scouting the trail ahead. You may run into them."

"Yes, we did see them earlier today. It looked as though they were getting ready to head back this way."

"I should have known that you would be aware of them," Jim said. "One of the things they were looking for is a band of Kiowa that have a Negro woman with them. We saw their camp a couple days ago."

"That band is a part of a larger group of renegade Kiowa. They do hold a few slave women. That is the reason they are no longer part of the main tribe. It is not allowed to own slaves. They must be set free or adopted into the tribe.

"This group can be dangerous," the chief continued. "We have tried hard to keep them from causing trouble with settlers and cattle drives. So, be very careful around them."

"That's good to know. Thank you."

With nothing more, they turned their horses and rode back following the same trail they'd come in on. After a bit, I turned to Jim, saying, "Now I'm hoping Grizz and Fini didn't find that band of Kiowa."

"Just thinkin' the same thing," he said. "Let's hope they're back pretty quick."

A little while after the Indians had left, we could see two dust clouds. One, we figured, was the two Cherokee. The other, a little to the west, we hoped would be Grizz and Fini. In a short while, we could see them riding toward us.

"Well, we found the campsite of the Kiowa from a couple days ago, and their trail that leads to the northwest from there. But, we decided not to follow it too far," Grizz told us.

"Probably a good thing you didn't," Jim said. "We just talked with some Cherokee that told us they were part of a renegade Kiowa bunch. And, it sounds like they're a little on the hostile side."

"What're we gonna do about Eustace's sister?" Grizz asked.

"We'll have to figure that one out tonight when we make camp," Jim said.

Chapter Twenty- Four

That evening, after circling the herd, I walked over to give Eustace a hand with his rope corral. As we finished, I asked, "Have you thought about what we should do to find Sophie?"

"Been thinkin' 'bout nothin' but that... all day long."

"Thought of any plan?"

"Yeah," he said slowly.

"Well," I said, after waiting a bit. "Gonna tell me?"

"Oh, yeah, sorry," he said. "A couple of us could trail 'em, an' when we get their camp in sight, we'll need t' find a place t' sit an' watch fer a while. When we knows which tent Sophie's in, an' when she's alone, I'll sneak up and whisper her name. When she knows it's me, I'll cut the tent skin, 'n she kin sneak away wit' me."

"Well, it sounds like a good idea. It may take some time, but it's workable," I said. "After some supper, let's sit down and talk to Jim about it." Later that evening, I said to Jim, "There are too many variables to really lay out a good plan, but I think Eustace has the right idea."

"How many days do you think before your back to the herd?" Jim asked.

"I think it'll be three days, maybe four, before were back."

"How many men are thinkin' of takin' with you?"

"I think just Eustace, me, and Fini, since he's pretty good with a gun, and the only one who can communicate with the Kiowa if needed."

"We've been mighty lucky so far, on this cattle drive," Jim said. "Let's hope we don't run short on luck this time around."

"I think we'll head out before daylight" I said. "Fini knows how to find their old campsite, and the trail heading northwest from there."

"Okay," Jim said. "And, like before, you'd better damn well be careful. I don't want to be hearing about any of our men ending up dead."

"Oh, we'll be careful all right," I said. "Don't care to face the wrath of a renegade band of Kiowa."

The next morning we were mounting up an hour before daylight. There had been a light rain that night, so we could ride at an easy gallop and not worry about any dust cloud. Duke fell into stride with Duchess, and was going to get a good workout for the next few days. In about two and a half hours, we found the place where Jim had seen the Kiowa camped before. We could see the trail headed northwest from there, and it looked like there were seven or eight horses. A couple of them were probably pack horses, with at least one pulling a traverse.

With the ground drying quickly, we rode slower to not raise a dust cloud. We didn't know how far ahead of us they were, but hoped they had made camp again not too far down the trail.

Late that day, as darkness began to set in on us, we decided to stop. We wouldn't build a campfire, so we looked for some protection of rocks and trees to sleep under. We found a good spot, and, as we began laying out our bedrolls, Eustace said, "I know I won't be able to sleep for a while, so I'm goin' on ahead t' do a lil scouting. Ahs gonna be quiet 'n careful, so no need to be worryin'."

"Okay," I said, "but get back here, and try get *some* sleep before morning."

He swung back in the saddle and quietly rode away.

The next morning, as I awoke and sat up, I heard him say, "Mornin' Mack."

"Mornin' Eustace," I said. He was sitting on his bedroll, and I asked, "Any sleep at all?"

"Yeah, 'bout two hours," he said. "I seen were the Kiowa set up camp again. Had a campfire goin' in front of two small tepees."

"Could you tell if she was there?"

"Didn't go close enough to see."

"How far away are they?"

"Little over two hour's ride. Longer at a walking pace."

By then, Fini was up, saying, "Señor Eustace, let us go to see if we can find your sister."

Eustace smiled softly. "Let's go," he said.

131

We headed out, keeping our horses at a fast walk, to keep the dust down. Eustace began quietly explaining what he had been able to see. "Dey built camp in a small ravine, so it's not gonna be easy to sneek up on 'em. I think there were a few bushes right behind the tepees, so if I can move in on foot and sneak into dose bushes, I can wait for a signal from you... dat da woman has gone in one of the tepees."

I nodded. "Let's hope it goes easy."

Chapter Twenty-Five

About four hours later, we could see smoke from a small fire. We guessed it was less than an hour ahead of us. We weren't worried about them having anyone standing guard in the area, since they were camped in the Indian Territory, and generally weren't concerned about anyone coming after them. We continued on at a walking pace, watching for their camp and checking the surrounding area.

When we were close enough to see the tepees in the distance, we decided to split up. Fini and I moved to the far left along a tree line, and Eustace moved to the right along a ridge heading toward their camp. We tied our horses to trees, and moved in on foot, keeping each other in sight.

When we were about ninety or a hundred yards from their camp, Fini and I moved farther to our left and found a good spot to sit on a ridge to have a better view of things. Fini whispered, "There... the woman's carrying water. There must be a stream down that slope."

I looked over at Eustace and pointed to the woman. He nodded and began sneaking toward where he'd get to the bushes that were behind the tepees.

I whispered to Fini, "There's about twenty yards of open space he'll have to cross before he gets to the bushes. He'll have to be careful not to be seen."

"Oh, I think he can do it, Señor Mack."

"I think you're right."

Earlier, talking about what we would do, I asked Eustace, "What if she doesn't want to go with you?"

"Guess there is that chance she doesn't want to come wit'. But when she hear my voice, an' see me... I's sure she'll want to go wit' us."

"And if she does come with you, and you manage to sneak up the slope, we're going to need to hightail it out of here," I said. "It won't take long for them to wonder where she is, and finally see the cut in the back of their tent."

"Yer right 'bout that. I figured when we get t' that stream 'bout halfway back t' the herd, we should take that north for a ways to try and lose them if they come after us."

Now, there was nothing Fini and I could do, but watch and wait. Eustace disappeared over the ridge, then we could see him on the slope of the ravine where he had to cross twenty or thirty yards of open ground to get to the bushes that were behind the tepees. He paused, and watched for a long while, then quietly hurried across to the bushes. As he sat there hidden, he watched the movement of the Kiowa, waiting to see if the woman was his sister. He looked at us and gave us a signal that it was Sophie. Now, the question was, would she come with us.

Our plan was to signal Eustace when Sophie was approaching one of the tepees. We watched for a long while and I began to wonder if it would ever happen. Finally, after nearly an hour of watching and waiting, she walked over and reached for the door flap on the teepee closest to us. Ducking behind the ridge, I raised my left arm to Eustace, indicating she was approaching the tent on his left. When she stepped in the tent, I gave him the sign that she went in.

134

Eustace had been patiently waiting for my signal, letting him know that Sophie was going into one of the tepees. When I gave him the signal, he moved from where he'd been hiding, to the back of the teepee on the left. Lifting the bottom of the tent wall, he said in a soft voice, "Sophie, this is your brother, Eustace, and I'm here to take you home wit' me."

For a long while there was only silence. Too long for Eustace. He whispered again, "Sophie?"

Then he heard movement, and saw the buffalo hide on the back of the teepee move as though a hand had pressed against it. "Eustace?" her soft voice asked.

"It's me, Sophie. Do you want to come wit' me?"

"Oh Eustace... that would be a very dangerous thing."

"Shhhh," he whispered, as he reached for his knife and began cutting the buffalo hide. When he'd cut it about three and a half feet up, he looked in at Sophie, who stood with her hand covering her mouth. He reached for her other hand, and gently pulled her to him. He held a finger to his lips, but she was well aware of the need to be quiet.

They quickly moved to his hiding place in the bushes, where he gave her a big hug. We could see them whispering to each other, as they sat holding hands. Soon, Eustace looked up at us and pointed in the direction of his escape.

I quickly shook my head "No." One of the Kiowa was walking toward our ridge and would easily spot them trying to cross the open space. The Kiowa stepped into a group of bushes, then, a few minutes later, returned to where he had been sitting in their camp. I guessed that he had answered nature's call.

I looked to see if Eustace was watching, and gave him a sign that it was clear. Taking Sophie's hand, they hurried across the open space and over the ridge where they could go without being seen. Fini and I hurried back to meet them.

Eustace had a big, strong horse that could easily carry him and Sophie. We rode hard until we came to the stream Eustace had talked about. There we took a minute to let the horses drink, and began riding northward in the stream, hoping it would wash away our hoof prints, and any sign of where we'd gone. I carried Duke with me on Duchess to save him the effort of running up the stream.

Where we'd leave the stream and head east, would be mostly guesswork on our part. I figured the herd would likely be about twenty miles north of us. So, as long as the stream continued north, and didn't veer to the west, we could keep following it. Our luck was holding strong, and the stream continued north, with an occasional bend to the east.

We stayed in the stream for more than an hour, and I calculated that, at a fast walking pace, we'd probably traveled about three miles. "We should probably head east now, and pick up the trail of the herd," I said.

"Think we've gone far enough up the stream?" Eustace asked.

"Yeah, I think so. Our best hope now is to catch up with the herd. Once we are back with them, I don't think five Kiowa would try to take us on."

"Even though we have a crew of twenty men," Fini said, "I think we will have to keep a wary eye out for trouble from these Kiowa."

Chapter Twenty-Six

We rode hard for the rest of that day, occasionally slowing to give our horses a breather. Late in the afternoon, we picked up the trail of the herd, and headed north. As darkness began pushing aside the daylight, we started looking for good place to make camp. Soon, Eustace was pointing, and we followed him to the right, up a long slope. We came to a small plateau, where there was a cave-like space to provide shelter, and a good, high ridge above it to keep watch. We decided to spend the night there.

As we dismounted, Eustace introduced us to his sister. He said, "Sophie, dis here is Mack... one of da best frens ah ever had."

"Pleased to meet you, Sophie" I said.

She smiled softly, nodded and lowered her eyes.

"And dis here is Fini. He's from Mexico, an' just joined our crew a couple days ago," Eustace said.

"It is my great pleasure to meet you, Sophie," Fini said, with a slight bow at the waist.

Again, she nodded and lowered her eyes.

We laid out our bedrolls, and it was evident all of us were worn out from the long day. We would take two-hour shifts standing watch at the top of the ridge. If the Kiowa were on our trail, we didn't want to be caught off guard. The night was calm and quiet. From the top of the ridge you could easily hear anyone approaching, and with the bright moon, you could see a long way down the slopes.

Eustace and Sophie had been talking, and catching up for most of the day on horseback, so they both were well aware of the need to sleep as much as possible that night.

Eustace said, "I think we should be catchin' up wit' da herd late in da mornin' tamarra."

"Tomorrow" I said slowly. "... catching up *with the* herd by late morning *tomorrow.*"

Smiling at Sophie, Eustace slowly repeated what I said, then added "Mack has been helping me learn to speak better."

"I will take the first watch," Fini said.

"Okay, Fini. But I'm sure I won't wake up to relieve you, so, in about two hours you come down and poke me."

"Si, Señor Mack. I'm sure I will be more than ready for sleep by that time."

I was sleeping hard when I felt a poke at my shoulder. "Señor Mack, it is time for your watch."

I sat up, rubbing my eyes, and said, "Fini, it can't be two hours already."

"Oooh, si, it has. It has been a little more than two hours. I was becoming afraid of falling asleep, so I come to get you."

"Okay, Fini," I said, still rubbing my eyes. He curled up on his bedroll, and I headed up the slope to the top of the ridge. Duke, eager and alert, was walking by my side. "Your job to keep me awake tonight," I told him.

I found a rock to sit on, and Duke laid at my feet looking up at me. For the next hour, I enjoyed the quiet night, whispering to Duke occasionally, which helped keep me alert. At one point, with his head resting on his outstretched paws, something caught his attention and he raised his head quickly. He starred and started a low growl.

"What is it Duke?" I softly asked, and turned to look in the direction he was growling. As I turned, I heard a hissing sound, then something stabbed me in the side. The sudden pain was excruciating, and I looked down to see an arrow sticking through my side. Immediately, I knew what was happening and raised my rifle. When I caught a glimpse of the silhouette, I fired two quick shots. I don't know which of the two shots hit its mark, but the silhouette fell hard.

I'm sure they used the bow and arrow for stealth and silence as they moved in on us, but the two shots from my rifle alerted Eustace and Fini. They grabbed their rifles, and soon were receiving fire from the other Kiowa below. I scrambled to see where they were.

The arrow was causing a sharp, burning pain, and I was bumping it every time I tried to move. I quickly laid the gun down and broke off the long end of the arrow, causing more pain than I could imagine. Finally catching my breath, I grabbed my rifle again, and began firing at the silhouettes I could see below.

By then, Eustace and Fini had been shooting as well. I think they could see the muzzle blast from the rifles of the Kiowa to make out where they were. The gun fighting, blind as it was, continued for the next eight or ten minutes, until one of the Indians was seriously wounded. Then, with one down and one injured, they retreated, and soon I could hear their horses riding away.

Duke and I hurried down the ridge to check on Eustace, Fini and Sophie. Fortunately, none of them were hit in the gunfire. When I got close enough to Eustace for him to see, he said, "Mack! You been hit!"

Nearly stumbling and falling, I grabbed his strong shoulder, and groaned, "Yup, I need your help."

Fini hurried over and helped hold me up, saying, "Eustace, I can hold him while you fetch your medicine pouch. Then we need to get this arrow out of him."

As he hurried to his saddlebag to get his medicine pouch, he looked at Sophie saying, "Can you tear up some pieces from that ground sheet for some bandages?" She quickly grabbed her knife and began cutting and tearing the ground sheet into wide strips.

Eustace hurried back, looked me in the eye, and said, "This ain't gonna feel good."

"I know. Just grab it and yank it quick as you can. The quicker the better."

Without saying a word, he grabbed hold of the arrow and pulled as hard and quick as he could. I let out a short, but loud scream, and felt my knees buckle a little.

"Sit down here on your bedroll," Eustace told me. "I've got to cook up some good poultice to put on your wounds. Meanwhile, Sophie, can you put pressure front and back with those strips of cloth and try to stop the bleeding."

Sophie quickly came over and put cloth strips on my wounds. It didn't feel good to have her hands pressing hard to stop the bleeding, but I knew it was necessary.

As I had learned before from the comments of Lefty and Jim with their injuries, the poultice Eustace applied to my wounds seemed to ease the pain. He smeared it in the wound, front and back, then used long strips of the ground sheet to wrap me and hold the pieces of cloth in place on the wounds.

He said, "You lay back and sleep. I'll stand watch in case they decide to return."

"Take Duke with you, Eustace. He'll give you an early warning if anything is in the area," I said, as I grabbed hold of his hand and he helped ease me to my back.

"Good idea. Come on Duke," he said, slapping his leg.

The next morning, I didn't wake up until about an hour after sunrise. Eustace said they wanted to let me sleep as long as I could. He and Fini had been taking turns standing guard, and, fortunately, the Kiowa never returned.

"Think you can ride this morning?" Eustace asked.

"Won't know till I try," I said.

"Okay. Time to see," he said.

Fini walked Duchess over to me, and Eustace helped me into the saddle. I felt considerable pain, but said, "I think I can do it. Let's go."

With Sophie on his horse behind him again, Eustace took the lead and we picked up the trail of the herd heading north. We figured that it would take five or six hours to catch the herd. I was hoping it would take less than that. I was also hopeful of making a comfortable spot to lay down in the back of Jack's wagon for the next day or two.

We stopped regularly to rest, and for Eustace to check on my wounds. He said, "I caught sight of a big dust cloud ahead. We should catch the herd in less than an hour. When we get near, I'm going to ride on ahead to find Jim and ask him to hold up and cut the day short. You need the rest, and I'd like to give Sophie a chance to meet everyone, and get settled in."

"Good idea, Eustace," I said. "I'll be glad to rest for a while."

Chapter Twenty-Seven

When we caught sight of the herd, Eustace spurred his horse into a full gallop. As he approached the herd, Jim, who'd been checking down the line and was talking to Whitey, saw Eustace and spurred Dunny to meet him.

They pulled their horses to a stop as they reached each other. "Glad to see you made it back already, Eustace. This must be your sister, Sophie," Jim said, tipping his hat and smiling to her.

"Glad t' be back," Eustace said. "An' yep, dis here is Sophie, my little sis." Then glancing back at Sophie, he said, "Sophie, dis here's Jim, our boss."

Sophie smiled at Jim, then, in her usual way, nodded and lowered her eyes.

"Fini and Mack are just comin' up t' the back of the herd," Eustace said. "That Kiowa band caught up to us las' night, and Mack took an arrow in his side. He's gonna be okay, but I's thinkin' it'd be good to make camp here, so he can get a long night of rest."

"You sure he's gonna be okay?"

"Yup. Poked a hole through his side, but didn't hurt anything but muscle. I think with a long rest, and maybe a day ridin' in the back of the wagon wit' Jack, he should be back in the saddle 'n doing good after that."

"Okay. I'm going to ride ahead and tell Jack to make camp as soon as he sees a good spot. Then we'll circle the herd and make a short day of it.

"Pleased to meet you, Sophie, and I hope you feel comfortable riding with us," Jim said, with a tug on the brim of his hat again. Then he turned Dunny and rode away.

Watching him ride away, Eustace said, "He's a mighty good man, Sophie. Like ah been sayin', he 'n Mack are two of the bes' men I ever knew. You're gonna learn t' like 'em da way I do."

"Yes Eustace, ah kin see it in them," she said, with a soft voice and soft smile.

Eating supper that night, everyone wanted to hear us tell of rescuing Sophie. Jim spread the word earlier, that she would need time to get comfortable with everyone, so not to ask her questions, or put her on the spot.

Fini gladly agreed to be the one to tell of our latest adventure. With his Mexican accent, and his flamboyance, he had the whole crew glued to his storytelling. By the time he was through, you'd thought we'd taken on half the Kiowa nation.

While listening to Fini's stories, Eustace made another batch of poultice to put on my wounds. "You're lookin' pretty good," he said. "I thought our hard riding to catch up wit' da herd might have done more damage. But dere's no sign of infection, and yer lookin' good."

"Thanks to you... *Doctor* Eustace," I said. "But I'm ready to crash and, hopefully, get me a long night's sleep."

"Good idea. Jim tol' me we won't start pushin' da herd 'til daybreak. We'll fix up a soft bed in the back of Jack's wagon for you to lay on, and I'll check on you before we hit da trail."

Layin' in the back of Jack's wagon wasn't as bad as I expected. It was plenty bumpy, of course, but Eustace had piled up enough blankets from the crew to soften the ride. By the time we made camp that night, I was more than ready to get out and walk around a bit. The pain and soreness wasn't too bad, mostly because of the poultice Eustace was putting on the wounds.

Climbing out of the wagon, I saw Eustace, as he was finishing with his rope corral. I had told him to let Sophie ride Duchess for the day, and walked over to give Duchess a brush down and check her hooves. Sophie had set my saddle, bridle, and saddle blanket near the chuck wagon, and was helping Eustace. He saw me climbing from the wagon, and walked over to check on me.

"How you feelin'?" he asked.

"Pretty good," I said. "Wasn't too bad riding in the back of Jack's wagon. Even did a little napping now and then."

"That's good. After some supper, I'd like to have another look at'cher wounds,"

"You got it."

Sophie sat with Eustace and me as we ate supper. I asked her, "How did you like Duchess?"

"She is a very fine and gentle horse. I'm sure none from my brother's remuda will compare."

"Yes, she is a wonderful horse," I said.

Eustace and I had talked about Sophie riding with him, and helping with his remuda for the next four weeks until we reach the railhead in Kansas. When we were done with the drive, and headed back to Texas, Eustace wanted to find a small place of his own. Jim said that about twelve hundred acres of his land lay across the Glen River from his main ranch. With no easy way to cross the river, the land basically went unused and he would be willing to sell it at a very reasonable price.

"I don't even know if I could afford that," Eustace had told Jim.

"Oh, I think we could work it out in a way that you could pay me over a long period of time. Getting small regular payments is better than getting nothing," Jim said. "And having that land just layin' there across the River has always been a sore spot. It would be enough land to get you started with a small herd. I could help you with that, too."

So, Eustace was excited about the possibility, and talked with Sophie about living with him for a while. She liked the idea, and said it may be for a long while.

"As long as you want," he answered.

Chapter Twenty-Eight

The next four days went well, as we headed north through the Indian Territory. I was healing and doing fine. Sophie was getting comfortable with the crew and they were impressed with what a hard worker she was. She helped Eustace with the remuda, and would help Jack with meals and cleanup. Jack treated her as an equal, and Sophie soon warmed up to him. She also asked to take a shift on night watch, which Jim agreed to.

I walked over to see if Eustace needed any help, as he finished staking his rope corral that evening. He said, "I'd like to have one more look at yer wounds, and put some poultice on them, hopefully fer the last time."

"Sounds good," I said. "It's feeling a whole lot better than I expected in this short time." Glancing around, I asked, "Where's Sophie?"

"Oh, she went over to help Jack wit' supper."

"Should've known," I said. "She is the hardest working woman I've ever seen."

"Yeah, she's used to lots of hard work."

That night she was riding the midnight shift with Eustace, me, Rocky and two others. We saddled up and rode out to relieve the others, then began circling the herd as usual. Everything was quiet, and the cattle were calm. Soon, I turned Duchess and rode in the other direction for a change of pace. Whenever I passed Eustace or Rocky, I would stop and visit briefly. Each time I passed Sophie, I would smile and nod to her, which she did in return.

After a while, I think it was about two o'clock, I saw Rocky's horse coming toward me. Problem was, there was no Rocky. I felt panic, as I knew he would never let his horse wander away from him. I urged Duchess into a gallop, and rode to catch the rider-less horse. I grabbed the reins, which were still back over the horse's neck... another thing that wasn't quite right.

I began scanning the area, looking frantically for Rocky. I began circling the herd, continuing to scan for him. Finally, up ahead, I could see what looked like a man lying on the ground and nudged Duchess again.

As I neared, I could see that it was Rocky, and my heart sank, fearing that he might be dead. Before Duchess had come to a full stop, I was off her and running toward Rocky. I saw an arrow sticking out of the back of his lower left shoulder, and gently grabbed his right shoulder, saying, "Rocky? Rocky, can you hear me?"

I heard a soft moan of, "Umm hmmm."

"Rocky... what happened?" I asked, though, instinctively, I already knew what had happened.

He tried to push himself up with his right arm, and I said, "Easy, easy. Let me help you."

I gently helped him to a sitting position, leaning against a small boulder that was next to him, then he said, "Think they got Sophie. Maybe shot Eustace, too."

"The Kiowa?"

"Yup."

"Did you see them at all?" I asked.

"Nope. Heard something, then felt the arrow knock me from my horse. I kin hold on here, while you go see if you can find Eustace to patch me up."

"Okay. I'll be back in a few minutes." I ran to Duchess, jumped in the saddle, and began searching for Sophie or her horse. I found an area where it looked like several horses had been milling around, then the tracks headed west. I sat studying the scene, and the only conclusion I could reach was that the renegade band of Kiowa had been trailing us, and had taken Sophie back.

I circled the herd, looking for Eustace. I found him on the far side of the herd, and told him what had happened.

"They get Sophie?" he asked, a little panic in his voice.

"Think so," I said. "I haven't seen her anywhere."

"Where's Rocky?" he asked.

"Follow me," I said, turning Duchess, and urging her into a gallop. As we reached Rocky, Eustace grabbed his medicine pouch from his saddlebag. He knelt and looked at the arrow in Rocky's shoulder.

"Looks like it missed your lung, Rocky. Gotta get it outta yer shoulder, though," he said. "Guess I'm not tellin' you nothin' you don't already know."

Eustace turned and asked me, "Kin you get a pan from Jack's wagon. Need one to make some poultice fer Rocky here. Somethin' to tear into rags, too. I'll get a fire goin' while you do that."

"Will do. Anything else you think you'll need?"

Eustace hesitated a moment, then looked at Rocky, "Do you like whiskey?"

"Sure do."

"Get that bottle of whiskey from Jim's saddlebag and bring it," Eustace said.

When I returned, Eustace had a small fire going and was getting ready to break the arrow. When he saw me coming, he hesitated and decided to let Rocky have some whiskey before breaking it off.

I handed Eustace the pot, and motioned toward Rocky with the bottle of whiskey. Eustace nodded, and I said, "Here you go Rocky. Take a couple hits off this."

After a few good drinks of whiskey, and about fifteen minutes for it to have some affect, Eustace said, "Gonna hurt a bit when I break this arrow, Rocky. Hang on." He snapped off the arrow, which brought a muffled scream from Rocky. What surprised both Rocky and me was that he immediately grabbed the other end of the arrow and yanked it out of Rocky's shoulder. This brought a louder, not so muffled scream.

"Man, Eustace, why didn't you let me know what you were gonna do?" Rocky asked, after a few moments of groaning through clenched teeth.

"Figured it's better to get it done all at once, 'n not have you gettin' worked up ova what's gonna happen," Eustace said. "Now it's done with, an' I'll get some stuff on there that'll make it feel better.

"Mebee so," Rocky said. Then he took one more slug of whiskey and handed me the bottle.

After getting Rocky patched up and back to camp, most everybody was up and waiting to hear what happened. "So you're sure they took Sophie?" Jim asked.

"Yup, nobody's seen her for at least an hour. About the same time Rocky took that arrow in the shoulder," I said.

After a pause, looking at Eustace, Jim said, "Whatever it takes... we're going to get her back Eustace."

"T'anks Jim," Eustace said, then stared down at his hands, letting his great concern show.

While Eustace was working on Rocky, we talked about getting her back. "I think Eustace, me, and Fini can go after them and get Sophie back," I said.

"Sure that's all you'll need?" Jim asked

"Yup. Unless they picked up more help, there's only four of 'em, and one was healing up from wounds."

"Okay," Jim said. "Getting' mighty tired of needin' to send people off to take care of problems like this, though."

"We all are," I said. "This one is going to be a little trickier than the others. These Kiowa will likely be on the lookout for us to come after 'em."

"Think yer right. But it's good you're thinking that way... might keep you from steppin' into a trap" Jim said.

"Hope so," I said. "They were likely ticked off that we had taken her from them in the first place. They'll surely be watchin' for us this time."

Eustace was finishing up with Rocky. "Good thing that arrow didn't hit me any lower," Rocky said.

"Yup. Likely would of taken out your lung," Eustace said. "Never dealt with anything like that. Not sure what I'd do about a punctured lung."

"Got a feelin' you'd figger somethin' out," Rocky said.

Chapter Twenty-Nine

The sky was just beginning to glow in the east, as Eustace, Fini, and I were headed west on the trail of the Kiowa. We had talked about following at a fast walking pace, mainly to keep the dust down, but traveling any faster, we could easily ride right into an ambush. By the time we stopped to rest, and have a little something to eat, we had no reason to believe we were any closer to the renegade Kiowa and Sophie.

"We're headed into rougher country," I said, "Looks like they're headed into the Witchita Mountains. I'm guessing they're headed for a canyon or place they can hole up in. A place they can watch for anyone approaching."

"I think you are correct, Señor Mack," Fini said. "We will have to be very careful as we go. It will get more and more dangerous, the closer we get to them."

"Let's move slow from here," Eustace said. "And keep watchin' fer any trouble up ahead."

"Aright, Eustace," I said. "In a few miles, we'll be headed into the rugged hills and canyons of the Witchitas. It's gonna be mighty tough not to be spotted by them."

"And they'd like to be where they could ambush us," Eustace said. "Think we should spread out a little 'n move slow."

We decided Eustace would stay on their trail, Fini would be to his left a ways, and I'd move to his right. We would keep each other in sight, and be on the watch for any kind of movement up ahead.

After about a half-hour, Duke, who was walking by my side, stopped and looked back down the slope. "What do you hear, Duke?" I asked, quietly.

He glanced up at me, then quickly back down the draw below us. We had been following the ridge along a draw that sloped down to our right, and Duke was staring far down the draw. Soon, I could hear what he was hearing. A horse was coming at a steady trot.

"C'mon Duke. Let's get up in those trees," I whispered.

Ten yards up the slope, to our left, was a group of trees and boulders. We hurried to get out of sight, and as we did, I waved to Eustace. He stopped and watched as we got behind the trees and rocks. I looked over to him, and pointed down the draw. He quickly found cover and motioned for Fini to stop.

In a couple minutes, I could see it was a lone horse and rider. He was a Kiowa, all right, but I didn't think he was one of the five Kiowa we had watched when we first took Sophie. He continued up the draw, not seeming to be aware of us, heading toward a canyon about a half mile ahead.

As he moved up the draw, he eventually went out of sight. I left Duke and Duchess where they stood, and moved up the hill to try and get a look where he was headed. I got to the ridge top where I could see him again, and waited.

The rider continued at a steady trot, until reaching the mouth of the canyon. There he stopped, looked up to the right, and whistled, sounding like a bird.

At the top of the canyon wall, I saw a Kiowa step from behind a boulder and wave him up the canyon, then duck back out of sight.

I hurried back down to where I'd left Duke and Duchess, jumped in the saddle and headed for Eustace. He saw me coming, and waved Fini over to join us. As I swung down from Duchess, Eustace asked, "What were you watching over there?"

"A lone Kiowa, riding up the draw," I said. "Not one of the five we had watched in their camp when we got Sophie, though. The question is, is he the only one that's joined them since we last saw them, or are there others."

I reached for my canteen, took a long drink, then slapped the cork back in with the heel of my hand. "From here," I said "you couldn't see the top of that canyon wall. They have a sentry posted there. We would have headed right into an ambush."

"Got any ideas?" Eustace asked.

"Nope. Not yet. We're gonna have to figure something out," I said, shaking my head. "This is probably as good a place as any to wait."

"The one standing guard at the top of the wall will probably head back to their camp at dark, since he would not be able to see anything anyway," Fini said. "Should we wait here until then?"

"Yeah, we might as well get comfortable for now, unless we think of something better to do in the meantime," I said. "We should just sit tight for what's left of the afternoon and into the evening, until dark."

"Sounds good," Eustace said.

We moved a short ways from where we stood talking, to a place where we were well hidden, but could see the top of the canyon wall. I took the first watch, while Eustace and Fini rested. After about thirty minutes, Eustace sat up, saying, "Can't relax at all, Mack. Thinkin' too much... about Sophie. Why don't you rest, 'n I'll watch."

"Okay, Eustace. As long as you're sure you're okay."

"I'll be jus' fine. You can rest easy."

I did, and I was more wore-out then I thought. In a short while, I drifted off to a deep sleep. What seemed like a short while later, which actually was two hours later, Eustace was shaking my shoulder. "Mack... Mack... wake up."

Startled, I sat up saying, "What is it?"

Fini was awake and watching with Eustace. Eustace said, "The one standing watch at the top of the wall, got up and walked away a couple minutes ago."

I stared at the top of the wall for a few moments, and Eustace continued. "Not sure if he left, or is just moving around."

"I think our best bet, is to leave the horses here and move in on foot," I said. "If we don't see anything of that guard for the next half hour, let's work our way to the mouth of the canyon.

As we sat watching the top of the wall, Eustace said, "Think it's been more'n a half hour. Let's move."

"Okay, let's go," I agreed. We spread out like before and moved slow. We didn't want to be spotted by the sentry if he returned.

From the ridge I'd been walking before, I could easily see the top of the canyon wall and figured I would be able to until I reached the mouth of the canyon. I didn't see any movement in the canyon or at the top of the wall, as we inched toward the canyon. The three of us came together in a thick stand of trees at the side of the canyon entrance.

"I didn't see any movement at the top of the wall," I said. "Did either of you?"

"Nope, not at all," Eustace said shaking his head back and forth.

"No," Fini said. "For some reason, I think the one standing guard went back to their camp. Maybe they are moving again?" he said with a shrug. "The good thing is, I don't think we have been spotted yet."

"I don't think we'll know until we move through the canyon," I said. "Ready?" I asked, looking at each of them.

Eustace nodded his head, and Fini said, "Let's go, mis amigos."

"I'll take the lead," I said. "Let's put a little space between us as we go, so we're not easy targets." They both nodded. Eustace waited a bit, then followed me. Fini waited a bit more, then took up the rear.

After what seemed like an hour, I reached a point where the canyon opened up wider and turned to the right. I knelt behind some scrub bushes, and waved Eustace up. It was hard to see what lay ahead, as the canyon curved more and more to the right. In the distance, I could see that it curved back to the left.

Twilight was overtaking the canyon. Soon darkness would push out the last of the light and take control of the canyon. "Maybe the darkness will work in our favor," I said. "We can keep moving on foot, and spot any campfire from a long way out."

Fini said, "Si, Señor Mack. I think you are correct. We should wait right here in these bushes until it is dark. I don't think we can be spotted here, with the canyon wall at our back and the scrub bushes in front."

We waited for only a short while, and it became so dark we couldn't see more than thirty yards ahead. The canyon floor continued to widen, as it turned to the right. Fini held back to bring up the rear, as I moved slowly along the right wall, and Eustace moved along the left. As before, we tried to keep each other in sight and watch for any sign of movement ahead.

We moved through the canyon slowly, anxiously, staring hard through the darkness and listening for any sound. We knew, eventually, we would see signs of their camp. Hopefully, there would be a campfire to give us early sign of where they were.

As we inched our way ahead, the canyon began to narrow again, and I could see by the moonlight and stars above that it was bending left up ahead.

We followed the canyon through a long, slow bend to the left. I could tell, as we moved ahead, that we were slowly climbing. The canyon was widening again, and would soon reach a point where Eustace and I, if we continue to stay close to the walls, could not keep in contact with one another. There was a clump of scrub junipers just ahead, and I waved for Eustace to join me.

I kneeled and Eustace moved in next to me. I said, "This canyon is opening up, wider and wider. And we're beginning to climb, steeper and steeper. It's going to get...." I froze, and pointed up the canyon toward a plateau.

"Did you see that?" I asked.

"See what?" Eustace said.

"Looked like someone is trying to start a fire."

We watched in silence for a few moments, then there was another small glow, and a fire was soon growing.

Eustace and I glanced back at each other, having a good feeling about knowing where they had made camp. We started to move slowly ahead toward their camp and, suddenly, that good feeling left us when we heard a voice from above and behind us.

"Drop gun's... put hands up," the voice said somewhat haltingly. It was the voice of an Indian, probably a Kiowa, who's English wasn't too good. But we got the point... loud and clear.

I laid my rifle at my feet, and took my revolver from my holster and did the same with it. Meanwhile, Eustace hesitated, then put his Parker shotgun on the ground along with his big knife. We both slowly raised our hands.

The Indian jumped from the ledge where he had been hiding. About ten feet up, the ledge was wide enough that we could not see him waiting up there. He walked toward us, saying, "Move," and motioned with his rifle for us to move ahead. Soon, a second Kiowa warrior joined him from the scrub Juniper just ahead of where we stood.

Eustace and I glanced at each other as we turned and started to walk. The look was that of, "What do we do now?"

As we neared the plateau where the campfire burned, we could see that this was not their campsite, but merely a campfire. I soon realized that they knew we had been following them, and had started the fire as bait for their trap.

Our only hope now was that they didn't know Fini was with us. We didn't know where he was, but knew he was somewhere behind us. I was hoping he had found cover, and was watching this whole thing as it played out.

Chapter Thirty

As we passed the fire on the plateau, two more Kiowa joined the two that were escorting us up the canyon at gunpoint. We walked for about a quarter-mile, then, rounding another curve, we were close enough to their camp to see three teepees dimly lit by a campfire.

Both Eustace and I were poked in the back by rifles, indicating that we weren't walking fast enough for their liking. We glanced at each other as we picked up our pace a little. The look on his face was the same as the one I felt inside... no idea what we'll do next.

As we got to their camp, one began shouting at Sophie. It was in their Kiowa tongue.

"They want you to undress. Take everything off," she said. Then she reached in one of the tepees and brought out two pieces of deer hide. "Get undressed and then wrap these around you."

The one shouted again, and Sophie said, "Don't try anything or they'll shoot me first, then both of you."

With the pieces of hide tied around our waists, we were pushed toward some stakes that had been pounded in the ground. Again, one shouted at Sophie. She nodded quickly, and pointed.

"They want you both on to lie on your back in the staked-out areas," she said, looking from the Kiowa, to the ground, then to us.

161

Soon, we were tied by our ankles and wrists to the stakes. The leather straps they used were wet and pulled tight. As they dried, they would get tighter still. Tonight in the canyon, with only the loin cloth, it would get very cold. Tomorrow, in the sun, it would get very hot.

As I lay there, thinking about our predicament, I thought about Fini. I wondered where he was, and if he was working on some kind of a plan yet. I glanced over at Eustace. He was staring straight up, an angry, menacing look on his face.

"You okay?" I asked Eustace in a whisper.

I saw him nod his head that he was okay. A few seconds later, one of the Kiowa stepped between us holding Eustace's knife. He spoke in Kiowa, with a slight grin on his face. Sophie said, "He says it is a very nice knife that my brother carries. If you say anything more to each other, this knife will begin to cut your flesh."

I looked at Sophie and nodded. Then she spoke in Kiowa, telling him that we understood... I think.

That night, as I feared, was very cold. I focused on the hottest, sweatiest day in the saddle I could remember, hoping it would help me through the cold. As the sun came up in the morning, I could see it inching its way down the canyon wall toward where I lay shivering.

I didn't dare give more than a quick glance at Eustace to see how he was doing. So far, it looked like he was doing better than me. At least he didn't appear to be shaking as much as I was.

Sophie was stoking the fire and cooking some fry bread and corn grits for the five Kiowa warriors. She was also cooking some meat, probably venison from the good smell.

Through the night, one of the Kiowa sat watch over us continuously. We hadn't heard or seen anything of Fini. I hoped he was planning to do something soon. Knowing Fini, I was sure he would do something to help us. I think his first instinct would have been to get help, but that would have taken three days or more to get back with help. I'm not sure we would survive two more days of being staked out like we were. Particularly, if the Kiowa decided it was time for a little torture.

Fini had been trailing us up the canyon, staying forty or fifty yards back. He stayed just close enough to catch glimpses of Eustace and me as we moved through the darkness. He froze when he saw the Kiowa jumping down from the rock ledge, soon to be joined by another Kiowa that came from the scrub Juniper ahead.

For a while, Fini followed us up the canyon. He soon decided, though, it was better to go back and check on the horses, feed them, water them, and see if he could figure out what to do next.

The horses were fine, and Fini decided to stake them out in a small open area for good grazing. I had left Duke behind to guard the horses. Duke would be able to scare away most any predator that might come looking at the horses for their next meal. Fini gave the horses a little grain from my saddle bag and some beef jerky to Duke. He made sure each had enough water, too.

With the animals taken care of, Fini sat munching on jerked beef, drinking from his canteen and wondering what his next move would be. He decided it was probably clear to move up through the canyon, since they had captured Eustace and me, and didn't seem to be out searching for any others. He would decide what to do when he reached their camp and saw what things looked like.

He gave one last glance at the animals, then turned to head up the canyon. Though trying to move quietly, and watch for anyone up ahead, he moved at a quick pace in the dark. He slowed a bit and glanced around when he passed the rock ledge the Kiowa had been hiding on. He'd seen or heard nothing to this point in the canyon.

He moved through about a quarter-mile of the canyon, where the canyon floor was climbing at a pretty good rate. Reaching sort of a plateau area, where the canyon curved back to the left, he could see the smoke from a campfire clouding the stars and moon. He guessed it was about a quarter-mile away. The area opened up fairly wide, with lots of scrub Juniper and a few pine trees growing.

He moved at a very slow pace, trying to stay hidden most of the time. He only crossed open areas when there was no other choice, and then, only after scanning the area for some time.

He was surprised, not to have seen any sentry along the way to their camp. Just as he was nearing the camp, he noticed a draw angling left up out of the canyon. He moved up the draw until he was high enough to look down at the Kiowa's camp. He saw us stripped and staked to the ground, and his heart sank.

Chapter Thirty-One

Through the last of that night, and as the morning glow entered the canyon, Fini sat watching the movement of the Kiowa in their camp, trying to figure out what he could do to set us free. It would not be easy.

He thought there were a total of six Kiowa warriors in the camp, along with Sophie. By the time the early morning glow turned to daylight in the camp, he saw three of the Kiowa warriors ride out of the camp, heading west. This greatly improved his chance of doing something, but he would need to move soon... not knowing when they would return.

Having his rifle, his Colt revolver, and his hunting knife, he decided to move as close to the camp as he could without being seen, then rush to cut Eustace and me loose from our bindings. He hoped he could get Sophie's attention before he had to rush the camp. He sure could use her help.

His hopes were dampened, as he noticed Sophie was tethered to a stake herself. She had about a thirty foot rope tied to her ankle, the other end tied to a stake. The rope allowed her to enter her tent, and move in the thirty foot circle around the camp. This didn't insure against her escape, but would give instant notice if she wasn't attached to the rope, which someone was checking continually.

His hopes were raised again, when he was able to get her attention, and she nodded to him, showing a slight smile. He knew she would do whatever she could to help when the time came. He decided there was no way to think he could outsmart the Kiowa, so all he could do was rush the camp and cut us loose. He would be ready to shoot any Kiowa that that made a move.

He watched for a while more, and decided it was time to move. Two of the Kiowa were in a teepee, and one was at the campfire with his back to Fini. He would have to pass the one at the campfire as he rushed to our aid, and, if possible, would knock the Kiowa out with the butt of his rifle. Hopefully, this would buy some time before the other two Kiowa were alerted, and rushed from the teepee.

Sophie noticed Fini moving toward the camp, and hurried inside her teepee. In a few seconds, she was coming out without the rope on her ankle. She quickly moved to the far side of the campfire, to get the attention of the one kneeling at the fire. Fini rushed ahead, quietly as possible.

Hearing something, the Kiowa warrior quickly rose and turned to look. The Kiowa raised his rifle, just as Fini swung with the butt of his rifle, catching the Kiowa full in the face and toppling him over.

Fini quickly drew his knife and slashed at the bindings holding our hands and feet. Sophie, seeing one of the Kiowa begin to rush from the teepee, ran and rammed hard into him, knocking him against the buffalo hide of the tepee. He began yelling loudly in Kiowa as he scrambled to his feet. By then, Fini took aim with his revolver and shot the warrior. The second warrior was coming out of the tent, rifle first, and Fini shot him as well.

Eustace noticed Sophie pointing at the Kiowa by the campfire. He was beginning to move. Eustace ran, grabbed him and drug him to where we had been staked out. With my help, he gagged and tied the Kiowa to the stakes where Eustace had laid.

"We'll see how you like it," Eustace said, almost under his breath.

Sophie rushed to embrace Eustace. As he held her close in his arms, Eustace looked to Fini and said, "So glad to see you, Fini."

"Me too," I said. "Didn't know what you were going to do to help us, but I knew you'd come up with something."

Fini smiled and nodded, saying, "Looks like they have three ponies and a pack horse. Let's vamoose amigos."

We hurried to where the ponies and pack horse were tied. The ponies had bridles and we weren't going to take the time to find saddles, if there were any, and put them on the ponies. The pack horse had a halter and lead rope, and Eustace said that was enough for him.

Sophie came on the run, our clothes tucked up under her arm. We all mounted up and rode hard down the canyon to where our horses and Duke waited.

Taking a few minutes for us to throw on our clothes, and to drink some water from our canteens, we decided to let the ponies and pack horse go. Sophie would keep the pony she was riding, so she didn't have to double-up and ride on the same horse with Eustace.

"Gonna have to ride hard again for a while," Eustace said. "Put some distance between us 'n the rest of 'em."

As we mounted up, Fini shouted, "Vamonos amigos."

We rode hard until we decided it was time to give the horses a breather. We knew there was a small creek ahead, where we could take a break and let the horses drink. We rode at a slow pace for about ten minutes, and finally came to the creek.

167

It felt good to relax for a moment, sitting by the creek, as we let the horses take a breather and drink their fill.

"I've been thinking a lot about you saving our hides back there, Fini. I sure am thankful for your courage," I said.

"I am, too," Eustace said.

"And me," Sophie said softly.

"Just glad it all worked out, my friends," Fini said.

Chapter Thirty-Two

For the next day and a half, we rode at a steady pace. We didn't feel the need to push the horses, as two of the Kiowa warriors were dead, and one was staked out for who knows how long. If the other three warriors didn't return soon, the staked out one would be dead, too.

By early afternoon the second day, we could tell we were only a short way behind the herd. For some reason, I felt really excited about catching the herd this time – more than all the other times of trouble we'd been through. And I think that was true for Eustace, too. Maybe it was having survived a mighty tough situation.

For Sophie, it was uplifting to say the least. As we neared the herd, and passed by members of the crew, we heard shouts of, "Hi Sophie, glad to see you!" and "Good job boys. Glad you're back with Sophie."

If she had any uneasiness before, it disappeared that afternoon. She felt part of the group, and felt that each one of the crew cared about her. I could see it on her face, the good feelings that were growing inside her. It was good, and surprising, to see these tough, trail weary cowboys care about this colored woman the way they did now.

Jim decided to make camp and cut the day a little short. He was so relieved to see Sophie again, and all of us returning unharmed, that moving the herd farther wasn't important right now. Naturally, the whole crew wanted to hear the story, and Eustace and I were more than happy to let Fini do the telling. And, with his accent and his flamboyance, he did a great job... again.

The next two weeks seemed to pass quickly, and without a hitch... or any incidents like we'd run into before. We made several river crossings – the Canadian, Cimarron, and Arkansas rivers – and had crossed the border into Kansas. That was two days ago. Abilene was only nine or ten days away, and we could just about see and feel the end of the trail.

Crossing the Cimarron River had been anything but easy. It was always a treacherous river to cross, with turbulent currents. Adding to the terrible morning we'd been having, there were big, black threatening storm clouds building in the west. They were filled with continuous flashes of heavy lightning that looked like long, jagged, hot strings of wire made of white gold.

"We gotta start pushing the herd fast," Jim said. "Even though that storm looks a long way off and movin' slow, when it dumps on the Cimarron, upstream from here, it'll send a raging torrent of water down on us. So... we better have everything on the other side before it hits.

"There's another reason to push things a little," he said, hurriedly. "In a couple hours, we'll have the sun in our face and you know how much I don't want that."

He had always wanted to make river crossings with the sun at our back, or at least to the side. Cattle are very skittish crossing a river, and if you put the sun in their eyes it gets that much worse to make them move. Jim's theory is that they can't see the land on the other side. With the sun reflecting off the water and into their eyes, they are hard to move and will sometimes try to turn back while crossing. We had maybe two and a half hours to get the herd across before the sun would be shining in their eyes.

"Jack should be able to get the wagon across with no trouble, so let's start pushing the cattle. I'll tell Eustace to hurry his remuda and lead the way across as usual." He reined Dunny around and galloped off toward Eustace.

We did manage to get the whole herd across before the heavy water came crashing down the Cimmaron. We had a couple of minor injuries to members of our crew, and a few of the cattle, but, after watching the flood of water rushing down the river from the storm, we were glad to be high and dry on the other side.

We pushed the herd for another six miles that afternoon, and as we were making camp and settling the herd for the evening, I saw the Dusty Walker riding toward me from a ridge to the west. As he neared me and pulled his horse to a stop, he said, "You gotta see this, Mack."

"See what?"

"C'mon, I'll show ya." He reined his horse around and headed back toward the ridge. I nudged Duchess to a gallop and followed close behind. As we neared the top of the ridge, Dusty slowed his horse and swung down.

I did the same, and I heard him asking, "Hear that?"

I could hear what sounded like a loud, high-pitched whistling sound. "What is that?"

With a wave to follow him, he took off his hat and moved slowly to the top of the ridge. As we neared the top, he knelt and whispered, "When we stand up to look, be quick about it. They may disappear in a hurry."

I was still a little puzzled as I stood and scanned over the top of the ridge to the range below us. The loud whistling noise became a roaring scream. I stared down at a wide range covered with thousands of dirt mounds that had been pushed up by prairie dogs. Most of the prairie dogs were standing on the mounds, screeching a warning of danger. I looked to the left, the direction all the prairie dogs were looking, and could see three coyotes sneaking through the prairie grass.

When the coyotes finally broke into a full run, the prairie dogs immediately disappeared into their holes. One of the coyotes managed to grab a stray prairie dog, and one tried to dig frantically where he had seen his lunch disappear.

"Ever seen such a big prairie dog town before?" Dusty asked, grinning a bit and shaking his head over the whole thing.

"Nope. Nothing even close to this before," I said.

"Sure glad we never run into anything like that with the cattle," he said.

"Oh man," I said shaking my head. "Nothin' but a lot of busted legs waiting to happen down there."

Chapter Thirty-Three

Two days later we were making camp and circling the herd, when Jim rode up. "In the morning, I'm going to ride over to the trading post in Wichita," he said. "Mr. McCoy asked that I send him a telegram from there, so he could know when we'd be coming in with the herd."

Joseph G. McCoy was the man buying the cattle from Jim. Last year, McCoy had purchased about 280 acres just to the northwest of Abilene, Kansas, and built the Great Western Stockyard. There he purchased cattle and shipped them by rail to Chicago, St. Louis, and other large cities.

"The trading post is only an hour ride from here, so you can start the herd north and I should catch up to you in three or four hours," he said.

"How 'bout I ride with you?" I asked.

"Well, didn't think I'd need anybody with me, but, on second thought, with the things we've run into on this drive, maybe it would be good idea."

"Good! That's what I was thinking, too. With the Jesse and Frank James gang, and others like them on the prowl in Missouri and Kansas... you never know."

At supper, Jim told the crew his plans, and that Rocky and Eustace would be in charge and get the herd started north at first light. "We should be catching up with you guys by 10 o'clock in the morning, and we'll be picking up some supplies for Jack. That'll mean better eating for our last seven days."

"I'm going to tell McCoy that we'll be there in seven days," he told Eustace and me as we ate supper. "My guess is, we'll be there by the end of the sixth day, but that's okay. I'd rather be there a little early anyway."

In the morning, Jim checked with Rocky and Eustace to make sure everything was okay. Then he and I headed for the trading post near the town of Wichita, just an hour's ride east. As we got to the post, we could see a sign above a door that read, "Telegraph Office." We rode over, tied our horses to the hitching rail in front, and walked in to send a telegraph to McCoy. For me, this was a brand-new experience. I had never sent or received a telegram before, so I hung back a little, watching and listening to Jim.

He stepped inside and told the operator that he would like to send a message to Joseph G. McCoy at the Great Western Stockyard. The operator quickly wrote this, then held his pencil ready to write the message. Jim said, "Dear Mr. McCoy. Will be arriving with my heard of 2900 cattle in seven days. Signed, Jim Clusky."

Digging in his pocket, Jim glanced at the list of charges on the wall and paid the operator $1.45 and we stepped out to our horses. "Let's find the dry goods store and pick up those supplies for Jack," he said.

In a short while, we had purchased all we needed, loaded it on our two horses, and were headed northwest to catch up with the herd. "I think we'll be catching the herd a sooner than I figured," Jim said. "No need to push our horses too hard."

By 9:30, we were passing Whitey and Tuck at the rear of the herd. They waved when they noticed us approaching and then pass them, headed for the front of the herd.

174

The next five days were the best we'd had on the drive. The weather was much cooler, we were traveling across gently rolling terrain, and the cattle were used to the trail and cooperative. As we made camp and circled the herd that evening, we all knew we were only a day away from Abilene and turning the cattle over to McCoy and his fenced stockyard. There was a definite uptick in everyone's attitude as we sat around the fire eating supper.

As Jack finished eating and began his usual cleanup with Sophie's help, he said, "More than any of you, I'm looking forward to tomorrow night and eating a good steak and a meal that I didn't have to cook." Then he smiled brightly and began to laugh, which brought laughter from most of the crew.

The next morning, everyone was up extra early and energetic. I think it was knowing that today was the last day on the trail. Tonight there would be bathhouses, saloons, and hotel rooms with beds to sleep in.

In the afternoon, about two o'clock, Jim rode over to say he was headed into Abilene and look-up McCoy at his stockyard. "I'll get things lined up and will know where to lead you when you get there. I'm guessing you'll be there a little before five o'clock, and I'll come out to show you where to bring the herd."

"Sounds good. No make that... Sounds great!" I said. "We've made it... end of the line."

"Yup, finally! Thinkin' about gettin' home already."

"I think everyone is," I said. "Some of the guys are planning on partying in Abilene for a day or two, but I think most are anxious to get back home."

"It'll be two weeks riding, maybe a bit more, to get back home," Jim said. "But that's much better than the two months it took getting here."

"Got that right. See you later this afternoon."

He waved as he turned Dunny and headed toward Abilene.

Chapter Thirty-Four

That last day, our sixty-fifth day on the trail since leaving Jim's ranch, seemed to be going very slowly. I'm sure it was because we were all more than anxious to see Abilene on the horizon, and leave these cattle in the capable hands of McCoy and his people.

Everything went smoothly and, at four o'clock in the afternoon, Rocky and I thought we could see a few buildings on the far horizon. "Got to be Abilene," Rocky said, and added, "Thank the Lord!"

"Yup, think your right," I said. "See that dust cloud? I'm bettin' it's Jim headed our way."

Soon, we could see it was Jim riding Dunny, coming at a steady lope. He gave us a short wave as he neared, then rode up, pulled Dunny around and fell into stride with our horses.

"You're right on schedule," he said. "I told McCoy that you'd be at their gates in an hour. When we get there, I'd like you two to find a perch by the gate and count our cattle as they come in. McCoy will have two of his people there also, to compare the count when all the cattle are in."

"Sounds good," I said. "Be glad when the last cow goes in and the gate closes on them."

"Me too," Jim said, showing a little grin. "Tell the boys to meet me at the two big trees in front of the stockyard office about twenty minutes after they close the gates on those cattle. I'll have their pay for them. You boys come in the office with your count soon as our last steer comes in."

"Is there a hotel with a bathhouse?" Rocky asked.

"McCoy has a new hotel called the 'Drovers Cottage.' They've got a bathhouse, and a dining room that's supposed to be pretty good."

"Can't wait," Rocky said.

"I reserved me a room for tonight," Jim said. "Wasn't sure what everybody else's plans were, but they said they've got nearly a hundred rooms and plenty of them available."

"I'm going to be one of the first in line at the bathhouse," I said. "Then I'm headed over to the Mercantile and buy me a new shirt and some new pants. This shirt and pants that I've been wearing for most of our sixty-five days on the trail, I'm going to pitch in the garbage."

"Same here," Rocky said, showing a big grin.

"I'm going to ride back and meet with McCoy," Jim said. "See you soon."

Rocky and I both nodded our heads to Jim, as he turned Dunny and rode off toward Abilene again.

"Never thought I'd be this excited about getting to Abilene," Rocky said. "I feel like a kid just making his first trip to the candy counter in the dry goods store."

"Been a mighty long haul," I said, "and with more than our share of troubles along the way."

"I'm not sure – only been on one other cattle drive before – but I think you're right," Rocky said. "We didn't run into near the trouble on that first drive I worked."

"Well, we made it and didn't lose anyone along the way," I said. "And... picked up a those extra cattle for our bonuses, too."

"Yeah. Our pay for this drive is gonna be somethin'."

The next hour seemed to fly by, and soon Jim was meeting us as we neared the stockyard. The cattle weren't the least bit slow in getting through the gate. I think it was because they could smell the water in the huge stock tanks at the far end of the corral the area.

Jim had given Rocky and I a pencil and paper to keep track of the cattle count. In the end, Rocky had tallied two thousand, eight hundred seventy-two. My count was two thousand eight hundred sixty-nine. When we'd met with Jim in the stockyard office, he told us that the men for McCoy had tallied two thousand eight hundred seventy-two and two thousand eight hundred seventy.

"I think we'll settle on two thousand eight hundred seventy. It's a nice round number and all four of you were close to that count," Jim said. "I'm going with McCoy to the bank and get cash for the payroll and a little extra. The rest they'll wire back to my bank in Glen Springs. His banker is waiting there to meet us, so I should be back in ten or fifteen minutes to meet with you boys by the trees."

Soon, the whole crew was stretched out in the shade of the trees, waiting for Jim to return. The only topics for conversation were bath houses, steak dinners, whiskey, and comfortable beds.

As we relaxed in the shade, I noticed three men ride out of Abilene at a full gallop. They were headed west, but I didn't give it much thought, as we had noticed lots of people coming and going.

"I wonder what's holding up Jim," Flap Jack said. "Been nearly twenty-five minutes we been waitin'."

No one answered, but I began to wonder a little myself, and sat up to look around. After five more minutes, I said, "Eustace... Rocky... want to walk with me over toward the bank? See if Jim is still there."

Without answering, they were both on their feet walking beside me. It was only a short walk to the main street of Abilene, called Texas Street, which ran the east and west through town. As we walked east toward where the bank was at the corner of Cedar Street and Texas, we passed the 'Alamo' – one of the two saloons in the town – that was across the street. As we passed, I noticed a man lying on the ground near the back corner of the building.

I stopped in my tracks. "I sure hope that's a drunk lying there," I said, "and not Jim."

We hurried across the street toward the empty lot next to the saloon. Before we were halfway down the side of the saloon, I could see it was Jim lying there. Glancing at Eustace and Rocky, I could tell by the look on their faces that they knew it was Jim. We ran the last twenty yards to him, and could see a big, bloody gash on the back of his head as we neared.

"My medicine pouch is back in my saddlebag," Eustace said. "Be right back," he shouted, as he turned and ran to get his horse.

I slowly turned Jim, and saw he was unconscious. "Rocky, would you run and see if they've got some water and a rag in the saloon?" Before I'd finished the question, he was running for the side door of the saloon.

180

As I held Jim, I could tell he was still breathing and tapped his cheek trying to bring him around. Soon, Rocky came rushing out the back door of the saloon carrying a pitcher of water and some rags. I grabbed a rag, soaked it in the cool water, and dabbed it around Jim's face.

Before long, Jim began groaning and slowly lifting his hand. "Jim," I said, tapping his cheek lightly. "Jim, can you hear me."

"Mack," I heard him say softly. "Mack... they got me from behind."

"Who did?" I asked.

"Don't know. They clubbed me from behind. I'm sure money is gone."

"Let's worry about the money after Eustace fixes this gash in your head," I said. As he was coming-to, I'd soaked the rag again in the cool water and held it against the gash.

Just then I could hear a horse coming and looked to see Eustace, as he charged around the corner of the saloon. Sliding his horse to a stop, he was out of the saddle and looking at Jim in no time at all.

"All I can remember," Jim said, "is two guys coming toward me on the sidewalk as I left the bank. They said 'Hi' and tipped their hats as they came toward me.... must've been a third one behind me."

"I saw three riders leaving town, heading west at a full gallop about the time you should have been back to meet with us. Didn't think much of it at the time," I said, "but I'll bet anything it was them."

181

"Looks like they might have hit you with the butt of a rifle," Eustace said. "The gash should heal up in a few days, but you'll probably have a world-size headache for the next day or two."

"Lift me to my feet," Jim said. "I've got to go talk to McCoy and his banker. Hopefully they haven't sent the wire to Glen Springs yet. I need some more cash to pay the men. Rocky, maybe you could run ahead to the bank and see if they're still there... at the bank. Ask them to wait."

"Will do," Rocky said, and he was off, jogging toward the bank. Soon he was back, saying they were waiting for us.

Jim slowly shook his head, saying, "They got me for five grand – the payroll for the crew, plus a couple grand."

"We're gonna track 'em down and get it back for you," I said. "You boys up for one more adventure?"

"Don't even have to ask," Rocky said. "Already figured we'd be doing that."

"Me too," Eustace said. "Flap Jack can see to your wound. I'll give him extra poultice to put on it every day."

Jim was silent for a long while, as he looked at each of us. "Don't know how to thank you enough."

"No need to," I said. "We're all family."

"Das right," Eustace said. "Never in muh life did I think I could say that 'bout white folk... all three-a-you are like family to me."

"Those three guys riding at a dead gallop out of town are the only thing we have to go on," I said.

"I'm gonna ride back and makeup some poultice to give to Jack. I should be ready to go when you get saddled up," Eustace said, as he swung into his saddle.

I helped Jim hike over to the bank, where we found McCoy and the banker patiently waiting for us. They hadn't sent the wire to Texas yet, so Jim asked to take five thousand more in cash.

Finally, we headed back to where the crew sat, anxiously waiting in the shade of the big trees. Eustace had explained where we found Jim, and said it would be best if they'd wait right there. "Better'n us getting' scattered all over," he'd told them.

"Don't know what they've been able to tell you so far," Jim said to the crew. "I got clubbed in the back of the head, and they stole my money. But I worked it out with McCoy and the banker, and will be able to pay all of you your wages and bonus."

"I say we go after those mongrels," Flap Jack said, jumping to his feet.

"You have to stay here with Jim and look after his busted head," I said to Jack. "Eustace is fixing up some stuff to put on it every day. He and Rocky and I are going after the ones that robbed him. Hopefully, we'll be back in the next couple days."

"Need any more help?" Lefty asked.

"No, I think the three of us can handle it. The rest of you can get busy with baths, haircuts, whiskey 'n such."

"Glad to help if you need it," Lefty said. "But I'll have to say, I don't mind the thought of the other things."

The men all gathered around Jim, as he paid each of them their wages and bonus. Every man on the crew thanked him for his generosity, and told him it had been a pleasure to work with him.

"Like I told Eustace, Rocky, and Mack, you boys have all been like family to me," Jim said. "So, let's see if we can manage a little fun in town for the next day or two, even though they're out risking their necks again." He looked toward us with a sad looking grin.

"That's right! That's the way we want it," Rocky said.

Chapter Thirty-Five

The trail heading west out of Abilene was covered with tracks. Tracks from stagecoaches, buggies, horses, cattle, and almost anything else could be seen in the dust. Every now and then, though, we could pick up the tracks of what looked like three horses running at full gallop.

These tracks followed the trail west for about two and a half miles, then angled southwest across the prairie. As they headed across the prairie, it was easier to tell that there were three horses and that they were moving fast.

After trailing them for several miles across the prairie, we slowed to give our horses a breather. "Looks like they might be headed for the Smoky Hill Buttes," Rocky said. "That's not too far from Salina, Kansas. Only a few hour's ride from here."

"Dark will be settin' in on us in a while," I said. "Let's be watching for a good place to camp tonight."

"I never rode through the Smoky Hill Butte area, but heard that it was not too rugged," he said. "Probably just rugged enough to find a good place to hole up in."

"Well, let's keep following the trail and watchin' for a place to camp," I said. "We probably have about an hour of daylight left."

Eustace nodded and spurred his horse, following the trail at a steady lope.

About forty minutes later, we spotted what looked like an abandoned barn near a grove of trees. "Place to camp tonight?" Eustace asked.

"Let's ride over and see," I said, turning Duchess. It was an old barn, used only occasionally by its owner. There was an old bail of straw laying on the dirt floor in the corner, and two bales of hay in the small loft.

"Looks like the loft would keep us high and dry," Rocky said.

"Think you're right," I said. "And we can keep the horses inside the barn, so no one spots them."

The three of us slid from the saddle, and led our horses through the open door. One of the hinges was busted on the door, but we were able to lift and swing it shut. I climbed to the loft and said, "Throw me the bedrolls."

Eustace threw all three bedrolls up to me, and I turned to check the hay bales. I grabbed a chunk and tore it loose from one of the bales. "This stuff ain't too bad," I said. "We could let the horses munch on this tonight."

After taking the saddles and bridles off our horses, we gave them some hay and climbed up into the loft. As we relaxed, leaning on the bales of hay, Eustace said, "Hope their trail leads us to Salina or those Buttes you mentioned. Either way, we should be on them before noon time."

"Let's hope so," I said. "Though, this may be as rough a situation as we've faced."

"Think it's best we leave that worryin' until we find 'em," Rocky said.

"You're right," I said.

Eustace just nodded his head, staring out the loft door at the darkening sky.

The night air turned cool, but we were very comfortable in the loft of the barn. I slept hard that night and, in the morning, decided it was because of the quiet – no noise from the herd that we'd listened to every night for the past couple months. Daylight was just breaking as I glanced out the door of the loft.

I was surprised to see the other two sitting up when I turned back. "Ready to hit the trail again?" I asked.

"Gimme a minute to wake up," Rocky said. "I slept hard last night, and no one waking me for my watch."

"Got that right," Eustace said. "Best night's sleep I've had since leavin' Glen Springs."

We saddled our horses and picked up the trail again. As before, it continued heading southwest toward Salina. Rocky figured we'd be there by ten o'clock that morning. After about two hours following their trail, we slowed to a walk to give our horses a breather.

"If there trail heads right into Salina, we'll just have to spend our time there trying to pick up any clues to these characters. Finding any trail that leaves the town will be near impossible," I said. "Our best hope is that these three figure no one could be on their trail, and they're free to spend the money and live the high life."

"Let's hope," Eustace said, his eyes fixed on their trail.

We came to the Smoky Hill River for the second time on our journey. We'd crossed it the first time when we left the main trail and angled southwest through the prairie. Now we were going to cross it a second time.

"When we cross the river this time, Salina is only a short ways away," Rocky said. "In fact, if you look through the trees," he was pointing now, "you'll see the roof of some of the buildings over beyond that rise."

"Yer right, Rocky," Eustace said, "I see 'em now."

"How we gonna work this?" Rocky asked.

"Let's split up and head into town alone. That way, no one knows were together," I said. "Then we just keep watching and listening for three guys that have lots of money to throw around."

As we crossed the river and reached the far bank, Rocky angled left and I angled to the right. Eustace held back and would follow me into town about five minutes behind. We decided to just keep moving on foot from place to place, watching for three guys that might fit. We'd each have our own lunch, and meet up at two o'clock behind whatever building was farthest to the south.

Walking the town of Salina didn't take long, as it was only about six blocks in length, with one cross street that extended about a block each way from the main street. I saw two saloons, one hotel with a diner and a saloon, and one diner that sat next door to one of the saloons.

At quarter to twelve I decided to get some lunch. I could see Carol's Diner across from me, next to the Bird Dog Saloon. I headed across the street, pulled the door open, and stepped into Carol's. I was surprised by how nice the place was. The tables were all covered with red and white checkered tablecloths, and the walls were decorated with prints from great Western artists like Charlie Russell and Albert Bierstadt.

I was pleasantly surprised, and impressed with the place, as I stepped to an empty table near the front window. I'd no more than sat in my chair, when a young woman walked up and asked if I'd like "coffee or something else to drink."

Pleasantly surprised, again, I said, "Sure, I'll have a cup of coffee."

When she returned with the coffee, she asked, "Are you having dinner today?"

"Yes. What are you serving today?"

"Meatloaf with mashed potatoes, gravy, and a dinner roll," she said, smiling at me.

"Sounds delicious! I'll have a plate, please."

"Yes Sir," she said, smiling again as she left.

I sat drinking coffee and looking around the room. There, eating his lunch was Rocky at a table in the far corner. He hadn't noticed me yet. I sipped the coffee again and thought *this is sure better than Jack's trail coffee.*

The waitress returned coffee pot in hand, asking if I needed a refill. Reaching toward her with my cup, I said, "Sure do, Miss. That's very good coffee."

"Thank you, Sir," she said, as she turned and stepped to the next table.

My food came, and as I began to eat, I noticed Rocky stand and turn to leave. He glanced my direction and I gave him a small nod and returned to my food.

The lunch was very good, and I was very hungry. I leaned back in my chair, finishing the last of the good coffee. I paid for the lunch, left the waitress a little extra, and headed out the door to tour the town some more.

As I walked past the door of the Bird Dog Saloon, I heard some loud shouting and paused to listen. As I peered over the swinging doors, I saw Eustace backed up against the bar, surrounded by four rugged looking hombres. As I stepped through the batwing doors, Eustace noticed me, then looked back at the one shouting at him.

I stepped toward the group saying, "Howdy boys. What kind of party we got goin' here?"

The biggest one, the loud one, jerked his head around. "Gonna give this troublemaker a little lesson in manners." He was a big man, mostly fat, and was missing a couple of his teeth. The rest were stained darkly from years of tobacco chewing.

"You know," I said loudly, "I've run into this one before and your right... he is a troublemaker." I walked directly toward Eustace, nudging my way past the fat one, and saying, "I owe this one plenty."

I moved closer to Eustace, winked at him, and said, "Know what I hate more than a troublemaking slave?"

"What's that?" The big one asked, then spit tobacco juice, managing only to hit the side of the spittoon.

"Ignorant slobs who always like the odds stacked in their favor." Before he fully realized what I had said, I whirled and buried my fist in his face, putting everything I had behind the punch. I heard bone snap in his nose, then saw the big hulk slump to the floor on his knees.

190

In the same instant, Eustace planted his big right fist in the face of the nearest thug, toppling him to the floor. Then before testing whether we could out-fight the other two, I drew my pistol, shouting, "That's it, boys." The remaining two slowly stepped backwards, raising their hands and looking as though to say, *Don't shoot. We're not gonna do anything. Don't shoot.*

"Take these two slop-hogs," I said, waving my gun at the two on the floor, "and get on out of here."

When they were gone, I turned to Eustace, saying, "Think I need something strong to calm things down."

"Me too," he said. "It's on me."

He turned and ordered two whiskeys from the bartender and dropped a five dollar gold piece on the bar. When he turned back, he handed me a shot and raised his. "Here's to fewer battles," he said, then downed his whiskey.

Downing my whiskey, I asked, "What started all this?"

"They figured I was paying too much attention to what those three in the corner were doing." He nodded towards a Faro table in the corner, as he turned and ordered two beers. He turned back, handed me a beer, and said, "Might be the three we're lookin' for." He took a long drink of his beer, then said, "When I first got here, one was laughin' and braggin' about the guy droppin' like a wet rag when he hit him on the back of the head. The other two were tryin' to make him quiet down, but were laughin' just the same."

"Let's go sit down at a table and listen some more," I said, turning and heading toward a table nearer the Faro game. We sat, relaxing and listening for the next thirty or forty minutes, not saying much to each other.

After listening to the three for a good while, I was convinced that Eustace was right... these were the three. "Why don't you go see if you can track down Rocky. If you don't find him, we're supposed to be meeting in twenty minutes at the south end of town. Bring him back here and we'll take these three back to Abilene with us." Eustace nodded, finished his beer, then headed out the door looking for Rocky.

I got a deck of cards from the bartender, and sat playing solitaire while watching the three to make sure they didn't leave without us knowing.

Chapter Thirty-Six

The next time I looked up from my solitaire, the three at the Faro table were gathering their money and stuffing it into their pockets. I quickly looked out the window of the bar, hoping to see Rocky or Eustace. I saw neither, and for an instant wondered what I would do if these three leave the bar. They finished their drinks, pushed their chairs back and walked away from the table.

I waited and watched and, when it was evident they were heading out the door, I stood to follow them. They headed across the street and down the boardwalk toward three horses that were tied at a hitching rail in front of the Smokey Hills Saloon. Probably the place where they'd started their drinking earlier that day.

Instead of trying to follow them alone, I decided to stop them right now, and hope Rocky and Eustace would show up soon. I pulled my revolver saying, "Hold it right there boys. Get yer hands up... NOW!"

The three stopped in their tracks. The one closest to me glanced back, while the other two stared at the ground, and slowly raised their hands.

"Hey, you... you hard of hearing? Get your hands up," I shouted as I aimed my revolver at his chest. "Yeah, I'm talking to you."

Seeing I had my revolver cocked and aimed at him, he slowly raised his hands.

"Okay, now each of you carefully take your gun from your holster and throw it in the street. You first."

Everything was going good, so far, as the one closest to me eased his gun from his holster with his thumb and first finger, and started to toss it into the street. What I hadn't planned on, was the one farthest from me being quick enough to know that my eyes would probably follow the gun into the street and give him a split-second to draw and fire.

I heard the gunshot, and felt the burning in my side spin me and knock me to the ground. I grabbed for my side, and could feel the warm wetness beginning to soak my shirt. Looking up toward the three, they were already mounting their horses. Before the horses moved though, I heard a shotgun blast and saw the farthest one topple over, hitting the ground hard.

Then, immediately, the other two quickly raised their hands. As I turned my head and looked up the street, I saw Eustace and Rocky coming quickly – Rocky with his rifle at his hip, aimed at the two, and Eustace with his sawed-off ten gauge Parker also aimed at them. I felt a great relief, in spite of being shot.

"You shot my bes' friend... so you better be real careful how you take yer guns 'n rifles 'n throw 'em down," Eustace growled, sounding very agitated. This time, both of them carefully took the rifles from their scabbards and tossed them into the street. The second one tossed his pistol.

"Now you two slide down from them horses... real easy like," Rocky said, hitching his rifle up a little to let them know they were covered. He waved his rifle, directing them out into the middle of the street. "Okay... on your knees, hands behind your head."

Then he said to Eustace, not taking his eyes from the two in the street, "I got these covered, Eustace. Why don't you see to Mack."

Eustace ran to me, knelt beside me and asked, "Mack... Mack can you hear me?"

"Yeah... I can hear you," I said, my eyes closed. "It's hurtin' somethin' fierce."

"Dat's good. Means you're likely gonna make it okay," he said, sounding relieved.

"*That's*" I groaned, correcting him as usual. "That's good." Pausing, I said again, "*That's* good."

For the first time in a while, I saw a grin cross his lips. "*That's* good," he said slowly. "I'm gonna run 'n get our horses... get my medicine pouch and canteen. You be okay for a few minutes?"

"Yeah, I'll be okay. Hurry it up though."

Again he grinned, and left on a run.

"You got things under control, Rocky?" I said as loud as I could.

"Yup, you don't have to worry about these guys no more. You just take it easy 'till Eustace gets back."

In what seemed like only minutes, I heard horse hooves coming up the street. I raised my head enough to see Eustace riding his horse, with Rocky's and my horse in tow. Again, I felt relief as I knew Eustace would take good care of my gunshot wound.

During the time since the shooting had stopped, some of the local folks had gathered around. Evidently, one was running to get to town sheriff, too. I could hear all kinds of talking and whispering going on now.

As Eustace slid from his saddle, grabbed his medicine pouch and canteen, he quietly said, "Kin you folks give us a li'l room?"

The people complied, and began moving back from where I lay. Eustace quickly knelt and tore open my shirt. Grabbing his canteen, he began washing away the blood so he could have a good look at the wound.

"You may be the luckiest soul I ever knowd," he said quietly to me.

"Why? Because I got shot?"

"No, because you take an arrow in one side and it tears through skin and muscle. Then you take a bullet in the other side, and all it does is tear through skin and muscle."

"Well...thanks for the analysis, and all the sympathy."

He smiled again, which made me feel a little better. Then he said, "I'll get you fixed up, 'n put some good poultice on there to ease the pain. I think you should rest for at least a day or day and a half, before we head back to Abilene."

"Why? I was riding again the same morning I got shot by the arrow."

"Yeah, but we were a li'l more worried 'bout the Kiowa comin' after us again," he said, as he cleaned the wound.

"We should send a telegraph to Jim, ease his mind and tell him we'll be back in a couple days," I said.

"Yeah, Rocky can do that when the Sheriff gets here and takes them two," Eustace said, glancing toward Rocky.

Helping me roll to my side, Eustace cleaned my back where the bullet exited. Glancing over at Rocky again, he asked, "What's he doin' over there?"

I grabbed Eustace's big shoulder and pulled myself up to have a look-see. "Looks like he's having 'em empty their pockets."

"Guess you're right. He's got quite a stack of money in his hand."

Just then we heard Rocky say to the two, "Okay boys, face down on the street. And don't try to make a move or you'll hear this rifle barking at you." Then he walked over to the dead one and checked his pockets, finding more money. Next, he checked the saddle bags on each of their horses and found more.

He glanced up the street to see if the sheriff was coming yet, and hurried over to put the money in his saddlebag. One person in the crowd asked, "What'r you doing with that money?"

"It's money they stole from us," Rocky growled. "Just getting back what's rightfully ours. After we count it, if there's any extra we'll give it to the sheriff."

Glancing at the two, who were still face down in the street, Rocky walked over to us. "Wanted to get Jim's money before the sheriff got here," he said quietly. "Otherwise, it might be tied up as evidence for days... maybe even weeks."

"Good thinkin'," I whispered, "don't want to have to sit here waitin' for the judge, so Jim can get his money and we can hit the trail for Texas."

"Got that right," he said. "How you doin', anyway?"

"Doin' all right, except for the ration of grief from Eustace," I said.

Eustace looked up at him with a grin. "Oh, I'm sure it's nothing you don't deserve," Rocky said. He slapped Eustace on the back, then turned and walked to where the two still lay face down the street.

I heard one of the locals say, "Here comes the sheriff and his deputy."

Softly, I said to Eustace, "Glad Rocky thought of the money. Better to have it in our hands instead of theirs. Like he said, it could be tied up for days or weeks."

In a short while, I saw Rocky talking to the sheriff. He was doing most of the talking, pointing at the two on the ground and the dead one over by the horses. Then the sheriff had the two back on their feet, with the deputy holding a shotgun on them. The deputy started walking 'em down the street – most likely to the local jailhouse.

I heard the sheriff say to someone in the crowd, "Would you go get Howard for me. Tell him we've got a dead man here for him to pick up."

Next, the sheriff and Rocky walked over to where I sat. The sheriff looked at me, and said, "I understand that these men robbed your boss of five thousand dollars, and that one of them shot you. How are you doing?"

"I'm doing pretty good Sheriff. I'll be better as soon as Eustace gets me all patched up."

Chapter Thirty-Seven

The sheriff looked at Rocky, saying, "Well, the good thing for you boys is the Judge will be getting into town this evening. Could you send a telegram to your boss, asking if he could come over here tomorrow?"

"I can do that right now," Rocky said. "I'm sure it won't be a problem for him."

"There is a stage that comes through Abilene at nine-thirty in the morning, and gets in here about three-thirty," the sheriff said, "if that's easier for him."

"Good to know. I'll tell him."

"As soon as you're patched up... Mack was it?" The sheriff asked.

"Yes sir, Mack it is," I said.

"When you're patched up Mack, could the three of you stop down at my office? You'll find our office at the north end of town."

"We'll meet you down there in a half-hour or so," I said, trying to hide the pain, "as soon as Eustace makes his poultice for my gunshot wound and bandages me up."

Eustace needed a fire, or a cook stove, to make the poultice, and I noticed Julie – the waitress that served me lunch in Carol's – had come out and joined the crowd of people that gathered. Just after the sheriff was done and walking away, I asked her if it would be okay for Eustace to use their kitchen stove, and explained why.

199

"Yes. Come with me, Eustace," she answered, waving for him to follow her.

Meanwhile, Rocky had grabbed the saddle bags off his horse and sat down beside me. He took the money from the saddle bags and began counting it. Five thousand dollars made for quite a pile of greenbacks – mostly twenties and fifties. Counting it out in stacks of one hundred dollars, then putting those together to have piles of five hundred dollars, he soon had ten piles totaling five thousand dollars.

"Somebody had some luck playing Faro I think," Rocky said. "There's an extra two hundred eighty dollars here. After their drinking and eating and gambling, I figured we would be lucky to come anywhere *close* to Jim's five thousand dollars."

"Surprised a little myself," I said. "I suppose we'd better bring the two hundred eighty dollars down to the sheriff's office when we go there. Don't think they'd agree with deducting three day's pay for each of us – the time wasted tracking those no-goods down and getting back to Abilene... plus our expenses, of course. "

Rocky smirked, then said, "No, don't suppose they would."

Looking at the pile of money on the boardwalk, he said, "I'm going across to that dry goods store and see if I can get some sort of sack to put this is in."

"I'll be waiting right here," I said. He glanced back at me, smiled, and headed across the street.

By now, the people who had gathered to watch went back to their lives. When the sheriff left, he said, "Okay folks, let's break it up... get back to whatever you were doing."

Before long, Rocky was coming back from the dry goods store, carrying a cloth sack. He waved, looking past me, and I turned to see Eustace coming out of Carol's, carrying a pot in one hand and some rags in the other.

While Eustace was patching me up, Rocky was putting the money in the sack. Then he said, "You know... think I'll put this in your saddlebag, Eustace. No offense, podner, but not many would think a former slave would be carrying this kind of money."

"Got that right," Eustace said, slowly shaking his head. "No offense taken."

In a short time, Eustace had me wrapped up snug, and said, "Give it a little time for the poultice to dull the pain, then we'll head for the sheriff's office."

Staring down at his work, I said, "Glad to!" Then, groaning loudly from the pain of trying to move, I put my hand on the boardwalk and laid on my right side to rest a bit.

I felt a light tug on my shoulder, then heard Rocky saying, "Mack." I guess I'd dozed off and had been snoozing for about twenty minutes.

"Time to head over to the sheriff's office," Rocky said, reaching out to help me sit up. "How's your pain?"

Grabbing his hand, I pulled myself to a sitting position and felt around my side – front and back. "Not bad," I said. "Feels like Eustace has worked his magic again." I reached over, slapped him on the shoulder, saying, "Thanks pard'. Thanks for everything."

He nodded, trying to hide a grin. "Glad I could help."

They each grabbed an arm and helped me to my feet. "Help me into my saddle 'n we'll ride down to the sheriff's office," I said.

At the hitching rail in front of the window that read "Saline County Sheriff", Eustace and Rocky helped me slide from the saddle and limp into the office. They parked me in the first chair they saw, just as the sheriff came out of his office.

Chapter Thirty-Eight

The sheriff looked up from a paper, as he walked out of his office. He stopped and waved, saying, "Come on into my office." Handing the paper to his secretary, he grabbed a chair from the front area and returned to his office. He set the chair by the two at his desk, and pointed for us to sit. Moving around his desk, he sat in his large, comfortable chair, saying, "Glad to see you boys."

Reaching for some papers on his desk, he said, "Two of the three men that robbed your boss – the two we have in custody – have active warrants on them for assault and robbery. S-o-o-o..." he said, drawing it out as he sat back in his chair, "I don't think it's going to be difficult to get a conviction from the judge in short order. Maybe during our first day in court."

"That's good to know," I said, shifting in my chair to get more comfortable. "Been more than two months since we left Glen Springs, Texas, and, now that were done pushin' cattle, we want to head back as soon as possible."

"I appreciate that," the Sheriff said and paused. "But... I'll need you here as witnesses to the shootings – the one that wounded you," he said, nodding at me, "and the one that killed the other robber. As I understand it, we have no witness to the robbery in Abilene, only the conversations you and Eustace heard in the Bird Dog Saloon. And, of course, the five thousand dollars they had in their possession."

"All of which points to a speedy conviction in your opinion?" I asked him.

"I think it does... it definitely does."

Rocky spoke up. "We stopped at the telegraph office, and I sent a message to our boss, Jim Clusky. We should be hearing back soon."

The Sheriff stared out the window, and said, "If he can get in here tomorrow, Wednesday, we can appear before the judge first thing Thursday morning. With no complications, we should be done by the end of the day." He sounded very confident in what he was saying.

"That would be great," I said. "We could hit the trail for Texas on Friday morning."

"The telegraph office is only a couple doors down from here," Rocky said. "Give me a minute to run over there and see if we've got an answer back from Jim."

"Okay, we'll be right here," the sheriff said. "Would either of you care for a cup of coffee? he asked, waving his finger between Eustace and me.

I was shaking my head 'no', and Eustace looked from me to the sheriff, saying, "No thank you, sheriff."

"Okay," the sheriff said, and went to fetch himself a cup. As he returned to his desk, Rocky hurried in to tell us that Jim would be arriving by early afternoon tomorrow."

"Good news," the sheriff said. "I'll put this case on the judge's calendar for the first thing Thursday morning."

"Where could we find a good room for the next couple nights?" I asked.

"Well, there's the Salina Hotel at the other end of town. Or Harriet's Rooming House... that's in the middle of town, just behind the barber shop."

Harriet had two rooms available. One was a large room with two large beds. "We'll take that one for the next three nights," I said to her. "And would you reserve the other for our boss who's getting into town tomorrow. He'll need that for tomorrow night and Thursday night. We won't know if we will be staying beyond Thursday night until sometime Thursday afternoon, if that's okay."

"That'll be fine," she said smiling. Then pointing next to the doorway, she said, "The meal schedule and daily menus are posted there."

"Thank you, Harriet," Rocky said, and handed her enough to pay for both rooms until Friday morning.

"Thank you, Sir," she said, bowing slightly and leaving the room.

Then Rocky looked at Eustace, saying, "I suppose this means you and I have to bunk together, since he needs pampering while he's healing."

I started to say something, and Rocky began laughing and poked Eustace with his elbow.

I shook my head, saying, "Grief... nothin' but grief from you boy's. I don't know how I put up with you two."

"Poor guy," Rocky moaned.

"I know. Things are tough all over," Eustace said, shaking his head.

I limped over to look at Harriet's meal schedule. Glancing through the next two days, I said, "Well, there is *some* good news."

"What's that?" Eustace asked.

"Tonight Harriet's serving my favorite... meat loaf and mashed potatoes. Tomorrow night is roast veal, boiled potatoes and vegetables. Pretty good eatin' I'd say."

"Almost two hours 'till she serves supper, so how 'bout we limp over to the Bird Dog 'n have a beer or two," Rocky said.

Out the door and down the boardwalk we went.

Chapter Thirty-Nine

The next day, early Wednesday afternoon, the three of us were walking back from Carol's Diner to Harriet's Rooming House to wait for Jim. We expected him in the next hour or so, and were going to wait on Harriet's large porch. Sitting there, we'd be able to see him approaching from a long way off. As we walked along, I noticed Julie – the waitress who served us lunch yesterday and today at Carol's – listening to a guy across the way, near the Bird Dog Saloon. The guy was pointing at three cards on his table.

"I'll catch up with you boys in a few minutes," I said. "I'm going to see if Julie needs any help."

I crossed the street, and as I neared Julie, I could hear the guy speaking. "Sounds to me that you had the misfortune of encountering one of those unscrupulous shills who would have the audacity to deceive and mistreat a fine, lovely person such as yourself."

Stepping up on the boardwalk next to her, I asked, "Everything okay, Julie?"

As she answered, "Oh, I think so," I stared menacingly at this fellow. He looked back at me with a look that said he'd been confronted by scarier people than me. Then he turned his attention from me back to Julie.

"I have no problem with your friend helping you in this challenge I've proposed," the guy said to Julie. "I would not endeavor to cheat or deceive you. I only offer you a chance to outwit me and win a nickel, a dime, or perhaps more if you begin to feel sure of yourself."

On his makeshift table were three blue playing cards laying face down. He flipped the cards over with a quick, fluid motion of his hands. The hands were slender, clean and soft, not the hands of a working man. The fingernails were clean and the hands appeared pampered.

Julie raised her head to look the huckster in the eye, then moved her hand over her purse, saying, "I'm not spending a nickel..."

"No, no my dear one," the man interrupted. "You don't have to bring out a penny. This is only a demonstration of my skills and a test of your powers of observation." Pointing once again to the queen and quickly turning the cards face down, he said, "As I move the cards around, your challenge is to find the lady in red – Le Fem Rouge, my French friends might say – and it's as easy as can-bee-see."

He began moving the cards quickly side to side, back and forth, up-and-down. As he dropped the last card to the table, he asked, "Do you know where she is?"

She briefly glanced at me, then pointed to a card. I looked at the huckster, and he said, "You're welcome to help the lady at any time."

When she glanced back at me, I smiled and nodded.

"This one," she said confidently.

He slowly turned the card. "Very good, m'lady. Your eyes may be quicker than my hands. Let's try once again." He held the queen up to show us, then dropped it to the table between the other two cards that were face down and began his quick movement again... side to side, round and round, over and back.

"Okay, m'lady, where does the queen lay now?"

Again, after a quick glance toward me, she touched a card. He flicked the corner of the card and instantly popped the queen over for us to see. With a sigh, he said, "Ma'am, your eyes may be far too quick for my simple magic. It may require the challenge of a nickel or two to smooth my nerves and defeat your gaze."

I gave her a questioning look as she reached in her purse. Then I thought, *a couple of nickels? What could that hurt?* "Go for it," I said.

Smiling at me, she took her hand from her purse and dropped two nickels on the table, saying, "Okay. Let's see your best, sir."

The huckster brightened, saying, "Now we're talkin'... so let's get these cards a-walkin'. Here they go, fast 'n slow. Up and down, round and round. Here and there while you stare." His quick hands were moving the cards back and forth. When he stopped, he asked, "Where has the red lady landed this time."

Julie was sure that she knew which one was the queen. Then, as she looked closer, she noticed that a corner of the card was bent ever so slightly. Glancing at me, she could see by my look that I had noticed too.

"This is the one," she said firmly, pointing to the card on the left.

When he flipped the card over for us to see, his body slumped noticeably, and he sighed. "The dreadful prospect of losing *my treasures* won't even let my hands defeat your gaze." He reached in his pocket and brought out two nickels, laying them next to hers on the table.

209

"Would you allow me one more chance to regain my losses... and my dignity?"

"Alright, let's go for the whole twenty cents," Julie said, smiling at me.

"Wow," the huckster said. "A feisty lady she is!" He flipped the queen and once again began moving the cards with a flourish. When he stopped, she pointed down at the center card.

"I think I've got you again," she said.

He turned the center card over. "Indeed you do," he said with a great sigh. "Indeed you do." Digging in his pocket once again, he brought out four nickels and placed them on the table by the others. "I would be wise to acknowledge that I've met my match, and cut my losses now," he said somberly, starting to gather the cards on the table.

"Surrendering so easily?" She asked, with a bit of smugness.

He gave her a long look, glanced at me, then looked back at Julie. "Well... as you may have guessed by now, gambling is my great weakness.

"S-o-o-o," he said slowly, drawing it out, "if you are willing to gamble a silver dollar, I'll race you one more time. If you take me once more, you'll have taken me for a dollar and thirty cents. A hard day's wages for most men, I might add. And a serious amount for me."

Without hesitation, she slid the forty cents from the table and put it in her purse. "One more time," she said, placing a silver dollar on the table.

"You're on, m'lovely lady," he said, replacing the cards. "Let the race begin." Quickly and smoothly, the cards began to move and he began to chatter. "Here they go, watch her closely. In and out all about. Up and down all around. Watch until they come to rest. Be good 'n ready with your guess."

When the cards finally stopped and lay side-by-side, he raised his hands asking, "Where does she reside?"

Julie looked a little unsure, as she pondered. *It must be on the right*, she thought. *And that's the one with the slightly bent corner.* Holding her hand close to her chest, she looked at me and motioned to the card on the right.

I gently wrapped my hand around hers, and asked, "Can I help you this time?"

The huckster started to object, but I held a hand up stopping him and saying, "You said I could help her at any time... did you not?"

"Yes, I guess I did, sir," he said, his shoulders sagging.

"It's the center card," I said softly to Julie.

"But..." She objected, quietly. "What about the bent corner of the one on the right?"

I nodded. "Yes, but it's the center card."

"But what about the bent corner?" she objected again.

"I know... but it's in the middle," I insisted.

She started to object again, then said softly, "Okay. I'll trust you."

Looking at the huckster, then back down to the cards, she pointed to the middle one. "It's right there," she said, tapping the card.

The huckster slowly, grudgingly turned up the queen. "I knew I should have cut my losses."

"Wow," Julie exclaimed. "How did you know."

I shrugged a shoulder saying, "Lucky guess."

"I have indeed met my match," the huckster said, gathering up his cards.

"I see the lady's dollar on the table," I said, "but I don't see yours there yet."

He reluctantly fished a dollar out of his pocket and threw it on the table. Julie gathered up the two dollars and dropped them in her purse, saying, "Thank you, so much, for your help Mack. That was fun!"

"That's for helping Eustace and me yesterday... when you let Eustace use the kitchen at Carol's." I said.

Chapter Forty

Thursday morning came, and we sat in the courtroom of Saline County. Sitting in a courtroom gave me a strange, eerie feeling. We sat whispering to one another about the sheriff, the courtroom, the two that were on trial, and the judge that we hadn't yet seen.

Soon, we heard a door open, and a voice say, "All rise." A tall man wearing a black suit walked in, climbed two steps and sat behind a large desk. I'm not sure if it was the courtroom, the suit, the desk, or the man himself, but he gave a definite sense of strength and authority.

The judge looked to his left at the man who had said, "All rise," and asked, "What's the first case on our docket this morning, Mr. Bauer?"

The man rose from behind his desk, saying, "The State of Kansas versus Lyle Raymond Archibald, and the State of Kansas versus William Ronald Jackson. Sheriff Babcock asks that we hear both cases simultaneously."

Looking toward the sheriff, the judge asked, "Is that correct Jonathan?"

The sheriff rose and said, "Yes, it is your honor. These two, along with a dead third party, are accused of one count of assault, one count of robbery, and one count of attempted murder, all in the same case. In addition, they have outstanding warrants for previous assault and robbery."

"Okay, I agree. Let's handle both of these cases at the same time," the judge said.

The day seemed to fly by quickly, and at quarter of three, the judge's gavel slammed loudly. The judge said, "This court finds you Mr. Archibald, and you Mr. Jackson, guilty of all charges. You are both sentenced to fourteen years in the Kansas State Penitentiary. This court is adjourned until nine o'clock tomorrow morning." He softly pounded his gavel again, then left the courtroom.

"Well," the sheriff said, as he stood, "that went about as good as we could have hoped for."

"I think you're right," Jim said. "We can head for Texas in the morning. Right?"

"Yup, you're free to head out anytime you like."

"Good! We'll be headed south at daybreak," Jim said.

Harriet was nice enough to fix an early breakfast for us and, as the first light began to glow in the east, we were swinging into our saddles and pointing our horses south, Texas strong on our minds.

Before the telegraph office had closed for business yesterday, Jim sent a telegram to Rebecca telling her he would be home in about two weeks. We figured it would take a strong two weeks to get back to Glen Springs, riding at a pretty good pace.

Along with the cattle, Jim had sold his remuda of horses – all but one, that is. He had asked Eustace to pick out the best horse in his remuda. That one, he gave as a gift to Sophie for all her work. She was so surprised by this, that she covered her mouth with her hand, and was unable to speak for a long moment. Then she gave a soft smile to Jim, saying, "Thank you... so much, Mista Jim."

Now, headed south toward Texas, there were seven of us – Jim, Eustace, Sophie, Rocky, Fini, Lefty and me. The rest of the crew were still in Abilene, and would be heading out at different times and in different directions from there.

The only concern we had on our trip back to Texas, was passing through the Indian Nations, and possibly running into that small band of Kiowa again. We decided to swing our route a little to the east, as we neared the place where we had encountered them. All along the trail back, we were trying our best to see different terrain and, in this particular area, avoid any contact with the Kiowa we'd had trouble with on the way north.

Two weeks of riding through broad valleys, narrow canyons, large flat meadows where the grass grows tall and crossing thirteen or fourteen rivers, the time seemed to pass very quickly. And, though all of us were trail weary as we neared Glen Springs, the site of Jim's ranch on the horizon immediately raised all of our spirits.

It was late afternoon on the fifteenth day since we'd left Salina, Kansas, and we were riding at a steady lope down a long, gradual grade north of Jim's ranch. We could see the buildings of his ranch against the horizon, with their long shadows stretched out to the east. Soon, we could see a dark chestnut horse and its rider coming toward us at a full gallop. Without a word, Jim spurred Dunny into a gallop and rode ahead to meet Rebecca.

By the time we approach them, they had been holding each other tightly for a long moment. Jim looked up at us, saying, "You boys go on ahead. We'll catch up to you at the ranch in a few minutes." As we rode on toward the ranch, I glanced back and saw Jim and Rebecca still holding each other, and kissing.

We rode up to the bunkhouse, unloaded our gear, and hauled it inside. Jim said we were welcome to stay in the bunkhouse for as long as we'd like. Looking around, Fini said, "This is a very fine bunkhouse Señor Jim has built." Then, flopping down on an empty bunk that Eustace had pointed out for him, he said, "And with very comfortable beds, too. I look forward to a good, long night's sleep here on this mattress."

His plan was to spend the night in the bunkhouse, then head south to his home, about twenty miles across the border from Laredo, Texas. He figured it was about four days of riding to get there, but said it would pass quickly... thinking of his beautiful wife, Estrella, all the way.

Jim had paid him very generously, considering he'd traveled not much more than half the way with our crew. And that generous pay, along with his pay from the first cattle drive he'd worked, gave him a goodly sum of money to bring home to his family in Mexico. He said it was enough money, so that he didn't have to work at all this winter in Mexico. He could spend all of his time with his family, and catch up with the work that needed to be done around their ranch. "My Estrella will be filled with joy to hear that I won't need to work this winter."

He'd told each one of us that we were invited as guests to his ranch if ever we were going to be in the area. "Please come to Mexico. I have a good bunkhouse – not quite as large and nice as this," he said, waving his hand around, "but, a very comfortable one. And you are welcome to stay there anytime you like. And, Estrella's cooking... oh Señor's, it is mouthwatering." The more he talked about it, the more the idea seemed like a good one to me. Maybe I'd head south in a week or two, and spend a few days with Fini and his family at their ranch.

Chapter Forty-One

The next morning, the six of us were treated to a delicious, home cooked breakfast by Rebecca and Jim. After the breakfast, and some time to enjoy visiting with each other, we said our goodbyes to Fini. He swung into the saddle on Domino, his beautiful Andalusian, and shouted as he rode off, "Adios amigos!"

"He's quite a character," Rocky said.

"Yes, and quite a cowhand," Jim said.

Shortly after Fini's departure, Lefty headed out for his family's ranch near Uvalde, Texas. He said he hadn't seen his folks or brothers in nearly a year, and he was looking forward to getting back home.

The rest of the morning, we spent working on little projects around Jim's ranch that needed attention. After a good lunch, Jim took us on a long ride south, across the Glen River, and back up to the land he'd told Eustace all about. "This is a nice chunk of land," Jim said, "but, like I told you, it's laid here for years unused, because of the difficulty getting back and forth across the Glen River."

During our two weeks riding from Kansas, Jim and Eustace had talked about this land a number of times. Jim had finally convinced Eustace that this was land where he could build a home and start a good cattle ranch. "If you ever outgrow it, and need more land, it means your business is doing mighty well," Jim said.

217

Ranch land in that area was generally selling at four dollars per acre. Jim agreed to sell this twelve hundred acre parcel to Eustace for three dollars per acre. In addition, Jim would finance the sale, with payments beginning in the third year when his operation should begin showing profits. Eustace thanked Jim, and said, "That's more'n any bank would do for me, I'm sure."

Eustace and Sophie had picked out a site to build their new home. It was on a knoll in the northeast corner of the land. Turning to Jim, Sophie said, "Jus' can't thank you enough for all this."

"You're more than welcome," Jim said. "It's not only helping you and Eustace, it's helping me. This land hasn't generated a single nickel of income for me until now, when you're able to start making payments that is."

"Awright if we start tomorrow?" Eustace asked.

"Start?" Jim asked, a puzzled look on his face.

"Our house... building a house," Eustace said, giving Jim a smile.

"O-o-h-h," Jim said, nodding his head. "Sure you can. You can start today if you'd like."

"That grove over yonder looks like it would have more than enough timber to build a small home," Eustace said, looking toward me, then Jim.

"I'm sure it would," Jim said. "I've got a small sawmill you can use... that will help you a lot. I'll get Jacob, our neighbor to the north, to ferry it across the river for us."

218

It was great to see the excitement in Eustace and Sophie as they looked forward to building their own home on "their own land." Something they would have never dreamed of as slaves, just a few years ago.

Rocky and I helped them every day, as we cut timber and began building their home. Jim helped whenever he had a little time from his own work. In a little less than three weeks, we had a small, very nice home built.

Eustace was putting the finishing touches on a front door. He had made the door by gluing several thick slabs of wood together, and then carving it into a beautiful six panel door. An impressive door that a slave would expect to see on the front of 'da big house.' "When I was a boy, I dreamed of one day having a door like this," he told us.

"Perfect," I said, as he installed it. "That's some nice work there. Your dream came true."

The home consisted of a large, central room with a kitchen area, living room area and fireplace; and two bedrooms – one for Eustace and one for Sophie. "We'll have to begin work on a bunkhouse eventually, too," Eustace said, "And..."

"Oh, I think you've got a little time before worrying about all that," Sophie interrupted.

Eustace chuckled, saying, "Yeah, guess my mind is racing ahead a bit."

"We need a table and chairs, and two beds built first," Sophie said.

"Tomorrow. We'll start on those tomorrow," Eustace said. "The rest of today, we'll relax and admire our new home. We deserve a little break." Sophie smiled and nodded her head in agreement.

It didn't take long for word to spread around town about Eustace and his new home. When Powell, Eustace's former owner, caught wind of this, he and two of his henchmen rode out to pay Eustace a visit. Luckily, when they rode up, Eustace had his twelve gauge Parker at hand, and suggested they, "Turn them horses around, leave and not come back."

"Well, Eustace, you still owe me 'n you're gonna pay up, or we'll take it outta yer hide," Powell snarled. Then he turned his horse and rode away, his henchmen following close behind.

After hearing this, I didn't tell Eustace or Sophie, but at sun up the next day I took a ride over to Powell's ranch. I found Powell and his two gunmen eating their breakfast when I strolled into Powell's dining room – not knocking on the back door first.

Startled, one of the gunman grabbed for his pistol. I drew and shot the man in the arm and his pistol dropped to the floor. Seeing that I was a lot quicker than they remembered, Powell and the other gunman eased there hands into the air.

"What'cha think you're doin', walkin' in my house like this?" Powell snarled.

"Just letting you know... if you ever bother Eustace or Sophie again, ever even come within a mile of their place, I'll hunt you down, kill you, and leave you for the buzzards to take care of," I said. "And, by now, I think you know I can and will do it."

Without waiting for a response from him, I backed out the door, swung up onto Duchess, and rode off, Duke running by our side.

220

Chapter Forty-Two

Over the coming days, we built the furniture Eustace and Sophie would need, and started the construction of a small barn. Eustace and Sophie had made a couple of trips to town to get the various supplies they'd need for their new home, including a bouquet of flowers Eustace had seen for sale in the Mercantile.

"They'll look beautiful on your new table, Eustace," Sophie said.

"On **our** new table," Eustace said, smiling at Sophie.

As a part of their deal, Jim had sold Eustace forty-seven young heifers, ready for breeding, and two bulls, both a year and a half old with strong confirmation. With these, Eustace will have a strong, growing heard in two years.

"The Glen River is too wide and deep right here to push this young herd across," Jim said. "But if we drive them down about two miles to where we've been crossing, we can get 'em across and bring 'em back up to your ranch."

The next day arrived with a bright morning sunrise. Eustace, Rocky and I were headed to Jim's to drive the small herd down to the crossing. A few hours later, we were pushing the herd across the Glen River without any problem, then up to Eustace's new ranch.

Tying our horses to the hitching rail near the barn that was under construction, Eustace said, "Looks like some of those heifers are ready for breeding right now."

"Yup," Jim said. "And those young bulls are ready to take care of it, too. Eventually you'll have to separate them, but for now I think it's okay to let them all run together."

Rocky and I were living in Jim's bunkhouse, and for the next few days we were sometimes helping Jim around his ranch, and sometimes helping Eustace with building his new barn. One morning as we were waking up, sitting the edge of our bunks, Rocky said, "Think it's time I head for my brother's ranch near El Paso. I been puttin' it off 'cause it's a long ride. But, I know my brother needs the help, and there is a girl in El Paso I'd like to see again."

"O-o-h-h," I said, stretching it out a bit. "You never mentioned the girl before."

"No, guess I hadn't. But she's a handsome woman, and I think she likes me some. Just hope nobody's taken her beautiful hand yet."

"What are you doing sittin' here then?" I scowled.

"Yeah," he said, slowly shaking his head. "Maybe Saturday mornin' I'll head west."

I stood from my bunk, walked over shook his hand. "It's been a great pleasure knowin' you, Rocky."

"Been great getting to know you, too," he said. "But, hey, we got two days before I leave, so let's not get too sentimental right now."

I laughed, and we headed over for breakfast with Jim, Rebecca, and a few of their regular hands. Rocky told them of his plan to head west on Saturday morning.

"It's been great workin' with you Rocky," Jim said. "Write me and let me know where I can reach you sometime next spring. Haven't made up my mind yet if I'm going to take a herd north next year, or not. If I do, and if you're available, sure would like to have you on our crew again."

"Don't know where I'll be a year from now, but I sure will write and let you know," Rocky said.

After breakfast, Rocky and I headed over to help Eustace with the roof of his new barn. By the end of the day, the barn was closed in and ready to use.

Sophie had decorated their little home, and it was very nice and very comfortable. I had no doubt that Eustace and Sophie would make a good-go-of-it as ranchers. I've never known a harder working pair.

Friday evening Rocky, Eustace, and I were headed to town for a few beers, since Rocky would be headed west in the morning. As we rode up to the hitching rail in front of JB's Saloon, I smiled to myself. Down the street I saw Powell and one of his henchmen. When they noticed us, they stopped, turned around, and headed for the saloon at the other end of town. *Must be heeding my warning*, I thought.

In JB's, we drank beer, laughed, and retold stories of the good times on the trail. Strange how a long, tedious job like a cattle drive can become fun in your memory. Finishing his third beer, Rocky said, "I'd better be headin' back to the bunkhouse and get some shuteye. Gonna head west after breakfast. Don't want to start out all hung over and feelin' ugly all day."

223

"Yeah, I probably should be headin' back myself," Eustace said. "Plenty to do tomorrow."

"Okay," I said, sighing deeply. "Can't have much of a party all by myself. Guess I'll head back with ya."

Chapter Forty-Three

The next morning we had breakfast with the Clusky's, and Rebecca gave Rocky a sack of food for the trail. "This should help you on the way to El Paso," she said. "There's a couple sandwiches, some beef jerky, a can of beans, and some apples. Ride safe, and maybe we'll see you next year."

"Thanks so much Becca. I look forward to seeing you guys again." Then he turned to shake Jim's hand, swung in the saddle and rode off, not wanting a lot of emotion.

"He's a good man to have around," Jim said, waving to Rocky as he left.

I nodded and paused a bit, then asked, "Need anything done before I head over to help Eustace?"

"No, we're in good shape," Jim said. "In fact, we're taking the weekend off and riding over to visit Becca's sister and her sister's husband. They're about an hour east of Glen Springs, just a little north of San Antonio."

"Hope you have a good weekend. Will I see you Sunday evening?" I asked.

"Yup, be back for supper Sunday. See you then."

I rode over to Eustace and Sophie's ranch to help with the finishing touches on their barn. When I got there, I saw Eustace at the back corner of the barn working on a large corral. He'd gotten a lot of work done since I was there just a couple days ago.

"In the coming days, I'll have to separate those two bulls," he said. "Figured a corral would keep 'em seperated for a while."

By the end of the day, we had most of the corral done, with only a gate left to be built. We heard Sophie shout to us, "Supper will be ready in fifteen minutes."

"Just in time," Eustace said. "I'm mighty hungry." We headed over to their well pump to rinse off the dust.

As we sat eating a delicious roast beef supper, I said, "I've been thinkin' about takin' a ride down to see Fini in Mexico. Never been to Mexico, and figured it was a good way to see some of their country."

"When d'ya think you'll be goin'?" Eustace asked.

"Probably Tuesday morning," I said. "Don't know how long I'll be down there, or when I'll be headed back this way, but I'll sure stop in to visit you guys when I'm back."

"You be sure and say hello to Fini for us," Eustace said. "Tell him we'd like him to come up with his wife for a visit sometime."

"You bet I will."

After supper, we relaxed on their porch visiting and watching a beautiful golden sun setting over the wide Texas range. I rode back to the Clusky's bunkhouse and, along the way thought, *I may as well leave for Fini's in the morning.* There wasn't any reason to hang around Sunday and Monday, so... why not?

I woke up early, left a note for the Clusky's on their dining table, and headed southwest on Duchess, Duke running excitedly at our side. Laredo was about four days away, and I hoped that I remembered the directions Fini had given me to his ranch from there. I know he'd said he was less than two hours from Laredo.

The days were long and boring, and in the early afternoon on the fourth day, I saw what I thought was Laredo on the south horizon. I was looking forward to a good bath, a steak, and a comfortable bed.

As we neared the town, I began looking for a livery to put Duchess up for the night. Toward the north end, I could see a large barn, with a corral off the back. *Has to be the livery*, I thought.

The man in charge seemed very capable and very pleasant. "Mighty fine Palomino you got there, sir," he said, as he bent down and petted Duke.

"She is," I said, "so I expect you'll take good care of her for the night."

"Want me to watch him, too?" He asked, glancing down at Duke.

"No, he'll stay with me. I'll be back to get her in the morning, probably not 'till at least eight o'clock though."

I started to leave, then turned back asking, "Where's the best place to get a bath and a good room?"

"Probably the Laredo Hotel, near the south end of town. You can get a pretty good meal there, too."

"Thanks, again," I said, waving as I turned to leave. "C'mon Duke. Let's go get me cleaned up."

227

As we walked down the street, I was checkin' out what looked to be a mighty fine town. It had most everything a man could think of in the way of goods to buy and stores to buy 'em in. I passed by "Crooked Nose Jake's" saloon, where there weren't more than five or six customers. Then, down the street a ways, I saw a large sign attached to the upper store-front, painted in pink. It read 'The Texas Rose.' As I neared it, there was music playing and plenty of noise; almost enough noise to drown out the music.

I decided that a shot of whiskey and a beer would wash away the dust in my throat. The bath to clean up the rest could wait for a while. I crossed the street and walked past a window with 'The Texas Rose' painted in pink, like the sign above. I stepped through the swinging doors, glanced around the room, then eased my way over to the bar.

"Shot of whiskey," I said. "Some of yer good stuff down below... not that rot-gut sauce you got sitting on the back shelf there."

The barkeep stared at me for a second, then reached down and brought up a bottle of whiskey. I threw a five dollar gold piece on the bar as he poured a shot. "I'll have a beer to go with that," I said, smiling.

I threw back the whiskey, enjoying the good, smooth taste. Then, as I drank a swallow of beer to wash it down, there was a big commotion over near a Faro table. I set the beer on the bar, and looked just as a man backhanded the woman he was arguing with. The backhand caught the woman's jaw, and spun her head sideways. She slowly turned back and glared at the man with fire in her eyes.

I quickly glanced around the room and it appeared no one was concerned with what had happened, or was going to help the woman. I let out a big sigh thinking, *Can't let him get away with that.*

I pushed my way through the crowd to where the woman and man stood glaring and about to start shouting at each other once again.

As I neared him, the guy looked at me and snarled, "You lookin' for a piece of me?" It sounded to me as though there was a bit of a chuckle in his voice.

"Nope. Just don't want to see you take another swing at this lady," I said, figuring the next swing would be coming my way.

"Okay..." the guy said. He was an inch or two taller than me, twenty pounds heavier, and seemed to have a real mean streak in him. "Maybe, *you* want it then." His shoulders quickly began to turn, and he threw a big right hand, roundhouse punch at my head. I stepped into him, slapping the arm with my left hand deflecting it, and struck him just above his beer belly – the solar plexus area – with the heel of my right hand, putting everything I had behind it.

The guy doubled over as though having a huge cramp, and was gasping for breath. I pushed him backward, tumbling him to the floor, then quickly looked around to see if he had help coming to his rescue.

"His boys are out eating supper," the lady said, rubbing her jaw. "Shouldn't be any more trouble... for now."

"You okay?" I asked.

"Yeah, I'll be fine," she said. "Thanks for helping. I'm Joey Carson... owner of the Rose. "

"I'm Troy MacAlan, call me Mack. And you're welcome. Glad to help. What's up with this guy anyway?"

"That's Pavel Johnovich. Figures he's gonna own this place after he pushes me out," she said. "I think he's behind the ambushing of my dad... his death is why I'm running this place now."

"I was just gonna look for a place to have a good steak for supper. Care to join me?"

She hesitated for a moment, then shouted, "Zeke, will you watch things while I go have supper?"

Zeke brought out a shotgun, laid it on the bar, and said, "Yup. I'll keep an eye on things."

She hooked her hand in my elbow, and began to walk me toward the door.

"Where to?" I asked.

"Let's go down to the Laredo Hotel. They serve a pretty good steak there," she said, giving me a soft smile. "And a pretty good drink, too, I'd have to admit."

"Sounds good," I said, squeezing my arm on her hand. "In case you haven't figured it out, I'm new to Laredo."

"O-h-h, I had that figured. Not likely you'd have tried to stop Pete, if you weren't a new-comer."

As we neared the door, I patted my thigh saying, "C'mon boy." Duke rose, stretched a little, and joined us as we walked out of the bar.

"That's a handsome looking dog. What's his name?" she asked.

"Duke. He's a great dog, and a great partner."

She stopped, bent over a little and said, "C'mere Duke." He moved in front of her, and nearly swooned over the attention she gave him; scratching behind his ears, stroking his fur and talking softly to him.

As she straightened up, she said, "Okay, Duke. Let's go." She grabbed my elbow again and gently pushed as she started walking.

"Why did you say that?" I asked. "That I wouldn't have tried to stop this Johnovich. Got a big reputation or what?"

"Yeah, and a bunch of mean riders that work for him that are usually all around him."

"Riders?" I asked.

"Hired guns... Henchman... Enforcers... Thugs... whatever you want to call them."

"And no one that'll stand up to 'em," I said.

"Not even the town sheriff," she said, disgustingly.

We walked toward the hotel, not saying much to one another for a long while. I thought about her predicament with this character named Pete Johnovich, and looked around at more of the town. Soon we were at the door of the Laredo Hotel. As we walked in, I said, "Mind if I see if they have a room for me?"

"Not at all," she said, as we turned toward the registration desk.

They did have a room, and I signed in saying, "Duke will be staying with me in the room. I hope that's okay."

"Oh, that will be fine sir," the lady behind the desk said, smiling down at Duke.

We walked into their dining room and found an empty table near a window. We were just getting seated, when a young lady came over asking if we wanted anything to drink.

"I'll have a shot of that Gosling Rum... in fact, make it a double. And a glass of water with it," Joey said, then looked at me.

"I'll have a beer."

"Thank you," the young lady said. "I'll be right back with them."

I looked out the window, and the evening was darkening. Looking back at her, I said, "S-o-o, tell me about this Pete Johnovich guy."

She hesitated, evidently not sure where to start. "He's a big... jerk, who hounded my father for the better part of a year to sell the Texas Rose to him. Then, about seven weeks ago, he had my father shot in the back while riding out to visit a friend at the friend's ranch east of town."

"You sure it was this Johnovich behind it?" I asked.

"Absolutely. The friend that my father was going to visit heard the gunshot, and rode out to check what it was. He found my father laying on the trail near his horse. My father's last words were, 'Tell Joey I love her.' She paused and her eyes welled.

232

"Not more than an hour after my father's friend brought his body into town, and told me what had happened, Johnovich was in the Rose saying, 'I'm sorry to hear about your father's death. I'd like you to know that I'll buy the Texas Rose from you, and even give you a higher price than I offered your father.'

"Now... how did he know my father was dead? We hadn't told anyone yet. Not even the Sheriff. But the sheriff says Pete could have overheard it, or who knows what else. That this wasn't proof that would hold up in court. Truth is the Sheriff just didn't want to have to deal with him."

"Sounds like you've got the Sheriff pegged," I said. "There was plenty there to bring him in for questioning, maybe even holding him in jail for a couple days while checking it all out."

"You're right," she said, "but everyone knows that he won't lift a finger when it comes to Johnovich. He's scared to death."

"Nobody else in this town will do anything about it, either? All of them too cowardly?"

"Nope. He has every man in the area afraid of him and his gang," she said, sadly, and stared down at the table.

"Well, don't know that I like the notion of going up against his gang with just you and me, but I'm certainly not afraid of him," I said. "Wish I had a couple of my good friends here to help us."

Our drinks came and changed the mood of our conversation for a bit. She raised her glass of rum, and clinked it against my beer as I held it up. "To better days," she said, and drank down a good portion of the rum.

I took a long, thirsty drink of beer, then set it down on the table. As I looked at her again, there was a soft smile on her face, and her eyes sparkled as they looked deeply into mine. She was a handsome woman. For a long moment, we were quiet and I began to feel a little uneasy.

"How would you like to work for me?" she asked. "Help me manage the Texas Rose for the next few weeks."

"Well," I said very slowly, "that wasn't the next thing I expected to hear. Not sure what it was that I expected, but definitely not that."

"Does that mean you don't want to?"

"No... not at all," I said, a little too quickly. Then I hesitated, stumbling over my thoughts. "I think it might be interesting to help you manage the Texas Rose."

"Does that mean you will?"

I laughed, saying, "You get right to it, don't you."

"Yeah... I guess I've been accused of being a little too blunt on more than one occasion. But, that's the way by dad was and I'm sure I learned and it from him." Her pride and love for her father showed in the way she talked about him.

"When would you want me to start?"

"How about tomorrow?" she asked matter-of-factly.

"I had plans to visit a friend tomorrow... but I guess that could wait for a while. What time tomorrow?"

"How about three o'clock. It would be three to midnight seven days a week for a while, until we figure out what Johnovich is going to do."

Chapter Forty-Four

As we finished eating our steaks, we talked more about me working for her at the Texas Rose. "I'm sure it'll mean regular run-ins with Johnovich, until he gets the point that were not going to roll over," she said, as though wondering if I'd be okay with what it would involve.

"I'm not worried about dealing with Johnovich. It's his gang of thugs that concerns me a little bit," I said, with a shrug. "I've been thinking about recruiting some help tomorrow morning. Would you be willing to pay four or five guys to help us over the next couple weeks?"

"Yeah, if you can recruit four or five guys to work with you, knowing they have to face Johnovich," she said.

"Well, I'm going to ride out to my friend's ranch in Mexico tomorrow," I said, "the one I was going to visit tomorrow anyway. I think he, and a few of his ranch hands, would be willing to come here and help me."

"Are they reliable?" she asked.

"Fini is as good as they come, and I would trust him with anything. He's saved my hide more than once."

"Alright," she said with some excitement. "Ride out in the morning and see if they will work with you. When do you think you'll be back?"

"I should be back at the Texas Rose by four o'clock tomorrow afternoon," I said. "With any luck, Fini and a few of his men will be with me... or close behind."

"Good. I'm sure we'll be hearing from Johnovich by tomorrow evening," she said, sounding relieved.

The next morning, I picked up Duchess at the livery and we headed for Fini's place. I remembered the landmarks he had told me about, and they brought me a right to his ranch. My only concern as we got closer was that I would find him at home.

Riding through a large gate and nearing the ranch house, I saw a lovely woman and two girls working in their garden. The woman shaded her eyes from the sun, and asked with a thick Mexican accent, "Can I help you, Señor?"

"Well, yes Estrella, I hope so. I'm looking for Fini. My name is Troy MacAlan and we worked together."

"O-h-h-h, Señor Mack! Fini has told me much about you," she said excitedly. "You will find him in the pasture south of the barn."

I tipped my hat, and turned Duchess toward the barn. As I rode into the pasture south of the barn, I could see Fini and a couple of men throwing up hay from the cut meadow grass. One of his men said something to him, and he gave a quick glance in my direction. There was a brief pause, then his head snapped back to look at me again. He began to laugh, as he stuck his pitchfork in the ground. As his laughter quieted, he spread his arms wide. "Señor Mack! What a wonderful surprise!"

I slid from the saddle, walked over to him, and we embraced for a long moment. Stepping back, I said, "Fini, you're lookin' great."

"Oh, you know," he said grinning, "some of us just have that certain something... Si mi amigo?" He was obviously joking, and soon began laughing at himself.

"I met Estrella when I came to your ranch house. She was working in the garden with two young girls. Are they your daughters?"

"Si, they are my beautiful daughters Teresa and Maria Elena. They are sixteen and thirteen years old."

"And Estrella, she is every bit as beautiful as you described," I said.

"She will be very pleased to hear you said that about her," he said. Then with a wave, he added, "Let's go to the house and have a cup of coffee, maybe with a nice big slice of Estrella's delicious pie."

As we sat talking, catching up on old stories from the cattle drive, I turned the subject to the Texas Rose. "Would you and three or four of your best men be willing to come and work with me for a couple weeks? The pay is very good, but the work will be very boring... and maybe a little dangerous. It will be mostly waiting for this Johnovich and his thugs to show up, looking to cause some trouble."

"Si, we will be happy to help you. And your timing is perfect. We are just finished with putting up some hay, and there won't be much going on here for the next couple weeks. I will choose four of my men that are best suited for this work. The rest can look after the ranch without us for a couple weeks. When would you like us to start?"

"If you could catch up to me later this afternoon at the Texas Rose... that would be perfect. Otherwise, tomorrow around three would be fine, too," I said.

"It sounds very dangerous for Miss Joey... I think we can make it this afternoon," Fini said. "We'll be at the Rose by four o'clock."

"That would be great, Fini, Thanks so much for being willing to help out. I didn't like the notion of facing that gang alone."

"I would help you with just about anything Señor Mack," Fini said, showing his big smile. "Besides, things have been so quiet lately, that my men are getting bored. It'll be good to go to Laredo and mix things up a little bit with this Johnovich and his thugs."

"I knew I could count on you, Fini. I'm going to head back, and let Miss Carson know you'll be helping us."

Chapter Forty-Five

At three o'clock, I walked into the Texas Rose and found Zeke, the bartender, cleaning and organizing the bottles and glasses behind the bar. "Things been quiet so far today?" I asked.

"Sure has, Mack... been good 'n quiet today."

"Miss Carson in her office?

"Yup. Catchin' up on her paperwork, and waitin' to see you," he said. "Your friend in Mexico gonna help us out?"

"He sure is," I said. "Should be here with four of his men in about an hour."

With a big nod of his head, he went back to his cleaning and organizing.

I found Joey in her office, head down working intently on some paperwork. I knocked lightly on the door frame, startling her a bit. "Oh, Mack," she said sounding relieved. "I've been edgy all day waiting for you to get back. I'm so glad to see you." There was a wonderful softness in her last words, and in the smile she gave me.

She motioned for me to come in, and pointed to a chair in front of her desk. "How about a beer... you've been on the trail a couple hours and must be thirsty."

"Sounds good," I said. "Sounds real good."

She shouted to Zeke, and asked him to bring me a beer, and her another cup of coffee. "Tell me about your friend. Is he coming to help us?"

"He sure is. He and four of his men should be here by four o'clock," I said. "Gives me some real peace of mind."

"Me too. I was mighty worried about you going up against Johnovich and his bunch, with only Zeke and me behind you," she said. We sat visiting for a while, me thirstily drinking my beer, and she sipping her coffee. She pointed at her desk, saying, "My dad... I loved him dearly... but he was the worst at paperwork that needed to be done for the business. I'm still catching up on the ledgers for this year."

There was such sweetness in the way she talked about her dad, that I found myself staring at her and thinking what a beautiful, sweet woman she was. She had sandy-blonde, wavy hair, that she sometimes tied back in a ponytail, but was always a little on the wild side.

I was lost in my thoughts about her, when I heard Zeke's loud voice bark, "You 'n your boys can turn right around 'n git from here."

Joey showed panic on her face, as I said, "Wait here," and hurried to help Zeke. He was standing behind the bar, his shotgun aimed at Johnovich. I quickly drew my revolver and stepped to his side.

"Do you really want to do this?" Johnovich asked loudly. "With our seven guns against your two?"

"Question is," I said, looking from man to man on each side of Johnovich. "Do *you* really want to do this? You're getting the first shotgun blast from Zeke, Johnovich. And which one of you wants to take my first shot, before the rest of you *maybe* gets us," I said, waving my gun.

"And make that *our* seven guns against *your* seven, mis amigos," I heard Fini's voice say loudly from the doorway, as he and four men slipped in the swinging doors of the Texas Rose, guns drawn.

Johnovich slowly holstered his gun, looking side to side, then saying, "Looks like we stepped in it pretty good, boys. Put your guns away, and let's ease back out of here... if they'll let us." Fini and his men stepped to the side and let the group of thugs leave the bar.

"That was mighty nice timing, Fini," I said, holstering my gun.

"I saw that group walk in here, just as we were riding toward the hitching rail. Then, when I slid from the saddle, I overheard some of the shouting," he said. "I wanted to wait just a little, until all of their attention was focused on you, amigo."

"Well, I'm sure glad to see you. C'mon in and have a seat," I said. "Can we get these boys a beer, Zeke?"

"Sure can," he said. "I'll bring them right over." He bent to put the shotgun on the shelf below the bar, then reached for some clean glasses.

Joey had been watching all this from the doorway behind the bar. As she walked into the barroom, she smiled and said, "I think we've met before, Fini."

"Si, Miss Joey," he said, smiling. "I have been in your fine bar a few times and visited with your father."

"Yes, you have, and I'm sure glad to see it's you that Mack spoke of," she said, taking a seat between Fini and me. As she sat, she turned and asked, "Zeke, can you bring me a beer, too?"

"Be right up," he said.

"And poor one for yourself," she added.

"Gladly, Miss Joey."

We sat in the Texas Rose, enjoying the beer, and our first small victory against Johnovich and his bunch. Joey said, "Fini, I will pay you and your men three dollars per day. That's nearly three times the typical wages for cowhands, but this is going to be more dangerous, too."

"That is very generous of you, Miss Joey," Fini said. Then looking at his men, he added, "And, as I told you men before, you will continue to collect your regular vaquero's pay while we're here (one dollar per day American money)." This brightened things for Fini's men considerably. Each day they spent in the employ of the Texas Rose, meant four times their normal wages.

I looked from Fini to Joey saying, "We need to figure out a plan. If we sit back waiting for Johnovich and his bunch to show up, we're likely to get bushwhacked."

"I think you're right," Joey said. "Upstairs, we have a room with a window facing west toward the street, and the door to the bar. There's another one overlooking the south side. Your men can take turns watching those windows, but I'm not sure where to put the other two."

"That would work great," I said. "I looked things over earlier, and I think two men on the roof could watch the other two sides of the building. That way we'll have early warning if Johnovich or any of his men are approaching."

"Juan, you and Santiago take the rooms upstairs," Fini said. "Diego, you and Pablo take the roof. We will rotate every two hours. I will relieve you Diego in two hours, you relieve Santiago, and so forth. If you see anything suspicious, you run down here to tell Señor Mack."

"We'll have to learn what each one of Johnovich's men looks like, so we can spot them on the street," I said.

242

Chapter Forty-Five

The next two and a half days went by quietly. By the evening of the third day, I was beginning to get a little nervous about what Johnovich might be scheming.

Our system of rotating Fini and his men seemed to be working well, and gave us a good feeling of security about not letting Johnovich or any of his thugs surprise us. That evening, Fini and his men left to have supper at five thirty, and returned at six twenty. Joey and I left for our supper about ten minutes later. "See you by seven-thirty," I said, waving to Fini as we walked out the swinging doors.

We strolled up the boardwalk, headed for the diner at the Laredo Hotel. We were enjoying light conversation, and even managing to make each other laugh... which we hadn't done much of for the past couple days. It was too late, when we realized guns were aimed at us and closing in.

I heard the hammer of a revolver pulled back, just as I felt the cold steel of a gun barrel press against the back of my neck. "Move real careful like, Mr. MacAlan. You too, Miss Joey. We're going to turn left between the buildings just ahead." I felt my gun yanked from its holster. I was certain they had taken Joey's as well.

I didn't dare turn my head, but from the footsteps and conversations, I figured there were four men with guns pointed at us. We walked between the buildings and there were two more men waiting with horses.

The thug walking Joey pushed her as we neared the horses. "Climb aboard... Miss... Joey," he said disdainfully.

The one walking with me, nudged me with his gun barrel, saying, "Mount up MacAlan."

We rode south for about twenty minutes at a steady lope, until I saw a small barn. They led us to the back door of the barn and, as my horse stepped in, I could see Johnovich sitting in a chair, smoking a cigar, and showing the slightest bit of a smile on his lips.

"Well, if it isn't my good friends from the Texas Rose," he said sarcastically. "Climb on down. Grab a chair. Make yourself comfortable." He took a long draw on his cigar and glared at us.

I swung down quickly, and moved to help Joey down from her horse and over to a chair. Just as she sat, one of Johnovich's men – probably the biggest one in the barn – gave me a hard push, saying, "Go sit over there."

"Miss Carson, I think you know what we are here to talk about," Johnovich said.

"Well, you're not getting the Texas Rose from me this way either," she said defiantly.

She had no more than spoken those words when a fist hit me so hard that I was sure it had loosened a couple of teeth. I shook my head, then looked to see where the punch had come from. There stood the big guy rubbing his fist and grinning at me. My face and jaw hurt something fierce.

Then one of their other guys dropped a rope over me and tied me to the chair. I looked over to Joey, and saw a guy tying her to the chair she sat on as well.

"You can end all this right now," Johnovich said, "by just signing this bill of sale for me."

I could see she was about to answer him, and interrupted saying, "Don't sign *anything*, Joey." I'd just got the words out, when I felt a hard fist again.

I didn't think he could hit me harder than before, but he did. This time, it spun my head so fast that I was sure it broke a bone in my neck, and it dizzied me to the point of feeling like I was about to pass out. I tried to clear my head without shaking it, as I was afraid of doing more damage to my neck. My mouth filled with the metallic taste of blood and my vision was blurred.

At the Texas Rose, Fini was talking with Zeke when he noticed two men walk through the swinging doors into the bar. "Aren't they a couple of Johnovich's bunch? he asked, watching them closely.

"Think yer right, Fini," Zeke said, as he moved down the bar to serve a couple customers. Then, finished with his customers and moving back to where Fini stood, he asked, "What'cha thinkin'."

Fini glanced at the clock and saw it was ten minutes to eight. "Señor Zeke, I'm a little concerned about Mack and Miss Joey. They said they'd be back by seven thirty and now it is nearing ocho... sorry, eight o'clock."

Zeke stared up at the clock. "You're right, Fini. Can you send a couple of your men to check on them at the Laredo Hotel?"

"Si, I will send Diego and Pablo right away."

The two men returned fifteen minutes later. "There is no sign of them at the Laredo Hotel, or anywhere in between," Diego said.

"Gracias amigos," Fini said. "You see those two men on the left end of the Faro table, go sit where you can keep a good eye on them for a while. They are two of Johnovich's and we do not want to let them slip away."

Fini and Zeke talked for a while, and finally Zeke said, "I say we take those two in the back room and see what they know about Mack and Miss Joey."

Fini hesitated a moment, then said, "Okay. I will get Pablo and Diego and we will meet you in the back room with those two."

In the back room, Zeke held his shotgun and asked the two what they knew of the whereabouts of Miss Joey and Mack. "Where are they?" he demanded again.

"Why the hell d'ya think we know anything," the one on the right smarted off.

Without hesitating, Zeke hit the man hard with the butt of his shotgun, splitting his lip wide open and spraying blood on his partner. Looking at the other guy, Zeke growled, "Maybe you want to try answering the question." As he said it, he cocked the butt of his rifle as though ready to swing it again, this time at the second one.

"Wait... wait, wait," the guy muttered, looking like he was trying to figure out the right way to answer. Finally, squeezing his eyes and flinching when Zeke looked like he was gonna swing the gun again, he said, "Out at the small barn... the one at the north end of Johnovich's place. That's where they are"

"Better shut yer mouth, Wilson," the other one growled. When Zeke heard that, he swung the butt of his gun again, hitting the first man on the other side of his face and spraying blood the other direction.

"You better get all four of your men and ride down there quick like," he said to Fini. "I'll take care of these two."

"How will I find it?" Fini asked.

"Easy. Take the main road south for about fifteen minutes, and you'll come to a big tree on the left that leans over the road. About fifty yards to the right you'll see the small barn sitting next a small grove of Desert Willow."

Fini and his men hurried to saddle their horses, and headed out of town at a full gallop. As they rode, Fini thought hard about what they would do when they got to the barn. As they neared, seeing the big tree leaning over the road on the left and the silhouette of the barn on the right, he said, "Leave the horses by the tree, and we will move in on foot."

Tying their horses and seeing no one standing watch around the barn, they quietly jogged halfway to the barn. Fini signaled for them to stop. "Santiago, you and Juan take this east side door," he said, pointing to the door nearest them. "Pablo, Diego, and I will circle around to the door on the west side. Check the door. If it's barred, get ready to smash in a window to shoot through. I'm going to fire a shot in the air when I think everyone is ready and it looks like it's time to do something. Swing the doors open or break glass quickly, ready to start shooting. If Miss Joey and Señor Mack are in your line of fire, shoot at the ground, but keep shooting until you hear or see my signal to stop."

With the light of the lantern inside the barn showing through the gap in the barn doors, Fini could see that the doors on his end were not barred. He whispered, "You two each grab a door ready to pull it open. I'm going to kneel in the middle ready to fire my rifle at the big one beating on Señor Mack." They nodded, and each grabbed hold of one of the barn doors, ready to pull on his signal.

Fini peaked back through the gap in the barn doors once more, and decided it was time to do something right now. What he saw was the big guy walking toward Mack with what looked like an ax handle in his hand.

Inside the barn, Mack was clinging to consciousness. Several times he had told Joey, "Don't sign anything." Each time he felt a fist rock his head.

Johnovich's big thug was rubbing both fists now, saying, "My hands can't take much more of this." Walking toward the corner of the barn, he said, "I'm going to use this ax handle leaning in the corner."

Grabbing it, he turned and started back toward Mack when a gunshot startled him. He dropped the handle and reached for his gun just as the barn doors swung open. In an instant, he heard the crack of a rifle, and before he could raise his gun to shoot, felt the bullet hit him high in the chest and spin him, knocking him to the ground.

Fini shouted, "Anybody reach for a gun and you will have bullets coming at you from all around this barn."

Evidently thinking he could out-shoot 'em, whoever *they* were, one of Johnovich's men foolishly grabbed for his gun. Santiago shot him from the window on the other end of the barn, and knocked him off his feet, while Juan fired several shots into the dirt floor to get their attention.

Now the other three, along with Johnovich, quickly raised their hands, afraid of more shooting. Fini, Pablo, and Diego slowly walked into the barn through the open doors, rifles at their hips. Juan and Santiago held their rifles in the broken windows they'd smashed, both aimed at Johnovich.

"Throw your guns in the dirt away from you," Fini growled. All four slowly did as they were told. Diego quickly untied miss Joey, and Pablo hurried toward me to do the same, and see how I was.

As soon as Joey was free, she rushed over to me, carefully caressing my head. "Mack... Mack..." she whispered. "Please Mack... please stay with us."

"I'm still here," I groaned softly. I tried to force a grin, but my face hurt way too much for that. I tried to open my eyes, to focus, to see something. Then, suddenly, everything went black.

When I came to, a couple hours later, I was in a doctor's office. The doctor, Dr. Martinez, was asking, "Can you hear me? Mack, can you hear me?"

I groaned a little, and tried to nod my head. It still hurt way too much to move, so I just waited a moment until I could say something. Finally I mumbled, "C-a-n hear you, Doc."

"O-h-h... Mack," I heard Joey's voice say.

Then I heard Doc Martinez speak again, this time with some urgency. "Joey, take it easy. Don't be grabbing at him until I can check to see if anything's broken.

"Okay, Doc, I'm just so glad he's come to and is able to speak," she said, with excitement in her voice. "I'll stay back and out of your way."

After nearly a half hour of him examining me, he said, "Well, luckily, you've only got a small fracture in your jaw bone, but I don't think any breaks or fractures anywhere else. That's the good news."

"And the bad?" I asked.

"It'll probably take three weeks before all the swelling goes down, the contusions start to heal, and the pain goes away," he said. Then he reached out and gently pushed me back down to his table, as he saw me trying to sit up.

"Stay put," he said emphatically. "Just try to take it easy. We've got to do more cleaning and bandaging before I let you up."

Later, with Doc Martinez nearly done and my head a little clearer, I heard Joey say from across the room, "When Doc is all done with you, you can come and stay at my house for a while."

"I don't want to be burden. You've got a bar to run," I mumbled.

"Nonsense," she insisted. "Zeke can look after things at the bar. I'll hire him extra help if he needs it for the next week or so. You'll stay in my guestroom until you're feeling better and back on your feet."

"If you insist," I whispered, looking up and trying again to smile a little bit.

She smiled softly. "I insist."

Chapter Forty-Six

For the next two days, I was sleeping much of the time. Whenever I'd wake up, Joey was there, saying, "Drink a little of this," or "Eat a little of this." I wanted to talk to her, thank her, say much more, but it seemed that after every little bit to drink or eat I'd slip back into a deep sleep.

Finally, in the early morning of the third day when I woke up, she was there, smiling as I pushed myself up and sat on the edge of the bed. Trying to clear my head, I asked, "What day is this?"

"Wednesday, third day since the beating you took... because of me," she said, hanging her head.

"No, not because of you. Because of Johnovich trying to steal the bar away from you. I'm just glad that you held up through it all."

"I held up?" she said, sounding like she was upset and trying to scold me. "I just...."

I raised my hand to interrupt her. "I meant that you didn't sign it. I asked you several times not to sign his bill of sale. It had to be hard, under the circumstances, but you didn't sign it."

"Oh you big... I wasn't the one taking the beating."

"No, but it's gotta be just as tough to watch."

She paused staring down at her hands, then said, "Well, yes, especially when it's someone you lov... I mean when it's a good friend that you care about." She stood quickly, looking a little embarrassed, and said, "I've gotta go get some water."

She returned, having gathered herself, and held a glass toward me. "Have a drink of this water."

"Thanks," I said, reaching for the glass. The water was cool and I was thirsty. I downed the whole thing, let out a long sigh, and gave her a soft smile. "No need to be embarrassed about anything, anything at all." Then, pausing and looking down at the polished wood floor where she stood, I finally looked up at her again, and said, "I care a lot for you, too."

"Oh Mack," she said with a sigh. "I could have cost you your life. I feel terrible."

I took her hand, gently pulled her toward me and softly kissed her. "Thank you," I whispered, after feeling the softness of her kiss.

She was surprised and pulled back for a moment. Then moved toward me again, leaned in and kissed me. She looked in my eyes and smiled a sweet smile.

I held up the empty glass between us, grinned and asked, "Could I have some more water?"

"Oh you..." she growled, trying to sound angry. From the side, as she left the room, I could see she was smiling as she slowly shook her head.

When she returned, she carried a fresh glass of water in one hand and a bucket and towel in the other. She handed me the glass of water and set the bucket and towel on the table next to the bed.

"Thought you might want to wash up, if you're going to get up for a while. There's some soap and a cloth to wash with wrapped up in the towel" she said. Then, pointing as she left the room, she added, "I got you a new pair of pants and a shirt. They're hanging on the hook over there."

Later, feeling better than I had in a few days, I was cleaned up and wearing the new clothes she'd given me. I stepped out onto her front porch, stretched and took a deep breath of the fresh air. I'd just settled in to one of the two wood rocking chairs on her porch, when she came around the corner of the house carrying the business ledgers from the Texas Rose.

"Hey there," she said brightly, "lookin' pretty good in those new duds."

"Feelin' pretty good, too," I said, looking down at the shirt and pants. "Thanks for these."

"Figured it was the least I could do, after yours got all bloodied 'n torn up."

"Well, thanks just the same," I said, then asked, "Been over to the Rose?"

"Yeah, I wanted to check in with Zeke, and make sure everything was okay." Then, hoisting the ledger she was carrying, she added, "And pick up the receipts for the past week and get my paperwork caught up."

"Why do you do such detailed bookkeeping?" I asked.

"Just to keep track of things, and for my own peace of mind. It lets me know if we're making a profit and, I think, keeps my employees honest, knowing I'm keeping track of every nickel," she said, then shrugged, as if to admit she wasn't sure.

"You're probably the hardest working business owner I know," I said, "and that earns you a great deal of respect from your help. I know it does with Zeke."

"Think so?" she asked, sounding unsure.

"I sure do," I said, nodding my head and smiling.

253

"That's good to know," she said, sounding relieved. "I've never been sure they liked working for a woman now." She climbed the steps to the porch, walked over and sat in the other rocker. She plopped the ledgers in her lap, let out a sigh and leaned back, slowly rocking the chair.

"I don't remember... where are Fini and his men? Are they still at the Rose?" I asked, slowly rocking my chair in rhythm with hers.

"No, I paid them, and they headed back to Mexico. They'd only worked a week, but I paid them two weeks wages. I thought they deserved it for coming to help us and saving you the way they did. The sheriff actually got up the guts to lock up Johnovich, and the men that were with him that night in the barn, so I told Fini that he and his men could head for home."

I nodded, saying, "I'm glad you did that. It was no small risk helping us the way they did. I think I'll ride down and visit them in the coming days."

"Can..." she started. Then, pausing a long moment, finally asked, "Can I ride with you?"

"You sure can," I said. "I'd like that a lot. And I think you'll really like Estrella, Fini's wife."

She folded her hands on top of the ledgers, smiled at me and said, "I'd like that a lot, too."

Chapter Forty-Seven

Tuesday morning, after an early breakfast, Joey hitched a horse to her buggy, and we headed south to Fini's ranch. We had been enjoying a wonderful visit at their ranch, when Lucas, Zeke's young helper from the Rose, came riding through Fini's gate at a full gallop. We were all helping Estrella in her garden, when Joey said, "It's Lucas. Wonder what he's doing here?"

I could see by the way the horse was lathered up that he'd been riding hard for some time. I dropped the garden hoe I held, and ran to meet him.

A little out of breath from the long ride, Lucas struggled to say, "Johnovich's men shot the Sheriff. Gotta get back to help Zeke right away."

"Easy Lucas," I said, as the others came near. "Take a couple of slow, deep breaths," I told him.

"What happened?" Julie asked, anxiously.

"Sounds like trouble with Johnovich again," I said. Lucas was calming a bit, so I said, "Slide down from that saddle, Lucas. Let's go over and sit on the porch and get you a drink of water, and a chance to catch your breath."

After a long, thirsty drink of water, Lucas sat back in his chair and tried to calm self. "Sheriff Jackson is dead," he said, sadly. "Two of Johnovich's men, that weren't locked up with him, shot him and his deputy this morning. So Johnovich's whole crew is on the loose again. Zeke told me to ride down here and get you as fast as I could."

Joey and I looked at each other, then I turned to Fini asking, "Can you and some of your men help us again?"

"Si, Señor Mack. But I think I better bring six of my men with this time."

"I think you're right, Fini. Can you come with us today?" I asked.

"Si, amigo. We can be ready as fast as we can saddle our horses, and throw a few things together."

"You will be able to travel faster than we can in the buggy," I said, "so Joey and I will leave right now. You just catch up as fast as you can."

Joey, Lucas, and I were about a half hour from Laredo when Fini and six of his men rode up beside us. Joey showed her great relief as she saw them and, I'd have to admit, I was very relieved myself.

We rode into town and up to the hitching rail at the Texas Rose. There didn't appear to be any trouble yet – looking from the outside anyway – but we rushed in, guns at the ready. I relaxed when I saw Zeke in his usual place behind the bar, serving two customers.

When he saw us rushing in the door, he turned and said, "Sure glad to see you. Lucas, you must have made good time riding down to Fini's place."

"No trouble from Johnovich yet?" Joey asked.

"No, none yet," Zeke said. "But I wasn't sure what would happen after they killed the sheriff and his deputy this morning."

"Well, you were right to send him down to get us," she said. "And I'm sure glad you did. Hard to tell what that varmint's next move will be. Hopefully we'll be ready for it, whatever it is."

Early in the afternoon, the mayor of Laredo called an emergency meeting of the City Council for six-thirty that evening. He sent word to Joey, asking that she and I be there for the meeting.

That evening, about quarter to seven, the mayor was pounding his gavel loudly. The courthouse, main level and balcony, was filled to standing room only, and the mayor was trying desperately to bring order to the room.

"Quiet please!" He pounded his gavel harder, then shouted, "Could we get quiet please, so we can begin our meeting."

The people gathered in the courthouse – there must have been nearly two hundred – were anxiously carrying on conversations about the happenings of the day, and what this meeting was going to be about. That, and the fact that the mayor himself was not a highly respected individual, left the crowd not paying much attention to him.

Finally, one of the city council members – a gruff old rancher whose family had lived near Laredo for almost a hundred years – turned in his seat, opened the window behind him, and fired two shots skyward with his revolver. This got the immediate attention of the crowd.

In the brief silence, the mayor pounded his gavel again, and said, "I call this meeting of the City Council to order." He'd barely gotten the words out, and the crowd noise began to grow again.

Harlan, the council member who'd just fired his gun, yanked it from its holster again and fired a shot into the floor near the outside wall. This time, when the crowd quieted, he shouted, "You folks gonna sit down and be quiet, or are we gonna need to boot y'all out into the street?" The crowd immediately answered the question by taking their seat and being quiet.

The mayor was pointing at the hole in the floor, and glaring at Harlan. "Oh, stop worrying about the damn hole in the floor... I'll patch it up," Harlan said gruffly. "Let's get this meeting started."

"As I'm sure all of you are well aware, we lost Sheriff Jackson and Deputy Larson this morning," the mayor began. "Funeral arrangements are being made for Saturday morning. I called this meeting of the City Council to begin the process of hiring a new sheriff. The toughest part of hiring a new sheriff is that his first order of business will be to hunt down and bring in Pavel Johnovich and his gang."

This brought on a good bit of whispering and soft talking among the people again. The mayor pounded his gavel, saying, "You folks be quiet so we can carry on with our meeting, or I'm going to clear the house." Silence returned to the court room.

"Now, we do have a name to recommend as our new sheriff, it's mostly finding out if he'd be willing to accept the position." As the mayor is saying this, he stood from his chair and was walking around the council table, toward where Joey and I sat. "A few of you have met him, and most of you have heard tell of the time, a couple weeks back, that he stood up to Johnovich at the Texas Rose."

A flush come over my face, as I felt lots of eyes focusing on me, and knew the mayor was about to single me out. He gave a polite gesture with his hand toward me, saying, "His name is Troy MacAlan. I am sorry if I am embarrassing you, Mr. MacAlan, but would you please stand for those folks who haven't seen you around town before."

I slowly stood from my chair, turned to face the crowd, and raised my hand to give a small wave to them. The applause was polite, but much louder than I expected. As it quieted, the mayor motioned for me to sit once again and turned to walk back to his chair.

258

"I'm sorry to spring this on you sudden like, Mr. MacAlan, but as I'm sure you know, we've got an unusual and urgent situation. We met earlier today, informally of course, and we literally have no one else to turn to; no one that we trust could get the job done anyway. We know that you may want a day to make your decision, but we sincerely hope that you will consider taking the job."

During the two-hour buggy ride back from Fini's, I'd given lots of thought to Johnovich, and what Laredo was going to do for a sheriff – one that would be able to take care of the problem. I thought with the right help I could do it, but I sure didn't want the job long term.

I raised my hand to get the mayor's attention. "Yes, Mr. MacAlan, you have a question?" he asked, pointing a finger toward me.

I slowly stood from my chair, and in a voice I hoped was loud enough for all to hear, said, "Mr. Mayor, yes I would accept your offer, but only if you and the City Council agree to two conditions."

"Well, I'm glad you are willing to give us an answer this quickly. What are your two conditions?"

"The first is that I would take the job on a short-term basis... only until Johnovich and his bunch are brought to justice. Meanwhile, you and the City Council continue your search for a new sheriff."

"I think that's very reasonable," he said, glancing around at the city council members, who were all nodding their heads in agreement. "And your second condition?"

"That the city be willing to hire seven deputies, men of my choosing, at a rate of two dollars and eighty cents per day, until such time that Johnovich faces a trial and is shipped off to prison."

259

This stunned the mayor slightly, and after a few moments of gathering himself he said, hesitantly, "I'm not sure we can meet that condition, Mr. MacAlan. I don't remember ever having more than two deputies working for the city. And I don't think we ever paid more than two dollars per day."

"I understand, Mr. Mayor. But you must understand that Johnovich has eight men in his gang, and most of them mean killers, as is Johnovich himself. If you truly want the job done, I think that's the bare minimum of what it would take."

"He's right!" came the shout of one man in the audience. Soon, several of the men in the crowd were shouting their agreement. Finally, one of the loudest voices shouted, "This isn't the time to be worrying about pinching pennies, Mr. Mayor."

Chapter Forty-Eight

The mayor and city council discussed the proposal I'd presented for about a half-hour. Then they passed a motion to hire me as Sheriff, at three dollars per day, and seven Deputies (to be named by me later) at two dollars and eighty cents per day. All duties to begin immediately.

Next morning, Fini and I were sitting in the Sheriff's office – my new office – compiling a list of names for him and his men to give to the city office. The mayor had told us to stop by his office and he would swear us all in.

"I think that takes care of the paperwork for you, me, and your six men to begin work... temporarily that is... for the City of Laredo," I said. "Let's walk it over to the mayor's office, then we can go have breakfast before we all meet back here and get to work tracking down Johnovich."

At around quarter past nine, Fini and I sat with his six men in the sheriff's office. We decided to begin our search, for Johnovich and his men, by spreading out and asking as many people as we could in Laredo, and the surrounding ranches, if they had any idea of where the gang was, or were they might be headed. We would meet back at the office at five o'clock that afternoon.

During the course of the day, I must've talked to at least forty-five or fifty people, and had no better idea of where to look for Johnovich than I had that nine o'clock that morning. I was beginning to wonder if there was any hope of finding a trail. I met up with Fini as I headed back toward the sheriff's office. His luck had been about the same as mine, and said, "I hope one of my men had better luck than we have, mi amigo."

We sat in the office, talking to each of his men as they returned. The result was about the same with each one. Finally, when Francisco came in, he brightened the day for all of us. He had been talking to ranchers who lived out near Johnovich's place, and had found one old-timer who lived on the ranch just to the west of Johnovich's. The man was eighty-some years old, and said that Johnovich had always looked to him as sort of a father figure, and spoke with him and asked advice regularly.

"This man was very concerned about Johnovich, and said that when they last spoke, just two days ago, that he and his men were thinking of heading toward Rio Piño for a while. The man thought that one of Johnovich's men has a ranch just a little ways from that town."

"Good job, Francisco. At least now we have an idea of where he's headed," I said.

"That is a long day's ride from here," Fini said.

"Sounds to me like we'd better start out at dawn tomorrow," I said. "Time to lock up this office 'n get cleaned up for some supper."

That evening, Joey joined us for an early supper at the Laredo Hotel, and we told her of our plan to head out for Rio Piño. "Not sure what we'll find when we get there, but at least it gives us a starting point," I said. "With any luck, we'll find him there and bring him back to Laredo without an all-out gun battle.

Next morning, the sky was beginning to glow with the hope of a new day, and we were in the saddle headed northwest. We weren't sure of how we would narrow down our search around the Rio Piño area in hopes of finding Johnovich, but we had a long day of riding ahead of us to work on that problem.

Late that afternoon, we saw a crusty old rancher repairing his wide ranch gate. We stopped, and I said, "Howdy. We're new to this area and were wondering if you could tell us how far it is to Rio Piño."

There wasn't much friendliness in him, as he looked us over briefly, then he pointed straight north, saying, "Little more than an hour from here."

Sensing that he didn't want visitors, not us anyway, I said, "Thanks," tipped my hat, and spurred Duchess into a trot. Duke, at our side as usual, glanced back as if checking to be sure he wasn't going to cause any trouble.

"Don't worry about him, Duke," I said. "He probably just doesn't like the company of strangers."

"That, or maybe he just doesn't like the company of Mexicans," Fini said, smiling.

"Maybe," I said, smiling back at him and shrugging my shoulders.

The old rancher had been honest with us. In about forty-five minutes we could see Rio Piño on the horizon. As we rode into the town, I saw a man sitting on a chair next to the open door of a barbershop. The candy-striped pole stood on the boardwalk on the other side of the door. I eased Duchess to a stop in front of where the man sat, tipped my hat and said, "Howdy. Are you the barber?"

"Sure am," he said smiling. "Chair's open."

"Well, I am in need of a cut and a shave, but won't have time till morning. What time do you open?"

"I'm usually here at eight in the morning. I can be here earlier, if you'd like."

"No, eight will be fine. See you then." I turned Duchess away from the hitching rail in front of the barber shop, then stopped and asked, "Say, you don't happen to know a guy named Pavel Johnovich do you?"

The man suddenly lost his smile, looked our group over, and asked, "Friends of his are you?"

"No sir, we're not. I'm Sheriff Troy MacAlan from Laredo, and these are my Deputies. We're looking for Mr. Johnovich to ask him some questions."

This seemed to ease his tension, and he said, "Good, the man's nothing but trouble whenever he's in town."

"You'll get no argument from me. Any idea where he stays when he's here?"

"He's got a friend named Anton Danko... got a ranch about three miles west of town," the barber said.

"Thanks. That'll help us a whole lot. See you in the morning."

"I'll be here," he said, his friendly smile returning.

In the morning, the barber – Don Anderson was his name – was finishing up with my shave and haircut. "I'm glad to help anyway I can," he said. "No one will hear from me that you're the Sheriff from Laredo, or that you're looking for Johnovich."

"That's great, Don, we sure don't want him getting any heads-up that were here lookin' for him."

"Well, good luck by golly. Hope you find him and haul him back to Laredo."

"We plan to," I said, handing him thirty-five cents for the shave and haircut.

I hiked down to the diner, where Fini and his men waited for me to join them for breakfast. As we ate eggs and bacon, and drank several cups of their good coffee, we talked about surrounding this guy Danko's ranch. I said to Fini, "I think you'll have the best chance of checking things out, by knocking on their door and saying you're looking for work. I don't think Johnovich or any of his men got a good enough look at your face to remember you."

"Si, Señor Mack. I can convince them that I am a hard worker, and looking for work. Hopefully, I will get a look inside and see if I recognize anybody."

As we neared Danko's ranch, Fini pointed to a ridge a hundred yards to the side of his house. We quietly circled back and around to the backside of the ridge where we could sneak up to have a look at things. Near the top, we took off our hats and laid on the ground with only our eyes sticking above the ridge.

We could hear sounds echoing up from the house. "Sounds like they are partying already this morning," Diego whispered.

"Yeah, or still partying from last night," I said.

"That would be good... yes?" Santiago whispered.

"Yes, that would be good. They would all be good 'n drunk," I said.

After looking the situation over, we decided to have three men sneak to the backside of the barn and get inside, two would ride a wide circle around to the granary on the other side of the house, and me and Pablo sneak down behind the stock tank in front of the house. Meanwhile, Fini would ride up and knock on the door. We would be watching for his cues on what we should do.

Fini knocked on the door, and I could hear someone shouting, "Hey, Danko, you got some Mex knockin' at your door. Want me to run him off?"

"No," a voice grumbled. Soon, a guy came to the door, saying, "You lost, stranger?"

"No, Señor, I am only hoping you have some work for me to do," Fini said, softly. "I did not mean to interrupt your fun this morning."

"Oh, now, you're not interruptin' a thing," the guy said, slurring noticably. "Didn't mean to make you feel bad. Come on in and have some mescal and beer with us." He grabbed Fini by the shoulder and pulled him through the door. "Mescal for my friend here," he shouted.

After nearly a half hour had passed, I began to get concerned about Fini. Was he going to get out of there in one piece? Finally, I saw him stumbling out the screen door, yelling, "No, I'm just going out to water the weeds a bit."

When he got clear of the house, he hurried to his horse, swung in the saddle and rode hard toward the gate. We all quickly backtracked, and found Fini below the ridge where we had left our horses, and left Duke there to stand guard over them.

A little out of breath, I asked, "What happened?"

"We gotta get back to Laredo... Fast Señor!"

"Whoa... whaddya mean?" I asked. "What's up?"

"I overheard one of the guys in the other room talking about Johnovich going back to Laramie for a couple days. Miss Joey will be in great danger."

"You're right," I said, "we're gonna have to ride hard."

266

I swung up on Duchess, turned her and spurred her into a gallop. Fini and his men were right with us. We rode hard back to Rio Piño. Along the way, I decided to send a telegram to Joey, hoping she would get the message from the telegraph office before Johnovich got there.

We rode hard, even though it would be late in the evening when we got back to Laredo. After about four hours of riding, we stopped at a creek to give the horses a breather and let them drink. Duke was more than a little wore out, too. He laid right down in the edge of the creek to cool his body and drink the fresh water in a leisurely way. After about fifteen minutes, we hit the trail again.

With the sun nearly set, and darkness overtaking the sagebrush prairie, we finally began to see lanterns burning in the windows of Laredo. We rode into town and up to the hitching rail at the Texas Rose. Jumping down from Duchess, I hurried in the swinging doors. Zeke was at the bar serving customers, and nodded when he saw me.

He seemed to have everything under control, so I relaxed a bit and waited for him to finish serving drinks. Soon, he walked over to me at the end of the bar, and said quietly, "Joey got your telegram. I told her to head out of town and hide somewhere until she hears from us."

"Good move, Zeke," I said, slapping him on the back. "Seen anything of Johnovich yet?"

"Nope. Nothin' yet."

Fini and his men were gathered around us. "Sounds like we can relax for a moment, Señor Mack," Fini said, glancing around the barroom.

"Maybe so... for a short while," I said. "How will Joey know that it's okay, or that we're trying to reach her?" I asked, looking back at Zeke.

"If she sees the old Texas flag is flying, she knows to stay away. If she sees the US flag flying, she knows it's safe."

"Okay! I did see the old Texas flag was waving when I rode up. Fini, would you take a couple of your men and ride out to Johnovich's place?" I asked. "See if there's been any activity out there."

"Diego," Fini said, "you and Pablo ride with me." Then looking my way, he said, "We will be back in no more than an hour and let you know what we find."

As promised, the three men were back at the bar in an hour. Fini nodded, as he said, "Johnovich and four men are out at his ranch house right now."

"O-k-a-y," I said, stretching it out and wondering what our next move would be. "Any ideas on the best way to go at this mess?"

"Well, maybe," Fini said.

"Whatcha thinkin'?"

"Like the men back at Danko's ranch, they are all drinking pretty heavy. If we wait a while, then go quietly to surround the ranch, and check if there's any one standing guard, I think they'll all be pretty drunk, or asleep. I think we can move in and take control... hopefully, without firing a shot." Fini sounded very confident in what he was saying, which gave me a good feeling of confidence.

"I like it. I like the idea of no gunfire," I said. "I guess we can relax a while. Got any coffee brewing Zeke?"

"I'll make a pot right now," he said.

Chapter Forty-Nine

Later that night, we headed for Johnovich's ranch, and things could not have gone better. They did have one man standing guard, but Diego found him snoozing against a pine tree. With the help of Pablo, they gagged him and tied him to the pine tree.

We surrounded the ranch house, where there were still a couple of lanterns burning, and found Johnovich and three others sleeping, sprawled on various pieces of furniture in his living room. Checking the other rooms, there were no others to round up.

With the eight of us surrounding them in the living room, our guns drawn, I tapped Johnovich lightly on the shoulder. He didn't budge or blink. So, I tapped him harder, and shouted, "Hey."

This startled him, and he bolted upright. Still in a fog, he mumbled, "What the hell...."

"Rise and shine, Pavel," I said, with just a little sarcasm in my voice.

Quickly reaching for his gun, I said, "Don't bother. We've already got your guns."

"What the hell's goin' on here?" he growled. "What you doin' in my house?"

"Placing you under arrest for the murder of Sheriff Jackson and Deputy Larson."

"By what authority?" he asked, still growling.

"By this authority," I said, smiling and tapping at the badge on my chest.

He rubbed both eyes, then stared at the badge. Then he huffed as though it were a joke. "You... you're the new Sheriff?"

"Give that man a prize," I said pointing, "for guessing right the first time."

By now, the other three were awake and wondering what was going on, too. They all sat up, a blank stare on their faces when they realized they had no guns, and that there were eight of us surrounding them with guns.

"You can all stand and put your hands behind your back," I said, loudly. "You probably have never seen these newfangled handcuffs before. They were just invented a couple years ago, by a man named Adams... I think. And the Sheriff's office just happened to have recently purchased six sets. Lucky you... you get to try 'em out."

It didn't take long to get complete cooperation from them. Six of us marched them out to the barn where we'd help them climb into their saddle. Meanwhile, Diego and Pablo rounded up the one they had tied to the pine tree and put him in handcuffs and on his horse.

We rode into Laredo, and up to the jailhouse. We would leave two guards to watch the prisoners, changing up every three hours. There was no one in town, that we knew of anyway, to try and bust out Johnovich and his men, but decided to have at least two guards on duty at all times.

When we rode back into town, there were still lanterns burning in the Texas Rose. "Fini, want to go with me and see if Zeke is still at the Rose?" I asked.

"Si," he said brightly. "Maybe we can still get a glass of beer from him."

"Bet we could," I said, nodding.

Zeke was cleaning up at the Rose, and gladly poured us a beer when we told him of locking up Johnovich. "Guess I can raise the US flag first thing in the morning," he said.

"You sure can," I said. "Should be safe for Joey to come back now. This time around there are eight of us to watch over them until they are convicted and sent to prison. I wouldn't be at all surprised to see them convicted and sent to the gallows."

"Think that might happen?" Zeke asked.

"Yup, I do," I said, "since it was a sheriff and a deputy that they killed."

"Hope so," he said, matter-of-factly.

The next morning I was at the Texas Rose shortly after Zeke unlocked the door. "Think she'll show up soon?" I asked, as soon as I stepped through the door.

"Oh, I think so," he said slowly. "I think she has someone watching the flag for her."

Sure enough, about an hour and two cups of coffee later, I heard a horse and buggy coming at a good pace. I walked to the window and looked out, and there was Joey pulling up to the hitching rail. She hurried through the doors, saw me and ran to give me a hug.

"Oh Mack, I'm so glad to see you're okay. Got Johnovich locked up?"

"Yes we do. Thanks to Fini and his men, we got him locked up last night... him and three of his boys. That leaves four, maybe five, of his men that are still up in Rio Piño. I'm sure they'll be headed this way as soon as they hear we got Johnovich locked up."

This thought set her back a bit, so I said, "Don't worry. We've got eight good men against their four or five. And, we'll be ready and waiting for them."

This seemed to steady her, as she moved to give Zeke a hug. "So glad you're okay, too. Thanks for all you've done."

"Glad to help, li'l sis."

She smiled up at him, then said to me, "Zeke is like the big brother I never had."

I smiled softly and nodded to him.

Chapter Fifty

The next couple of days were spent taking turns watching Johnovich's bunch in our jail. The whole town felt a good sense of relief with them behind bars, so there wasn't much trouble or much "sheriffing" to do. Our only concern was when the gang from Rio Piño would get here, and how they would show themselves.

Most of the time – except for the overnight hours where we had changed things up to have four men watching the jail, and relieving each other every four hours – there were usually five or six of us there at any given time. With each passing day, we were more on guard for the rest to come into town looking to free Johnovich. We had three more days to go before the circuit judge would arrive.

As it turned out, Danko and the rest of Johnovich's bunch almost outsmarted us. They filtered into town one at a time, not gathering up as a group until sunrise the next morning when they surrounded the jail. Anton Danko, evidently their leader with Johnovich locked up, shouted from outside the jailhouse, "Let Pavel and his men go, and you'll live to see another sunrise. Otherwise...."

I waited to hear what would come after the "otherwise," but there were no more words. Only a gunshot, followed by six more that, one by one, circled the jailhouse. "Must have recruited some more help," I said. "Thought they only had four or five left up at Rio Piño. Hope our boys are done with breakfast soon."

Grabbing rifles, Pablo, Diego, Francisco, and I each hurried to kneel by a window where we could watch all directions from inside. "Don't fire 'til they try to make a move on us and you have a good open shot."

I hoped Fini and his other men were done with breakfast and on their way soon. "Keep an eye on the rooftops," I said, as much to reassure myself as anything.

Fini, Pablo, Santiago and Alejandro had just finished breakfast and stepped out onto the boardwalk, when they heard the gun shots. Fini immediately stopped, thought for a moment, then said, "Mount up and grab your rifles. Pablo, you and Alejandro take the backside, Santiago and I will take the front side. Ride hard so you are not an easy target, and see how many there are... and where they are. We will meet up at the far end of town."

He turned Domino and spurred him into a full gallop, the others following close behind. Pablo and Alejandro swung between two buildings and circled wide behind the back of the jailhouse. There were some scrub junipers and a few boulders where men could hide, so they swung wide of those and saw three men, who quickly turned and started firing at them. They both leaned over beside their horse's neck so they were small targets. They urged their horses on and rode toward the far end of town.

Meanwhile, Fini and Santiago were doing the same up the left side of Main Street. They saw four men ducked behind two water troughs across from the jail, so they swung left between two buildings and around to the far end of town to catch up with Pablo and Alejandro.

As the four regrouped, Fini said, "We can get on the roof behind the troughs. What about the backside?"

Pablo said, "There are some boulders a couple hundred feet behind where the others are hiding . "

"Okay," Fini said showing a slight grin. "We can pinch them in a crossfire between us and our boys inside the jailhouse. Get in place, and open up as soon as you're ready."

Pablo and Alejandro swung their horses wide, hoping to be out of site as they circled to get to the far side of the boulders. Fini and Santiago climbed the back stairway of the building. It brought them close enough to where they could stand on the handrail and help each other to the roof.

As they neared the front edge of the roof, Fini could see me looking up at him through the window of the jailhouse. He nodded, and pointed at the troughs down below. I nodded back to him.

"Fini and Santiago are on the roof across the way, above the troughs," I said. "Pablo and Alejandro must be somewhere on the backside. Be ready... when they start shooting, we do the same."

The next thing I heard, though, was a buggy coming down Main Street at a good pace. I leaned as far as I could to see through the window at an angle and up the street. My heart sank, as I saw that it was Joey coming in her buggy.

I wanted to scream, "No-o-o," but knew she would never hear me from inside the jail, and over the noise of her horse's hooves. I froze, feeling helpless as she continued toward us.

"Joey's coming down the street. Open fire. We've got to get their attention away from her," I said, and began shooting at the trough where I thought Danko was hiding. The others with me in the jail started shooting, as did the four outside. The shooting startled Joey, and she pulled her horse to an immediate stop.

Soon, one of their men on the backside was badly wounded, and one of the four in the front was slowly beginning to raise his hands, knowing he was caught in a bad place with guns shooting at him from the roof and from the jail. It looked as though we were going to get this bad situation under control quicker than I figured.

Just as I'm thinking that, Danko stands, turns, and fires a rifle shot at Joey, knocking her sideways in the buggy seat. It almost seemed as though a small grin crossed his face as he shot her.

Immediately, I took aim, fired, and hit Danko in the middle of his chest. Small clouds of dust rolled away from his body, as he stiffened and hit the ground hard.

"Cover me," I shouted, heading out the door and running toward Joey. I could hear layers of gunshots coming from the jailhouse, the roof top, and somewhere out back, as I ran to her.

I grabbed her as gently as I could, and eased her to the ground. "Joey?" I said softly, trying to get a response.

I heard a soft moan, then she opened her eyes just a bit, raised a hand and touched my cheek, and whispered, "Oh Mack...."

"Don't try to talk. We'll get you over to Doc Martinez right away."

"Take the gold chain and cross from around my neck, Mack. I want to have it."

"That can wait..." I tried to object.

"No," she interrupted, holding her hand to my lips. "I want you to have it. My father gave it to me and said it was because he loved me so much and always wanted me to know. I want you to have it now, Mack. Please take it."

I gently unclasped the gold chain and slid from around her neck. "Thank you," I whispered. "Now I'm getting you to Doc's office."

"Not going to make it, Mack. I can feel it. Only wish we could have shared a life together," she said weakly.

I felt life slide from her body as I held her close, the gold chain and cross held tightly in my hand. "Oh Joey," I said softly, tears running down my cheeks.

As I sat on the ground holding her, and looking at her beautiful face, my body began to tremble violently. I suddenly looked toward the sky, wondering why this feeling seemed so familiar. In moments, I had the sensation of being pulled from my body. I was rocketing upward, seeing Joey shrink in the distance below. Then, in an explosion of light and speed, I was rocketed through space and time.

As things slowed, I found myself waking in a hospital bed, wondering where I was. Near my bed, my beautiful wife, Sonja, lay sleeping in another hospital bed, covered with her knitted blanket that she always snuggled in.

Lying there, watching her sleep, the confusion began to clear and I remembered a violent accident with a pickup truck. *How long have I been out,* I wondered.

I lay there watching Sonja for what seemed like hours, until she finally stirred from her deep sleep. "You awake?" I asked, barely above a whisper.

Her eyes popped wide open. "Mack!" She said in a whisper that was almost as big as a scream. "Oh Mack!" She said again, as she scrambled from her bed, trying to get to me as quickly as she could.

"Hi Babe," I said, as she began hugging me and kissing me all over my face.

"How long have I been out?" I asked, when she'd kiss me enough times.

"You've been in a coma for nearly two weeks," she said. "They didn't know if you're going to make it through this time, but I never gave up hope."

"This time?" I asked.

"Yes... This time," she said emphatically. "Twice, after gunshots almost did you in, and now this time a car accident almost take you away. Your comas are going to be the death of me."

Feeling a little bad, for sounding like she was trying to scold me, she hugged me again and said, "Oh Mack, I love you so much."

"I love you, too, Babe," I said softly. By now the morning sun was peeking through the window blinds, and caught the beautiful tones of her wavy auburn hair, and her striking green eyes.

"I love you so much," I said, thinking of the beautiful life we shared, and our three wonderful sons.

"Where'd you get this beautiful gold chain and cross?" she asked, looking down at my hand.

Looking down and slowly opening my hand, I said, "Don't know. Thought maybe you had given it to me."

"No, wasn't me," she said, sounding a little puzzled.

Feeling a little bewildered myself, I shrugged my shoulders, saying, "Huh... I don't know either, Babe."

www.ingramcontent.com/pod-product-compliance
Lightning Source LLC
Chambersburg PA
CBHW061550170626
46811CB00001B/159